OUTBREAK: THE HUNGER
SCOTT SHOYER

Severed Press
Hobart Tasmania

OUTBREAK: THE HUNGER

Copyright © 2015 Scott Shoyer
Copyright © 2015 by Severed Press

www.severedpress.com

ISBN: 978-1-925225-94-5

Praise for Outbreak: The Hunger

Every once in a while, some writer or critic will make the claim that horror's true purpose is to shine a light into the darkness so that the obscenities lurking there cannot flourish in our own souls. Or some such crap as that. I call bullshit. When I was a kid, I gravitated to horror because it thrilled me. It made me say, "Wow, this is really cool!" Well, that's what Scott Shoyer's Outbreak: The Hunger did for me, and for that, I thank him. It has been way too long since I said, "Wow, this book got it absolutely right!" However, that's what I did with Outbreak: The Hunger. I sat there, reading, with a huge smile on my face and the gooseflesh popping out up my arms. This is why we read horror. This is the dark gold we hope to find when we go to the bookstore. I wolfed Outbreak: The Hunger down. From front cover to back, I was turning pages as if they were on fire. Not only is it the kind of wild ride you expect from good old fashioned horror, but it is a zombie novel with a truly original take on the genre. I guarantee you, the story has not been told this way before. I envy you getting to read it for the first time.

- Joe McKinney, author of the Dead World Series

PROLOGUE

1

Present Day – Just Outside Austin, TX

He looks down at his watch as it turns 12:11 A.M.. Jason is dressed all in black and is carefully watching where he steps as he slowly approaches the Hudson Research Laboratory. Part of him can't believe he is doing this. Sure, he isn't alone. His friends from *Animal Rights First* are here with him. He just can't believe he is physically going to break into this medical testing lab and free a bunch of animals. He keeps telling himself that he's doing it for the animals, but deep down, knows he's doing it to impress Lisa and show her how "hardcore" he is. Funny thing is that Lisa isn't even here. She already had plans and couldn't make it.

Jesus Christ, Jason, he thinks. *What the fuck are you doing out here?*

He looks to his left and right, and sees Sean and Vicktor. They never had any doubts about doing this "liberation." He's not solely doing this for Lisa. He truly cares about the animals, and the thought of those poor, innocent, defenseless creatures being exposed to God-knows-what kind of experiments gets his blood boiling. However, Sean and Vicktor take it too far. The way they see it, the Earth belongs to the animals and creatures, and human beings should consider themselves lucky enough to be allowed to co-exist with them. *Well*, he thinks. *The group's name is* Animal Rights First.

They approach the back entrance. This isn't going to be some amateur break-in where they just smash a window, set off all the alarms, and have time to free only a few animals before the cops get here. Sean was their inside man in the lab. When they heard about the various tortures being done to the animals, Sean took a job there as a janitor, sweeping the floors and hosing out the cages of dead animals. He was physically and emotionally disgusted by the way these so-called 'doctors' were treating the animals. There wasn't any make-up or shit like that being tested. From what Sean could gather, the animals were being injected with various strains of one virus. He had even heard the phrase "mutated strain" spoken on a few occasions.

"It's probably some new fucking Botox strain," he would tell us after his shift in the lab. "They're infecting all those animals just so some rich cunts can get rid of the wrinkles around their eyes."

Sean was only guessing the injections were Botox, but you could see how angry and upset he was after every shift.

"Why the fuck do they need so many animals there?" he would ask. "They have four different types of monkeys, rats, rabbits, dogs and cats, a fucking lion and tiger, and chickens. Why the fuck do they have chickens?"

He would rant and rave for a few hours after every shift. Jason couldn't blame him. He didn't think he'd have been able to watch those animals being tortured every day.

They creep closer to the back door. Last night, Sean was able to steal a key card off one of the doctors. He made a copy and then put it back in the doctor's lab coat so it wouldn't be reported stolen. They aren't too high tech at *Animal Rights First* and Jason was surprised the doctor didn't notice the fake key. They were probably too preoccupied killing monkeys.

"Everyone stop," Jason whispers loudly, as he points up to the security camera. "You never said the back door was monitored by a camera, Sean."

Sean looks puzzled. "Dude, I swear that camera wasn't there last night."

"Well, it's here now," Jason hisses back. He's trying to think of a new plan on the fly, but he's not some combat-experienced soldier. Jason works at Starbucks during the day. Devising a plan while ten feet from the lab isn't his specialty.

"What the fuck are we gonna do?" Vicktor asks.

Studying the cameras, Jason notices they sweep from left to right, and aren't that fast. "Look how slow the camera moves back and forth. If we time it right, we can run straight to the back door and the camera will never even see us."

"Are you fucking crazy?" Vicktor asks. "I don't wanna take that chance."

"What do you think, Sean?" Jason asks as he turns to meet his gaze. "I think we can do this. We've come this far and there's no fucking way you can go back to the lab for work tomorrow. They're also gonna realize that a key card was stolen, so all the locks and access codes will be changed. This is our only shot at helping those animals." *Fuck you, Lisa*, Jason thinks, smiling. *This really is about the animals.*

Judging by the look in Sean's eyes, Jason already knows what his answer will be. "You haven't seen what they're doing to those animals, Vicktor." Sean's voice is cold and stoic. "There's no way in hell I'm turning back now. I'm doing this."

"I'm in," Jason says. "Vicktor?" They both look at him.

"Yeah, what the fuck," he answers. "Someone's gotta help those animals."

2

They time how long it takes the camera to make a full sweep from left to right. They have eight-seconds to avoid being seen.

"See," Jason says rather smugly. "That's plenty of fucking time. We're only, like, ten to fifteen feet away from the back door and the camera doesn't even look like it monitors the door."

"Who's gonna go first?" Vicktor asks nervously.

"Whoever goes first needs to open the door with the card key," Jason points out.

Vicktor and Jason both look at Sean at the same time, but judging by the look in his eyes, he doesn't want to be the first to go.

"Fine," Jason says angrily, "I'll go first. Gimme the goddamn key card."

Sean hands over the credit card-sized access card. "What's the code I need to push in after I swipe it?" Jason asks Sean.

"Swipe it and then punch in 092170," Sean says.

"Really?" Jason asks skeptically. "This lab is protected by a six-digit access code?"

"What the fuck do you want from me?" Sean says defensively. "I didn't create the security here. I just stole the fucking card."

"Calm down, Sean," Jason whispers. "I'm not questioning you. It just seems like a really lame security system."

This was all beginning to seem a little too easy. "Even if this lab was just testing out some new Botox formula," Jason says, "you'd think they'd have better security."

"If you're gonna be a fucking pussy, gimme back the key and I'll go first." Sean seems to be getting very worked up.

"Calm down, Sean," Jason says, matching his anger, "I'm not pussing out. I just wanna know exactly what the fuck we're getting into. We all need to have level and clear heads."

Jesus, fucking Christ, Jason thinks. *I'm about to break into a lab with a hot head and a pussy. I need to find some new friends.*

Jason watches the camera sweep to the right. Just as it is about to stop and sweep back to the left, he runs toward the door. Looking down at his watch, he sees that he has made it in six seconds. Jason swipes the key card through the magnetic lock and punches in the code.

He stops his mental celebration quickly.

There is a digital beep and then a panel to his left slides up. Now Jason is staring at either a handprint or retinal scanner. His blood boils instantly. He turns to make sure the security camera was facing away before running back to where Sean and Vicktor are.

"What the fuck are you doing?" asks Sean.

Jason pushes him up against the tree, hard. "Unless you have that doctor's hand or eyeball in your pocket, I think you better shut the fuck up," he growl.

Sean can see how pissed Jason is and meekly asks, "What happened? Doesn't the card work? Fuck, did they already change the access code?"

"No, asshole," Jason shoots back. "That code was only the first layer of security." Then, remembering the outside camera, he corrects himself. "Scratch that," he says as he nods at the camera, "the second layer."

"What's the next layer?" Vicktor asks.

"It's either a handprint or retinal scanner," Jason answers.

"How are we gonna get around that?" Vicktor asks.

"We aren't, you idiot," Jason replies, angrier than was necessary. "This has quickly turned into a cluster fuck, you guys." to Sean, he asks, "Are there any other surprises we should know about?"

He is about to shout something back, but decides he has no ground to stand on. "How the fuck was I supposed to know about the scanner on the door?" Sean sheepishly replies.

"Well, for one, you could have watched someone open the goddamn door." Jason rolls his eyes and looks away from them in disgust. He takes a deep breath to let his anger subside and then continues, "The way I see it, we have two choices: we either call it a night and go home utter failures, or we go break a window and try to free as many animals as we can before the cops show up."

Jason looks at them both, awaiting a reply. "You guys are pathetic," he says.

"Fuck you, Jason," says Sean. "I was the one inside that fucking lab five times a week watching all those animals suffer. So I missed a few details. It's easy for you to stand there and criticize."

"A few details," Jason yells back. "You call an external security camera and a handprint recognition pad a few details? If you focused on the bigger picture when you were in that lab and didn't break down every time you saw a fucking animal being mistreated, you'd have noticed all this shit. Now we're standing in it up to our knees. Fuck you, guys. I'm gonna finish what we came here to do."

Jason picks up a softball-sized rock by his foot and starts walking toward the window next to the back door.

3

It all seems pretty surreal as the three of them hurl rocks through the window . Jason expects it will be loud, but Jesus Christ, it sounds like a shotgun blast. Once the window is broken, he doesn't hesitate. He uses a rock to smash out the rest of the window and clear off the frame. Jason jumps through the window and lands on the broken glass. He doesn't even turn around to see if Sean and Vicktor are behind him.

"Jason," someone whispers behind me. "Slow the fuck down."

"We don't have time to slow down," he yells back, not even bothering to turn around. "We have ten to fifteen minutes before this place is crawling with cops."

Sean yells back, "For fuck's sake, Jason, just stop walking and listen for a goddamn second."

Jason is about to turn and lay into Sean again when he hears it. Well, actually, it's what he doesn't hear. "There's no alarm. What the fuck's going on?"

"I'd say it's our lucky day, guys," Sean quips back. "I told you all this new security wasn't here yesterday. They must still be installing it. I bet that outside camera isn't even being monitored. Now we can take our time and do this right."

Jason hates it when Sean gloats.

"No way, Sean. Something weird is going on here. If anyone was walking by the lab when we broke the window, I guarantee they heard it. The cops could still be on the way." Jason's gut is telling him something issn't right.

"Why the fuck isn't there an alarm going off loud enough to wake the dead?" Jason asks them.

"Who cares," Vicktor finally chimes in. "Let's get in there and do what we came here to do."

That is all Jason needs. "Sean, lead the way. That is, if you took the time to learn where the animals are." Sean looks at me and is about to say something, but realizes he's dropped the ball and turned this into one huge cluster fuck.

"Fuck you, Jason," Sean finally says as he takes the lead.

They held their breaths as they walk past the security desk and as Sean uses the key card. He swipes it and punches in the numbers and they go right through. Sean is noticeably relieved that the card worked. They just might be able to salvage this liberation mission after all.

After walking down a few more long hallways, they get to the main lab where the testing occurs.

Five minutes have passed.

Sean is swiping the key card again when Jason asks, "Are you sure this is the right room?"

"Of course it's the right room. I swept in here every day, five times a week, for the last month. Would you just get off my ass? I fucked up outside, but now we're back on track."

"But listen," Jason continues. "I don't hear anything. Shouldn't the animals be raising hell?"

"They're probably asleep," reasons Vicktor. "Either let's do this or get the fuck outta here."

Vicktor is right. "Let's do it," Jason says.

Eight minutes have passed.

As the door to the lab swings open, the first thing Jason notices is how large the room looks and how deceiving it is from the outside. They must've built onto the room from the outside. Thinking about that really pisses Jason off. These scumbags went out of their way to make sure they had space to torture the animals.

Looking around the room, they see various sized cages. Some are small enough to house one cat, while others are so large that there is enough room for a tiger to pace back and forth. Yet, no animal is pacing, moving, or even breathing from the looks of it.

Ten minutes have passed.

"Guys, this is fucking bizarre. Are all these animals dead?" Jason asks. They are all looking in various cages. "Did you ever find out what they are testing in here, Sean?"

"No," is all he says. "I think it was a secret, so none of the scientists ever talked about it when I was in the room."

"Seriously?" Jason asks as he glances up at him. "That didn't seem odd to you that there was no talking when you were in the room?"

"Well I..."

Sean never gets to finish his sentence. There is a sudden, violent burst of energy from one of the cats Vicktor is looking at as it jumps up from its dead-like slumber and bites him on the finger.

"Son of a bitch," Vicktor screams as he yanks his finger away. "Fucking cat just bit me!" he says as he sucks on his finger to alleviate the pain.

"Okay guys," Jason says, getting annoyed. "Enough is enough. Let's start opening some cages."

Thirteen minutes have passed.

Vicktor starts opening cages housing various cats and dogs. "I should leave this fucker locked up," he says, looking at the cat that bit him.

"Hey, ya can't blame these animals for not trusting human beings, dude," Sean says. "They've been tortured for so long, they probably think we're here to do the same."

"Okay, I can see that," replies Vicktor. "But why are they all just sitting there looking at the opened cage doors?"

Vicktor is right. By this time, Jason has opened a bunch of the monkey's cages. Vicktor opens all of the cat and dog cages, and Sean gets the majority of the chicken, hamster, and rat cages open. However, all the animals are just sitting in their cages and looking around. Poor things are so scared that they don't know what to do.

Sean goes to liberate a hamster when the hamster turns its head and bites him on the thumb.

"Mother fucker," screams Sean. He then shakes the cage, displacing his anger for the hamster onto the metal bars.

As the noise echoes throughout the lab, all the animals seem to come out of their daze at the same time. Even the animals that look dead jump up as if they suddenly realize they were being liberated. All hell then breaks loose as the animals become alert and violent, trying to get out of their torture cells. The odd thing Jason notices is that none of the animals are attacking each other. Cats and dogs pay no attention to one another, and even the rats seem oblivious to the predators around them. Nevertheless, they all definitely notice the humans.

Fifteen minutes have passed.

"It's time to get outta here, guys," Jason says. He is nervous. Besides the way the animals are sizing them up, the noise obscures any sound that may be coming from outside. The cops could be driving a tank up to the lab and they wouldn't hear a thing.

"What about the larger animals?" Sean yells over to me. "We gotta get them out too."

"Dude, if you wanna open the cage for the lion and tiger over there, be my guest," Jason says. "But keep in mind the reaction the hamster gave you."

Sean looks around and sees some rope. He ties one end to the cage doors and then walks to the opposite end of the lab. He is planning to pull the rope, freeing the large cats at a distance.

Jason freezes. He swears he heard talking in the hallway.

Sean and Vicktor see Jason stop moving and look at him questioningly with furrowed eyebrows.

Sean breaks the moment: "What are you..."

The door on the far side of the lab bursts open. Five men dressed in military fatigues with full gas mask gear, battle packs, and assault rifles swarm inside.

"Freeze!" The lead soldier fixes his rifle on us. "This is a restricted laboratory."

As the soldiers quickly fan out, covering the entire lab to secure the room, they notice all the animals running around. They even see some of the animals start to dart out the room through the door they kicked in.

The lead soldier, the one with his gun fixed on us, yells to the others, "We have a Code Five breach!"

Without hesitating, the other soldiers immediately start shooting at the animals trying to escape. The noise is deafening as they sweep their assault rifles back and forth on full automatic.

What the fuck are they doing? Jason thinks. He wants to stop them, but thinks better about it.

"They're getting out," one of the other soldiers says. Jason swears he heard an edge of panic in his voice.

With that, the lead soldier takes his gun off us and starts sweeping the floor with a rain of bullets. "Get the flame thrower, *now!*" he yells to no one in particular. The soldier closest to the door runs outside to retrieve the weapon.

"Are they fucking serious?" Jason asks, looking at Sean and Vicktor.

"I don't wanna find out," replies Vicktor. "We need to get the fuck out of here now."

There is a chance. All the soldiers are so busy trying to contain and kill the escaping animals that they seem to have forgotten the three liberators. They've become a secondary concern. As they step back, the lead soldier bolts towards them.

"Where the fuck do you think you're going?" he says. He reaches out for us and grabs Vicktor's arm. It is then he notices Vicktor's bleeding finger. The soldier quickly retracts his hand. "Were you bit by one of the animals?" he asks as he placed the barrel of the rifle inches away from Vicktor's head.

Jason doesn't know if Vicktor is going to shit or go blind first. He manages to stammer out an answer: "Yeah, a cat..."

Those are the last three words Vicktor would ever speak. The soldier pulls the trigger. There is a wet cracking sound as the back of Vicktor's head shoots across the room and lands inside one of the cages. A white lab rat notices the fragment of skull and pounces on it, tearing away at it in a frenzy.

Sean and Jason stand frozen.

"Were either of you bitten or scratched?" he asks, turning to us.

We shake our heads as Sean slowly slips his still-bleeding hand into his pocket.

The soldier returns with the flamethrower and immediately starts dousing the floor with short bursts of flame. The soldier who seconds ago was interrogating us backs away to watch the flames. It is then that he sees Sean holding the ropes tied to the lion and tiger cages. Before he can tell him to drop them, Sean yanks on the ropes. The large cats immediately come storming out of the cages, straight for the soldier who killed Vicktor. The tiger pounces on him, and in one fluid motion, sinks its teeth into the soldier's neck. Blood squirts and gushes between the beast's teeth and through the corners of its mouth as he tears the man's throat out.

As if working together, the lion attacks the soldier with the flamethrower. He sees the beast coming at him and aims the nozzle at the charging lion. He manages to fire off one burst of flame. The lion almost seems to duck out of the way, but isn't fast enough, as its mane catches fire. That, however, doesn't slow the beast down. It jumps toward the soldier and latches onto his right forearm. With one vicious tear, he takes the soldier's arm clean off at the elbow. The soldier slams to the floor, immediately going into shock.

The lion isn't finished yet. It looks at the maimed soldier on the floor, then goes on to attack the next healthy soldier.

Jason shakes Sean out of his daze.

"SEAN!" Jason yells. "We need to get the fuck out of here, NOW."

We race out the door behind us and into the hallway. There we see another soldier dead on the ground, the monkeys still tearing and… it can't be… but it looks like they are *eating* parts of the body. One monkey uses its sharp fingernails to dig out the soldiers eyes. Another is chewing on the soldier's fingers as if they are some kind of exotic beef jerky.

As they try to step around the dead soldier, one of the monkeys sees them and lunges at Sean. It lands on Sean's leg and immediately sinks its bloodied teeth into his calf muscle. Sean's eyes become wide with pain as he screams. He tries to shake the monkey off, but it has a vice-like grip around his leg.

Jason looks around for something he can use as a weapon. He spots the dead soldier's rifle lying in a pool of blood, entangled in his unraveled intestines. *These fucking monkeys are crazy,* he thinks. *They aren't just killing these soldiers. They're mutilating and eating them.* The monkey responsible for the evisceration is now feasting on the intestines.

Jason slowly approaches the blood-drenched monkey. Sean is behind him, still howling in pain. As Jason reaches for the rifle, the monkey turns and stares straight into his eyes. He thinks he's going crazy, but it appears it was sizing him up, trying to decide if he was a threat. It stops chewing for a second, as if debating on whether to attack or not. It then turns and starts feasting on the soldier's insides again. Jason quickly grabs the rifle and runs back over to Sean.

By now, Sean is almost in shock. The capuchin monkey isn't just biting him; it is tearing away parts of his calve muscle. Without hesitating, Jason swings the rifle as hard as he can. He catches the monkey in its ribs and it doesn't even respond upon impact. He turns the rifle around and jabs it hard in the ribs, trying to stab it. The barrel is too blunt, but it's enough to piss that bastard off. Without a warning, it leaps off Sean's leg and is going for Jason's throat. Instinctively, he pulls the trigger. A deafening roar sounds from the rifle. He hits the monkey square in the chest and sends it sliding across the floor.

"Sean, *Sean!*" Jason screams. "Are you okay?" Even as he speaks, he knows it might be the dumbest question he ever asked. Trying to correct himself, he asks, "Can you put any pressure on your leg? Can you walk?"

Sean looks at him in a daze. *Great*, Jason thinks. *He's going into shock.* Then Sean shakes his head. His mouth slowly opens as he looks over Jason's shoulder.

Jason doesn't want to look at what is happening behind him. Sean just had a fucking monkey chewing on his leg, but whatever is happening behind Jason is enough to make his jaw drop.

He slowly turns. "You gotta be fucking kidding me," he whispers. The monkey that took a round in the chest is sitting up and looking at us. He starts to stand when a random burst from the flamethrower brushes across him. It doesn't move. The flames engulf the monkey and it just sits there, staring. It finally stands and starts walking in Jason's direction.

"Oh come on," Sean says in disbelief. "What the FUCK did they do to these animals?"

They are in awe. There's no other word for it. They stand there, watching a fucking flaming monkey walking toward them. About halfway to them, it collapses face down. The last thing it does is raise its head to look at them.

"Okay," Jason finally says, breaking this surreal moment. "We really need to get the fuck out of here."

The adrenaline coursing through Sean's body allows him strength, despite the fact that a money was chewing on his leg no more than a few moments ago. It was fight or flight time. They run through the winding corridors, not really knowing where the fuck they are going. Finally, they see an emergency exit. "If this isn't an emergency, then I don't know what is," Jason yells as he reaches for the door.

As they push through the emergency door, an alarm sounds. *The back door to the lab wasn't alarmed but the fire door was? That makes no sense*, Jason thinks. Then he realizes that the back door WAS alarmed. It has a silent alarm on it that went straight to the local military base or private security force. He runs as fast as his legs will carry him.

Why, Jason wonders, *would this lab need such a high level of security?*

The last thing Sean and Jason see as they run around the block are the animals scattering. He should've felt good about the liberation, but he thinks back to a movie he saw not too long ago, *28 Days Later*, and remembered feeling that they had screwed up. That they had screwed up real big.

CHAPTER ONE

2003 – Austin, TX

Wake up, John. Everything is hazy, almost like I am swimming in a very thick fog. I can almost see the surface of consciousness. Trying to remember where I am is difficult. I can't focus my mind on any one thought. It almost feels like I was drugged. Drugged. Yeah… I think I was drugged. But why? By whom?

Swimming to the surface of consciousness, I can hear my breathing. It sounds labored. Am I dying? Why isn't anyone helping me?

I swim closer to consciousness. I feel hands on my body. Are they holding me down? What the hell is happening to me? I think I'm on a bed. Not the bed that I share with my wife, but some strange bed. My wife. Where is Sarah? Why isn't she helping me? We've been married for about a year now. She's always been by my side even during those times when I was a real pain in the ass. She's always supported me in all my decisions and choices, even when I quit the world of academia to become a professional cook. I was young when I got my Ph.D., so I figured I better get out of a profession that I hated and give my passion a shot. That was a great decision, but where is she?

I grip the sheets on the bed tightly. I'm almost to the surface. I hear a strange voice telling me to remain calm. Oh, God… I must have been in some terrible accident. The doctors must be working on my mangled body, but I don't remember being in a car accident. Was it a random shooting? Why can't I remember anything?

My heart starts beating harder as I panic. One of my eyes is open and I can see four doctors around me. One is hunched over my chest and is working on my eye. What the hell is happening?

Wait. My eye. I remember now. I'm in eye surgery to get a corneal graft. I was diagnosed a year ago with Keratoconus, and when my sight started to deteriorate, my doctor said it was time for 'the procedure.' All forms of light began hurting my eyes and my vision was really poor, but why is the doctor waking me up? He's still working on me. That sadistic mother fucker. Or maybe he's just a really bad doctor.

I try to talk but my tongue is too thick from the anesthesia. My heart beats even faster. I can hear it on the monitor.

"Just relax, John," the doctor finally tells me. "I need to bring you back to consciousness in order to get the stitches in your eye. You won't feel any pain, but I need you to move your eye when I tell you to. Do you understand me?"

I groan out an affirmation and start to relax. For the next hour, I move my eyeball in whichever direction the doctor tells me as he stitches in my new cornea. He could have warned me about this part of the surgery. It's a very odd sensation to see stitches being put into your own eyeball. I wonder if this is the kind of shit Lucio Fulci dreamed about. I start to relax but my hands still grip the bed sheets tightly, just waiting to feel the searing pain of a needle being pushed into my eyeball.

When it's finally over, they send me on my way, hopped up on Vicodin, with my wife pushing me out of the hospital in a wheelchair. My eye is bandaged and throbbing. I still can't talk due to the anesthesia hangover. I want to tell Sarah how I was awake when they put in the stitches. It's kind of a macho story that I'm sure I'll be telling anyone who will listen to me. I've always been worried that people look at me and see a man who always plays it safe. Growing up, I was afraid of heights, hated roller coasters, and preferred team sports where I could rely on other people to carry the team. I was always unsure of myself and within the past 4-5 years, I began to wonder if I had what it took to be heroic, whatever the hell that is. If the chips were down and something bad was happening, would I freeze up like a deer in headlights, or would I take control and give in to the adrenaline and prove myself to be a Man? I don't know. Getting my eye operated on while conscious seemed pretty cool, but then again, I had no choice in the matter. The doctor just woke my ass up and told me what to do. Hhmmm. Do I have what it takes to be a hero? If the events ever presented themselves, would I be able to stand up and be brave? I don't know. I like to think I have the balls, but being honest with myself, I just don't know.

That's one of the reasons I went into cooking. It's one of the most macho professions I could think of where I had a chance to prove myself. You work under tremendous pressure, its hot as hell on the line, you're dealing with smoking hot pans and extremely sharp knives, and sometimes it's just two of you on the line trying to keep up with the orders. If you go down, you look and feel like a huge pussy. If you keep up and dominate the line, you feel like a conquering barbarian. I've felt both ways.

I get home and Sarah puts me to bed. Most nights I try not to dream. I guess it's really not my choice whether I dream or not, but I at least try to guide my dreams in a certain direction. I focus my mind on one thought and try to put that into my subconscious, but with all the Vicodin, I can't focus on anything. So I began to drift off, unfocused and vulnerable.

1980 – Philadelphia, PA

"Come on, John. Pass it to me. Stop being such a fucking hog," says Dave.

I still get shocked when someone uses the "F" word. Just the other weekend, my dad took Dave, my brother, and I to a drive-in to see the movie *The Boys in Company C*. That was the first movie where we all heard the word "fuck" being used in everyday conversation. Even my dad was getting a little uncomfortable with the amount of "F-bombs" that movie dropped. After that, "fuck" was Dave's favorite new word. He worked it into every sentence he could. I liked using it too, but I was a little more select. My restraint kept me from getting punished. Dave, on the other hand, was always getting busted for using that word.

We are 10 years old and our game of choice is street hockey. That's what happens when you live in Philly. We have a great hockey team, but no one knows how to skate worth a fuck. So we take to the streets in the safety of our Converse shoes and pretend we're all skating.

I pass to Dave and he immediately shoots at the goal. Steve is in goal, and no matter what team he's on, Steve always plays goalie. The fat fuck. He could just stand up straight and no one would be able to get anything past him. Fat fuck. Dave winds up and nails a slap shot right into Steve's nuts. That was everyone's strategy: If Steve's in goal, aim for his nuts. You'd think he'd have caught on by now and started wearing an athletic cup, but Steve goes down howling. Everyone is laughing their asses off. I run over to Steve. He's all curled up in the fetal position.

"Dude," I say, looking down at him. "When the fuck are you going to start wearing a cup? You get nailed in the balls every game."

Steve just looks at me with his big, red, bloated face. I can't help it and start laughing again. He stands, thrusts his hand down his pants to adjust himself, and gets back into goal.

"Are you sure you're up for being back in goal?" I ask him.

"Are we gonna play, or are we gonna talk about my balls?" he answers.

We start playing again. This is the first time Steve has ever gone back into goal after taking a shot to the nuts. I think everyone is wondering the same thing. Is Steve's crotch off limits now, or is it still fair game? Moreover, is anyone going to attempt a nut shot again?

Dave passes the hockey ball to me. I get about five steps with it and fumble over my feet as the ball is taken away from me. I've always been tall for my age. Last year, when I was nine years old, I grew five inches in one summer. My whole body ached. My joints always felt like they were on fire. I also looked like a scarecrow. I was so lanky and skinny, but over the last year, I have been playing a lot of sports and trying to eat better. So I look a bit better than last summer, but I still haven't grown accustomed to my body. Whenever I play basketball, soccer, or street hockey, I hate when I have to be the one pushing the play. Just let me stand under the basket or next to the goal and pass it to me. I'm that fucking klutz that loses the ball almost every time.

Derek takes the ball from me with ease, but I chase after him, lower my shoulder, and drive into his back. He goes flying and Dave gets the ball. He runs toward the goal. Dave is a great athlete. No matter which sport it is, he always seems to excel at it. He gets close to the goal and we can all see the anxiety in Steve's eyes. Dave pulls his stick back for the shot and wails it. It bee-lines right at Steve's chest. Steve just stands there and takes the shot in the chest. He stumbles backward into the goal, but keep the ball from going in. We all stopTime almost seems to stand still for a second, like when a baby hits his head and waits to see if he's hurt or not. We waited for what seemed like forever to see if Steve is all right.

Steve just rubs his chest and says, "You shoot like a pussy, Dave."

Everyone laughs nervously. We all know Steve is hurt but he won't give Dave the satisfaction. Steve is a tough fucker when he wants to be. Dave apologizes about nailing him in the chest, but we all knew that he aimed at him. Dave is fiercely competitive and wants to win at everything he does. It can be sports, board games, schoolwork, whatever. If he is doing something that other people are also doing, he needs to be the best.

I, on the other hand, am not a very competitive person. Oh, I liked to win, but I never feel like I have what it takes to be a winner. My body is awkward and too tall, and it seems that whenever it is "up to me" I always fail and let down the others on my team. That's why I prefer team sports to the individual sports like tennis, golf, and swimming. In those sports, it is all up to you. You compete against yourself. If you lose, it is entirely your fault, and yours alone. In team sports, you can spread the blame among your teammates. I'll score once in a while to feel like I'm contributing to the game, but ultimately, it's someone like Dave that will win it for the team.

"Well, at least I didn't hit you in the nuts again," Dave yells over to Steve.

Steve just glares at him, picks up the little hard ball, and throws it down the hill. We all groan.

"Goddamnit, Steve," Dave yells. "Why the fuck did you do that?"

"Go fuck yourself, Dave," Steve returns. "Go chase it. I hope a car hits you in the nuts."

We all laugh. Steve never is any good at putting someone down. I run off with Dave to get the hockey ball. I figure it is a good time for us to get our game plan together for the sleepover tonight. We slept over at each other's house almost every other weekend. This was the time before the Blockbuster video stores dominated the scene and the 'ma and pa' corner video chains were the only places to rent movies. My parents were pretty cool, and set it up with the owners of the local rental place where my brother and I could rent anything we wanted to as long as it wasn't porn. Man, my parents were naïve! I would rent the craziest, bloodiest videos I could find and Dave and I would watch them until early in the morning. The weekend we rented *Cannibal Ferox,* we stayed up until five in the morning. We watched it three times in a row. I figure we could finalize our selection for the evening now.

Steve had a hell of an arm. The ball had rolled down the entire hill and disappeared into some bushes.

"You should ease up on Steve when we're playing," I say to Dave. "You're lucky that he has no idea how strong he is. He could easily kick your ass," I tease.

"Whatever," says Dave. "I would kick that fat bastard's ass." We laugh. We make our way through the bushes looking for that ball.

"Where the fuck did it go?" asks Dave.

"Beats ..." I never get to finish my sentence. A dog comes bursting through the back row of the bushes. I don't know if we scared him or if he is just an aggressive dog, but he means business. He takes us both by surprise. I am standing upright, but Dave is crouched down looking for the ball. I guess I am lucky. Maybe if I was the one bent down...

That dog just jumps on top of Dave and knocks him over. Dave is a flurry of arms, legs, hands, and feet. He manages to get his hands around the dog's throat, but that dog is crazed. The first taste that dog gets is of Dave's forearm. I see those teeth as they clamp into Dave's arm. Dave howls and does the worst thing possible: he pulls his arm back. This results in the teeth tearing through the meat in Dave's arm in a jagged, bloody mess. The dog immediately sinks its teeth into Dave's hand, which is right in front of its mouth. Like a bear trap, those teeth clamp down hard, and takes Dave's pinky, fourth, and middle finger clean off. I can see the look on Dave's face. He is going into shock from the brutal attack. Until that moment, I thought the dog was just snapping at whatever body part was right in front of its mouth, but in the next moment, I learn the dog's true intentions.

With Dave stunned and going into shock, I think the mutt would just go away. As Dave's two-fingered hand falls from the dog's mouth, the dog lunges straight for his exposed throat. In a flash, the dog has its jaw clamped onto his throat and is biting down hard. He isn't just happy with sinking his teeth into the flesh; he starts to thrash around in order to get a deeper penetration. Dave's eyes are wide open and glazed over. I think he knows that dog is going to kill him.

This whole time, from the moment I saw that dog jump through the bushes, I am frozen with fear. I can't move. It's not just the fact that I am afraid the dog will choose me (although that thought did pass through my mind); I am paralyzed with fear. There is even a tree branch right at my feet. I can see it clearly, as it was practically resting on my foot. I want to bend down, grab it, and beat the shit out of that dog, but I just can't get my body to follow what my brain is screaming. I am petrified. I know that if I don't do something, the dog will kill my best friend.

The dog is in a blood lust, violently shaking its head. Blood is dripping out of the dog's mouth, down its throat, and onto my dying friend. All the fight is almost gone from Dave. He lays there as the dog continues its assault.

I just stand there in absolute fear.

I am so scared I am beyond action. With one last violent tear, the dog tears out Dave's throat. Dave's eyes bolt all the way open. Death is coming soon for my ten-year-old friend. The dog stops for a second and releases Dave's bloodied trachea. That son of a bitch dog looks like it is actually trying to make eye contact with Dave in some bizarre dominance ritual. All I hear are gurgling noises coming from Dave's mangled throat.

As quickly as the dog stops, it seems to get that blood lust in its eyes again. It pounces on top of Dave and goes for his exposed abdomen where his shirt rode up during the attack. It sinks its teeth into Dave's soft belly and opens him up as if it is gutting a

fish. Dave's eyes are glazing over now and soon, he will pass on.
I am crying now, watching this fucking dog butcher my best
friend. Each bite gets deeper as it tears into his stomach. When it
reaches Dave's intestines, it begins pulling them out of him and
unraveling them like some gory spool of wire.

The tears are burning my eyes. I can hardly see anything
through them. Just then, a man comes bursting through the
bushes. He sees the bloodied, now-dead body of Dave and kicks
the dog hard in the ribs. I hear a couple of ribs snap. I want
nothing more than that man to keep kicking that fucking dog until
it is as bloody and dead as my friend is lying in the dirt.

"What the hell happened here?" the man screams.

I must have blacked out, because I wake up in the hospital with
my parents and brother around me. I passed out from shock and
for a split second couldn't remember what led me to the hospital.
Then, in one shocking instant, I remember. Remember my
friend's bloody corpse, remember my friend's chewed up trachea
lying next to his neck, and remember my friend's intestines
splayed out in the dirt.

I remember how I was paralyzed with fear as I watched my best
friend get murdered before my eyes.

I cry.

2003 – Austin, Texas

"Wake up, John," my wife says quietly. "You're having a bad
dream."

It was no dream. Twenty-eight years ago, I watched my friend
being torn apart by a dog while I stood there paralyzed by fear.
There were no heroic actions that day.

CHAPTER TWO

1

Present Day – Austin, TX

"Come on sweetie," I say, trying to urge my five-year-old daughter, Fiona, to eat faster. "We still have a 30-minute drive to the zoo."

We are having breakfast at Waterloo Ice House, our regular spot. We've been eating breakfast there two to three times a week for the last two years. I tell myself it's because Fi (we always shorten her name) likes staying on some kind of schedule. However, the truth is, I love going there with Fi. It's "our place." We've had some great times there and the morning wait staff love seeing her each week. Hell, they've pretty much watched her grow up for the last   two years.

"Are you sure you wouldn't rather go someplace else today?" I ask. Every week I try and get Fi to branch out and go someplace different for our weekly Daddy-Daughter day. We've been going to the Austin Zoo once a week for three years, but she loves that zoo. Maybe Fi does like a schedule.

"No, Daddy. I wanna see the animals again," she says.

How can I resist? With that cute little voice and her pouty lower lip, she already knows how to get exactly what she wants from Daddy. Truth is, I love going to the zoo for the same reason I love our breakfasts at Waterloo: it's our spot, and we've done a lot of bonding there. I already think about when she gets older and doesn't want to go to the zoo anymore. That'll be a sad day.

"Well, okay then, sweetie. We need to finish up so we can hit the road."

"Okay, Daddy," she says as she finishes her pancake. "All done." We say our goodbyes to the waitresses and head out the door.

It's a beautiful April day, and a little warmer than usual for this time of year, but the sky is clear. Considering the zoo is pretty much unpaved dirt, I welcome the warm weather with no rain.

As we get to the car, I open the door for Fi and she climbs in. At five, she is tall for her age. She comes up past my hips, and I'm six-feet four. Fi also has these electric blue eyes and beautiful blonde hair that flows down past her shoulders. She's a beautiful girl and is the spitting image of her mother. I know I'm in for a lot of trouble when she starts dating. She's always been so mature for her age, walking at ten months, beginning to mimic our words at a year, and putting basic sentences together shortly thereafter. I'm sure all parents think their kids are "advanced." Maybe Fi is, but all I know is that, along with her mom, she is the love of my life. I'd do anything to protect her and make her happy.

"I wanna buckle my own seatbelt, Daddy," she says as she climbs into the car. "And then I wanna close the car door myself." We go through this every time we get into the car.

"Alright, sweetie. Just make sure you pull the door hard enough." As she pulls the car door, I give it a little push, unseen to her eyes, to make sure it closes properly. I can't help it. I'm an overprotective father.

As I climb behind the steering wheel, I check my pockets to make sure I have my eye drops. Since my eye surgery six years ago, I'm pretty dependent on the drops. I had a corneal graft--so, essentially, have a piece of plastic serving as my cornea. The human body doesn't take too kindly to having foreign, inorganic things in it, so for the last two years my body has been trying to reject the graft. I take six different drops a day to hold back the rejection. If I miss one or two drops, my eye becomes very cloudy, like trying to see through a very thick fog. You can see the shapes of objects, just not any details.

"Goddamnit," I say a little too loud. I realize I forgot my eye drops.

"You shouldn't say that, Daddy," says the little voice from the backseat.

"You're absolutely right, sweetie," I say apologetically, "but I forgot something important at home."

I am trying to decide if I need to go back and grab the drops. Fi usually only has a two hour trip in her. That would get us home by noon. I think I'm good.

"Do we need to go home, Daddy?" Fi sounds concerned.

"And miss the zoo? No way. Daddy'll be okay until we get home," I explain.

The car ride to the zoo is pretty uneventful. I play all her favorite music on the iPod and she sings the entire way there. As we drive down Rawhide Trail, approaching the zoo, the air seems to become very still.

"We're getting closer, sweetie. Can you see the sign?" I ask.

"Ooohh, I see it. There's a monkey, a bird, and a giraffe," she says as she sees all the different animals on the zoo sign.

"I think we might be the first ones here today," I say. I always try to time it so we get to the zoo by ten o'clock AM and get a nice long morning there.

As we pull into the parking lot, I see that we aren't the first one's here. There are already six cars in the parking lot. We pull up alongside a black Hummer. Fi always carries along her *Dora the Explorer* backpack with a change of clothes (just in case of accidents) and her pretend make-up case. I walk around to her side of the car and open her door. I hear the 'click' as she unbuckled her seatbelt. As she slides out of the car, I open the trunk to get her backpack.

Fuck, I think as I open the trunk. Beside her pack are two knives I forgot to take out of the car. One of the perks of being a chef is that you can get your house knives and the knives in your collection sharpened free of charge. I have a guy come around to the restaurant every two weeks to sharpen the kitchen knives and every so often, I throw in some of my personal knives. This past week, I got my seven-inch Ka-bar and my eight-inch Gerber knife sharpened. I hate driving around with those things in my trunk. If I ever got into a fender bender and the cops look in, well, I'd hate to try and explain that.

I quickly took the Ka-Bar, shoved it into Fi's backpack, and stash the Gerber under some dirty work coats.

"I'll carry your backpack today, sweetie," I say, feeling like an idiot.

"That's okay, Daddy. I like carrying my backpack."

Great. My five-year-old daughter is carrying around a sharpened combat knife. Father of the year material here.

2

As we walk around to the entrance of the zoo, I notice that everything is very quiet. Usually there's a lot of noise from the animals, but today, everything is very still. There's usually a few cats running around the gift shop looking to be petted. Today, they're absent.

We approach the counter. "Hello," I say. There is usually a zoo volunteer at the register taking admission. "Is anyone there?" I look into the small office behind the counter. No one. Fi is looking at all the stuffed animals, already deciding which one she wants to take home.

I take an envelope from the counter, put the money in it, and write down our names. My gut is telling me that something's wrong here. There's definitely something strange going on, but that doesn't mean it is dangerous. Let's face it: I don't think anyone would be dumb enough to rob the Austin Zoo (which is, in fact, a non-profit animal rescue).

"Come on, sweetie," I shout to Fi as she is looking at the stuffed monkeys. "We can go in now."

"Yay!" she yells as she tosses the monkey aside. "I wanna see the monkeys first."

"Don't we always see the monkeys first?" I ask. "They're your favorite."

We exit the back of the gift shop, which leads into the zoo. To the right are the bathrooms and up to the left about fifty feet is where the monkeys are.

"Do you need to go to the bathroom before we get started?" I ask, knowing what the answer would be. She is way too excited to pee.

"No, Daddy. I'm good."

At the monkey cages, I finally see some people walking around. There are a few families already checking out the monkeys. That makes me feel better. I guess there are no terrorists attempting to take over the zoo today. I look down at Fiona, smile, and give her a big hug.

"Why did you hug me, Daddy?" she asks.

"Oh, your daddy's being a big dork," I reply, smiling.

As a family of four walks by, I hear the parents rambling on about some kind of excitement going on by the barn. The barn is a structure built to house the petting zoo. There are goats, llamas, and other harmless animals within. I can't hear exactly what they are saying, but it sounds like something big is happening over there.

I look down and see Fiona smiling at me with her wrinkled little nose. I think to ask the family what is going on, but figure it couldn't be too exciting or dangerous, else they would have closed down the zoo. The first cage we come to is the Ring-Tailed Lemurs.

"Here they are, Daddy," she says enthusiastically. "Hhmmm, there's only two of them today. Where did the other two Lemurs go?" she asks.

"I don't know, sweetie." I didn't even realize that the cage was minus two lemurs. I really need to be more observant.

"Maybe they're on vacation," I say jokingly.

"Where would a Lemur go on vacation, Daddy?" she asks.

Before I can answer, I notice something odd about the Lemurs. They aren't their usual playful selves today. They're usually running around, climbing and jumping. Today, they're just sitting on their swings. Looking closer, I see that the Lemur nearest to us has some kind of marking on its fur. It looks as though the fur is matted down. I approach the cage to get a closer look. It almost looks like dried blood on its fur.

As I look up, I notice the Lemur is looking right at me. Then, in a flash, it jumps out of the swing and latches onto the cage right in front of us, and begins shaking it violently. I swear it wants to attack us. Realizing it isn't going to break out of the cage, the lemur jumps away and runs into the enclosed part of the cage. I turn to look at the other Lemur and see that it, too, is scampering off.

"They're mean today, Daddy," Fi says. "Do you think they are tired of being in their cages and want to get out?"

"Maybe, sweetie," I respond, keeping my eye on the far end of the cage. *It's more like they wanna get out and take a bite out of our asses*, I think. I am still trying to process what I saw on the Lemur's fur. It couldn't have been dried blood. The volunteers here would never let one of the animals walk around injured. I wonder if the two lemurs were fighting. After seeing how violent the one was, I wouldn't be surprised.

"Let's go, Daddy," Fi insists as she pulls my hand. "I wanna see more monkeys."

I shake out of my thoughts. We continue to walk down to the next exhibit. As we approach the cage, we both noticed that there was nothing in it.

"Where is he, Daddy?" she asks.

"I'm not sure," I responded as I looked at the sign for the name.

The Colobus monkey is a pretty big animal, about five feet tall. If it was in there, we'd definitely see it.

"Maybe they're gonna clean out its cage later today and they have it in a back-up display." Even I don't believe my own bullshit.

"I think you're right, Daddy," Fiona says, pointing to the floor of the cage. "The cage is really messy."

I see what Fi was pointing at. It looks a little like blood. I step closer to get a better look. "What the fuck is going on here?" I whisper.

"What did you say, Daddy?" Fi asks. Fi is a very sensitive child. Not in the way that her feelings get hurt easily, but in the way she can sense what other people are feeling. Looking into her eyes, she could tell I am worried about something. Before she can ask the inevitable question, I smile. It doesn't work. She is about to say something, but before she can, we heard the monkeys in the next cage running around and screaming.

The noise breaks the moment. "Let's go, Daddy," Fi says excitedly. "They sound like they're being playful today.

Walking around to the front of the Patas monkey cage, we hear a lot of clamor. The Patas monkeys have the largest cage of all the monkeys in the Austin Zoo. There are usually six of them in the cage playing, swinging on the tire, and hamming it up for the people walking around. Once again, as we walk up to the cage, we both notice that there were only two monkeys in there today.

The Patas monkeys don't look like your average monkey. Their bodies resemble the build of a greyhound dog: long legs, narrow body, a defined rib cage. The sign on the cage says these are the fastest of all the primates, being able to reach speeds of thirty to thirty-five miles per hour.

Just as we are walking around the corner, a monkey sees us and lunges like a bullet. The only thing that stops it from jumping on us is the cage. It grabs onto the mesh about six feet off the ground and shakes the metal hard. Fi jumps behind me. I stand my ground, trying not to look upset or concerned. I even manage to force a smile onto my face.

"These monkeys seem just as angry as the Lemurs, Daddy," Fi observes. "Why are all the monkeys in bad moods today?"

I look down at my little girl. I could have lied and made something up, but I think she would have seen right through me.

"I don't know, sweetie," is all I could say. "Maybe they are just having a bad day." *Bullshit*, I think. *Unless by a 'bad day' they want to kill us.*

Then, something catches my eye at the back of the cage. Up on the hanging tire is what looks to be blood, but this time there is no mistaking it. It is blood, pooling in the bottom of the tire from the rope that fastens it to the top of the cage.

Okay, I think. *What the fuck is going on here today*? This is the third cage we've seen that has had some trace of blood in it.

By this time, the other monkey has joined its buddy on the mesh. Both are rattling the metal links, screaming, and trying to get to us. I take Fiona's hand and step away from the cage.

"Come on, sweetie," I calmly say. "Let's go see some other animals."

As we back away from the Patas monkeys, I bump into a man standing behind us, also observing the crazed monkeys, and step on his foot.

"Excuse me, sir," I say apologetically. "I'm very sorry, but I didn't hear or see you standing there." He is wearing the same safari-brown khaki shirt and pants that all the zoo volunteers wear. I saw the name on his shirt. "Sean."

"That's okay," he says, never taking his eyes off the monkeys.

"Do you work here?" I ask foolishly. He has a lean frame, stands about five-foot-eight, and has sandy hair and very distant eyes. He is still fixed on the monkeys. "They have some energy today, don't they?" I ask, trying to force another smile. Fi is watching me very closely.

"They certainly do," says the man. "The question is where they got that energy from." His voice is distant and detached. He may have been standing right in front of us talking, but his thoughts had him a million miles away.

He suddenly snaps his head around to us. "You notice that the animals are more aggressive today? he asks.

"It's kind of hard to miss," I say. "We come every week and this is the first time the animals have acted aggressive." Fi is hugging my leg. She looks at the man I am talking too and notices his cane.

"What's that for?" she innocently asks him, pointing.

"I'm sorry," I apologize. "Fi doesn't mean anything by it. She's just at that age where she notices the differences between people."

"It's okay," he says as he smiled at Fi. "This is a cane. I was… in an accident a few days ago, and now I need this cane to help me get around."

I look down at his bad leg. He is wearing long pants, but I swear I can see an indent in his calf. Almost like part of it is missing.

"I've been walking around all morning feeding and checking in on the animals. I'm a little concerned with how aggressive they're behaving today. I'm sure there's nothing to be worried about."

Sean is a terrible liar, I think. He knows there's something wrong with the animals. That much I can see in his eyes. But why he is acting so mysterious? *He probably just really loves animals*, I try to reason.

"Nice to meet you, Sean. I'm John. What else is strange," I offer, "are the odd markings I noticed on most of the animals' fur."

This brings him and his thoughts back to earth. "Markings?" he asks. "What markings?"

"Well, we saw that several of the Lemurs and Patas monkeys have some kind of odd red marking somewhere on their bodies. It kind of looks like blood, and with them all being so aggressive, we figured they had been fighting. You said you noticed they aren't fighting with each other." We both turn to the Patas monkeys. They are still on the cage, shaking it violently and screaming in our direction. "It kind of seems," I continue, "like they want to attack us."

"You think they want to attack us?" he repeated.

"Look at them," I say, pointing to the monkeys. "It sure doesn't look like they wanna be our friends. In the Colobus monkey cage, the monkey isn't even there, but there's a pool of that red stuff in its cage."

Sean quickly limps up the incline to the Colobus monkey cage. He presses his face right up next to the metal.

"See?" I say, pointing to the spot on the floor. Moving closer to Sean's ear, I whisper, "It sure looks like blood, doesn't it?" Sean is again in a far-off place, lost in thought. "What do you think it is, Sean?"

He slowly turns to me. The color in his face is gone and he genuinely looks scared. "Sean," I say, concerned. "Are you okay?" He just stares into my eyes. My instincts tell me to grab Fi, run back to the car, and get as far away from the zoo as I can, but is that what a hero would do?

"Talk to me, Sean," I say as I raise my voice. I actually consider slapping him. What the hell, it works in the movies. I put my hand on his shoulder and shake him a little. This seems to bring him back.

"I... I didn't know," Sean mumbles. "I thought I was helping them. I only wanted to save them."

"Save who, Sean?" I ask, confused. "What are you talking about? What didn't you know?"

Sean looks me straight in the eyes, and in a voice barely above a whisper, say, "I think we're all in trouble. We didn't know what they were doing in that lab..."

Before he can get another word out, three men dressed in full combat and containment gear rush out of the nearby thicket of trees. "Everyone stand where you are, hands over your head, and no one move an inch."

The men surround us, their assault rifles at point blank and fingers on the triggers. I grab Fi and drop to the ground, covering her with my body.

"Don't any of you move," shouts one man through his gas mask. Another of the men pulls out a picture, looks at it, and points to Sean. "That's our subject." The third man places his hand roughly under Sean's chin and pushes his head up to get a better view.

"Are you sure it's him?" asks the soldier with the gun in our face.

"Positive match," says the man with the picture.

The soldier then pushes Sean to the ground. His face hits the dirt and knocks the air out of his lungs. I look up to see them cuffing his hands behind his back.

"What the hell is going on here?" I yell.

The lead soldier moves his gun away from Fi and me. "Sir," he says in a very stern tone. "I need you to stand up." He takes a step back, encouraging me to stand. I start to ask him what is going on again, but he has his agenda and is sticking to it. "Sir, how long have you known this man?" he asks.

"I met him like five minutes ago," I say. I look over and see that the soldier that cuffed him still had his foot on Sean's back, keeping him firmly in place.

"What kind of contact did you have with this man?" the soldier continues.

"Contact? What the hell are you talking about?Who are you guys? What the hell is going on here?" I'm surprised that I am so angry. I'm scared shitless, but feeling Fi hugging my leg so tightly inspires a fear that I have never felt before. I'm angry and scared that I have absolutely no control in this situation. I have no weapon and no information. Nothing.

"Sir, we need you to answer these questions quickly and concisely." There is not going to be a give-and-take exchange here. He wants information from me and he was going to get it. A crowd of people start to gather around us. The soldier who holds the picture of Sean places it back inside his pocket and turns to the crowd.

"I need everyone to remain where they are," he yelled at the crowd. "This is a private matter and the quicker we can talk to these people, the quicker we will be finished." He has his rifle pointing to the ground, but something tells me that he won't hesitate to quell the crowd with force if it comes to that.

"Look," I say, trying to keep calm, "I just met him five minutes ago. We were looking at the friggin' monkeys. I saw that he works here, so I was asking him some questions. That's it."

"What kind of questions did you ask him?" I can't see his eyes underneath the gas mask, but I can reasonably guess that he is shooting me a stone-cold glare.

"I don't know," I say, trying to remember. "I was asking about the animals."

"What about the animals? What did he say about the animals?"

"I asked him if he noticed how aggressive the animals were acting today. He told me he did."

"Is that all?" he asks as he turns to the soldier with his foot still on Sean's back.

I debate whether to tell them about Sean saying he thinks we're all in trouble and that he looked scared. I figure that these guys found who they were looking for, and it doesn't really matter what I say at this point.

"Yeah that's all," I say, my anger rising. "That's all until you guys came outta the trees waving around your guns in mine and my daughter's face."

The soldier stares blankly at me.

"Who the hell are you guys?" I manage to ask. "Why the hell is the military ambushing a volunteer who works at the zoo?" The crowd around us grows larger. The soldiers all look around and then nod at each other.

"We aren't military sir. We're a private security firm. This man," he says as he nods to Sean, who is now standing, "is wanted for acts of domestic terrorism."

Then Sean, who just moments ago was on the ground, grows a pair and retorts, "Domestic terrorist? Are you fucking serious? If you call trying to liberate a bunch of ani…"

That's as far as he gets before the soldier gags Sean's mouth.

Without saying a word, the soldiers start leaving with Sean in front of them. I look at the crowd and see a few people trying to use their cell phones, I'm guessing to call 9-1-1. From the looks on their faces, I'd say they either can't get a signal, or they can't get a connection.

I kneel down to hug Fi. This whole time she's just stood there, hugging my leg tightly. She hasn't shed one tear. I sure hope I've put on a brave front for her.

"It's okay, sweetie," I say unconvincingly. "They're gone. We're okay now."

"What about that man," she asks. "Is he going to be okay?"

"Well, that man may have done some bad things and those other guys are going to take him back and ask him about those things." I don't think she's gonna let this drop that easily.

"Don't policemen usually come and arrest the bad guys?" she asks. I start to answer her and really didn't know what to say. Yes, the cops usually do the arresting, especially for civilians. Who the fuck were those guys? I think they were telling the truth when they said they weren't military. I didn't see any military rankings or branch insignias on their uniform.

I have to tell Fi something. "You're absolutely right, sweetie. The police usually go and get the bad guys, but sometimes if someone does something really bad, the police need some help." What bullshit. Sean looked about as dangerous as a house cat.

The crowd starts to break up and go back to the displays. I look down at Fi and ask, "Do you want to go home sweetie?" immediately regretting giving her the option of staying.

"No, Daddy. I wanna see more animals."

I knew she was going to say that. "Okay, Fi, but let's get out of the monkey area. Let's go see the lions and tigers." I'd be damned if I let this incident take over and replace all of the good memories in Fi's mind that we've had at the zoo together.

She agrees, saying she's seen enough monkeys for one day.

CHAPTER THREE

1

Animal Rescue Shelter, Hyde Park
Julie wakes up late to the high-pitched sound of her bedside alarm clock. She was up late the last few nights trying to care for the new animals she took into the shelter. She couldn't believe how many animals those two guys brought around. They had the typical house cats, dogs, ferrets, white rats and hamsters, as well as some not-too-popular house pets like snakes, baby alligators, and even three bats. When she asked the guys where they got all these animals, they told her they used to work for a group of veterinarians who went out of business. These animals, they told her, came from about four different vet's offices. She didn't believe a word of their bullshit. She suspects the animals came from some university or other kind of research lab, but at the end of the day, doesn't care. She is about helping and rescuing animals. They needed a sanctuary, and she would going to provide it for them no matter where they came from.

She slips out of bed and into the bathroom. She looks at herself in the mirror and almost doesn't recognize the face staring back at her. As exhausted as she is, Julie knows that she is pretty. She stands five-feet-ten and has long legs that she feels are her best attribute. As she brushes the dirty blonde hair out of her face, her emerald green eyes hit the bathroom light. *Okay,* she thinks. "*Maybe my eyes are my best feature.* She smiles.

After a quick shower, she feels revived. She grabs a quick cup of coffee and heads out to the animal shelter. She can't help but think about the odd animals those guys brought around. It isn't so much the types of animals that are odd; it is more their behavior. She's never seen a group of animals behave in such a way. When she or any of her helpers weren't around, the animals seemed calm and almost comatose, but as soon as one of them walked into the room, the animals would lose it and all hell would break loose. Against her better judgment, she could swear the animals wanted to attack her and the other helpers. She laughs. "What the hell is an eight-pound house cat gonna do even if she has the opportunity to attack me?"

Yet, she couldn't help but feel creeped out every time she walked into the main room where the animals were kept in the shelter. She could almost feel their eyes on her. Then, in unison, they would all lose their fucking minds and go into attack mode. It was creepy.

For as long as she can remember she has loved animals. She got along with them and understood them. They never wanted anything from her except to be fed and to feel safe. Men, on the other hand, always wanted something. The trail of losers she's left behind in her past is proof of that. She's always felt, from a very young age, out of place in her own skin. She has a tomboy mentality encased in a model's body. She wants the companionship of a man, but isn't willing to sacrifice herself or her ideals for it. Her animals come first. Most guys can never accept that. One of her exes actually accused her of fucking some of the animals. Thinking about that asshole makes her blood start to boil.

Julie makes the short drive to the shelter and pulls into the driveway. The shelter is, in fact, an old converted house in the Hyde Park section of Austin, TX. Her father told her she could get a good deal on some of those older houses. His intention was for his daughter to buy a house at a young age and build good credit and equity. Her intention had been to buy a cheap house and convert it into an animal rescue shelter. Animals always came first, even before her needs.

She pulls into the driveway of the two-story wood and brick house. When she gets out of the car, she is struck by how quiet it is. It is past the usual time she feeds the animals and they should all be clamoring in their cages to be fed. Luckily, she lives on one of the older streets away from the majority of houses. She rarely gets any complaints about the noise, and when she does get angry calls, she explains what she does, and that usually shuts up the pissed off caller. It's good to live in a liberal city.

Julie walks into the house to find her four tabbies walking around and jumping off the counters, hungry and mewing up a storm. She feeds them, scratches behind their ears, and apologizes for being late. As she starts to walk into what was the family room before it was converted into the main part of the shelter, she can't help but wonder why the group of new animals aren't raising hell to be fed. She figures they were abused and probably beaten by their previous owners,

As soon as she walks into the room, she gasps. "Jim... *Jim!*" she yells. "Get in here!" Jim comes running in. Jim has been a part of this rescue shelter since the beginning. He helped renovate it and kept it running by looking for donations and doing the handy work around the place.

"What's wrong, Julie?" Jim questions, running into the room. He stops on a dime the moment he looks around. "What the fuck is this?"

Around the perimeter are cages of all sizes housing all different kinds of animals. What has them spooked is that every animal is standing at attention and quietly staring at them. The animals make no sounds or noises. Tails aren't wagging, and tongues aren't hanging out of mouths panting. The animals just sit there, staring at the two of them.

"What the fuck is going on, Julie?" Jim asks. "Why are they all just sitting there? They don't even look like they're breathing." Julie notices that, too. She'd thought that her mind had been playing tricks on her.

"I don't know, Jim. When I walked into the room, they were all laying down. I thought they were dead. They weren't moving or breathing. Then they all stood up, faced me, and started doing that." She points at them. "They're seriously freaking me out."

"I told you three days ago I didn't like these animals. Those guys who brought them were full of shit about that clinic going tits up. These animals are seriously fucked up." Jim physically shakes as he looks around at the animals.

"Well, what could we do, Jim?" Julie asks, becoming more animated. "Those guys may have been shady, but those animals needed our help."

"Look, I checked around with my buddies at the university and there were no recent lab break-ins. I have some friends in those animal liberation groups and none of them know of any recent liberations." Jim is facing Julie. "I have no idea where these animals came from, but looking at them, I don't feel safe around them. I'm actually worried for the other animals we have."

Julie had placed all the new animals in a separate room, away from the ones that' were already housed here. She knew those guys who dropped them off were feeding her a line of bullshit. She suspected, even then, that the animals had come from some lab, and hadn't wanted to take the chance of them infecting the others. If that were true, they could have been testing anything on those poor animals.

"Okay, okay, Jim," she agrees. "I agree that there's something odd about these animals, but what can we do? They still need our help."

Jim shivered. "They are freaking me out."

"Well, let's get them fed. Maybe that will get them back to acting normal." She suspects it won't.

They both go to the cabinets to prepare the food. Once it is all portioned out, they return to the cages. With a bowl of food in his left hand, Jim reaches out to unlock a cage that houses five cats. Just as he lifts the latch, all five cats attack his hand. The closest sinks its teeth into the tender flesh between his thumb and forefinger. Jim yells and drops the bowl,trying to pull away. By this time, the others have taken advantage of his fingers. All five cats are attached to his hand, sinking their tiny, needle-sharp teeth into his fingers and thrashing their heads around. The ones that come away with flesh seem satisfied they will feast on their prize.

The cat that has him by the hand has already ripped away two chunks of flesh and is coming back for a third. This sets off all the other animals in the room. They are all thrashing against their cages, trying to get out.

Jim screams. He can't pull his hand out of the cage. To Julie, it looks like the cats are pulling him further into the cage. She grabs his arm around the elbow and tries to pull it out of the cage. She can't believe the grip those cats have. Finally, the main cat must have had its fill. It releases John's hand and darts out of the cage. The other cats follow, leaving behind a bloody cage filled with bits of Jim's flesh.

Jim grabs a towel and wraps it around his bloody hand. Julie noticed that he looks pale and is worried he would pass out. "Let's sit you down," she says as she walks him over to the office chair.

In the other room, Julie hears the screams and screeches from her four tabbies. She runs in to see the cats that had just attacked John have cornered and are attacking her tabbies. For a second, she freezes in fear. The largest of the cats, the one that had captured Jim's hand, has taken down one of the tabbies as if it were a mouse. It immediately goes for the throat, and in a fast, fluid motion, tears out the cat's windpipe. The cats are completely oblivious to Julie being in the room. They are focused on the tabbies and won't stop until they kill them all.

Looking away from her dying tabby in horror, she turns to see that another of the feral cats has already taken down and is eating another tabby. Tears fill Julie's eyes as she watches the cat tear into the tabby's stomach, but these cats weren't just killing; they are eating their fallen prey.

Julie grabs a nearby broom and runs at the cats. They don't seem scared at all by Julie's threatening advances. She gets to the cat that has torn out her pet's throat and smacks it hard with the broom. It doesn't even move. It keeps eating her tabby. She pulls the broom over her head and brings it down hard, but that only makes the cat look up at her. It stares at Julie as she is about to smack it again, but this time, flees and runs out the door. The other four cats follow.

Julie looks around and sees that all four of her tabbies are dead. Those fucking cats tore her tabbies apart, fed on their insides, and then ran off.

Julie starts crying, but was interrupted when she hears Jim moaning in the other room. He is still sitting in the chair, holding his hand. The animals are going absolutely fucking crazy, almost like they picked up the scent of blood and wanted a taste.

"What the fuck is going on here?" Julie screams. She reaches for the phone to call Austin Animal Control. She hates herself for doing it, but there is something very wrong with these animals. They didn't want to eat dog and cat food. They wanted to eat flesh.

"What the fuck is going on?" she repeats as she dials the phone.

2

"Austin Animal Control, how can I help you?" the bored voice on the phone asks.

"I need to get a few guys out here with cages and trucks. I have some very odd acting animals over here." Julie tries to remain calm, but even she can hear her voice trembling. Jim is in the other room, passed out from the pain of the attack. It is killing Julie to have to call animal control, because these people are the ones that put animals to sleep. After what she has just witnessed, she is scared shitless.

"Could you please tell me the nature of the problem?" asks the operator.

"The nature of the problem is that I have a room full of psychotic fucking animals and I need help removing them." She can't believe what she is doing or saying. If someone had told her five years ago that she would one day be on the phone with the city begging them to come out and take a bunch of animals, she would have rolled her green eyes and walked away laughing.

"I need you to remain calm, please." She hears him typing on the computer. "I need to know the exact nature of your problem. How many animals are involved, what types of animals are they, and has anyone been injured?"

Julie takes a deep breath. She is about to fucking lose it. "I run an animal rescue shelter in Hyde Park. A guy came around a few days ago with a ton of runaways and strays that needed help. There's about a total of fifteen to twenty-five animals." She can almost hear that bastard yawning on the line. "This morning when my partner and I went to feed them, they attacked him. It's pretty bad." That seems to have gotten his attention. She can almost hear him bolt upright in his chair.

"The animals attacked you?" he asks, concerned.

"Yes. Well, just the cats. When he went to open the cat cage to feed them, they jumped on his hand and really tore him up. Then those cats killed four of my house pets." Julie hears nothing on the other line. After a few minutes, she hears the man typing and talking into another phone.

"Please hold the line," he says, very sternly and to the point.

Ten seconds pass before another man answers the phone. "Thanks for holding. This is George. You say you work at a shelter with a lot of aggressive animals?"

The hair on Julie's arms stand up. She couldn't explain it, but this guy sounded like he was military.

"Yes," she answers hesitantly.

"Can you tell me where you got the animals?" George asks.

"A couple guys brought them by a few days ago. I told all this to the first guy. Who are you again? Is this still animal control?" George ignores her questions. "All the information you can give us will help us help you quicker." Something in the back of Julie's mind tells her that 'George' isn't all that interested in helping her.

"Look," she finally says. "Are you going to send someone over?"

"They're already on the way."

"Already on the way? I never gave you my address." Julie trembles. "Who the fuck are you? Look, I need some help. My friend is hurt really bad and I need to get these goddamn animals out of here."

"You have a hurt friend?" George asks. "Was he injured by one of the animals?"

"Yes. Look, I told all this to the other guy. What the fuck is going on here?"

George ignores her. "Was your friend attacked by the animals? Was he bitten?"

Julie hangs up. She sits there for a minute, staring at the phone. She picks it back up to call for an ambulance when she sees a figure walk by the backdoor. She only catches a glimpse, but she could have sworn he was wearing green army fatigues. She freezes. There is definitely something fucked up here. She runs into the other room and tries to wake up Jim.

"Jim," she loudly whispered, shaking him. "Get up, Jim. We need to get out of here." Jim doesn't budge. Julie hopes that he has just passed out and isn't in shock. She sees more people running in the backyard and decides she needs to get out of here. "I'll call the police and an ambulance for you, Jim. Just hang in there."

The old house she bought has a trap door in the main room. When the original house was updated with new plumbing, the owners included it just in case they ever needed to do repairs under the house. As soon as she runs into the room with the animals, they all go crazy. They start thrashing and clawing at their cages, trying to get out and, she assumes, at her. Julie doesn't stop. She runs over to the trapdoor and jumps through it.

Just as she is closing the door, she sees a group of five men dressed in full combat gear kick through the front and back doors in unison. Two of the soldiers, one at the back and one at the front, carry flamethrowers. One of the men grabs Jim and throws him to the ground. Then, without looking, the soldiers unleash hell into her house. They spray streams of fire all around and especially toward the cages. Her first thoughts are about Jim, but then she sees one of the men laying Jim on the ground and placing him in something that looks like a body bag, except with the face exposed so he can breathe. The soldier then fixes a contagion mask with an odd symbol over Jim's face and carries him out of the house.

The house goes up quickly. There hasn't been rain in Austin for almost two months and the house and lawn are dried out. The last thing she sees before she closes the trapdoor are the men walking to the cages and spraying streams of fire into each. She hears one man yell that he's found more animals in the back. Julie's heart stops. Those animals aren't sick. They were normal, whatever that meant. She knows those men are going to kill and burn any animal they find in that house. What really strikes her is that the sick animals aren't freaking out. They just sit in their cages, as if accepting their doom.

She starts to cry, but quickly remembers that she is underneath her house, which she is sure the soldiers intend to burn to the ground. She needs to make a move, but knows they'd be looking for the woman who made the call.

Julie crawls to the far left side of the house. She has a clear path to run straight into the woods. She is about to dart out when she hears one of the men on the radio. "We are neutralizing the problem right now. The majority of the animals here are the house pet varieties. No sir," he then answers. "There were no large cats or bears found at the site." The soldier pauses. "Yes sir, we will completely neutralize and cleanse this site. We have a male subject who was bitten by one or several animals. No sir, we haven't found the one who made the call. We will, sir."

The soldier motions to the others. "You know our orders," he says. "Neutralize and cleanse. Nothing living gets outta here." He then turns to the soldier to his right and says, "Find the female subject who made the call. We need to bring her in." Then he cups his hands around his mouth and shouts, "Nothing living gets through the perimeter." As they run into the controlled blaze, the last thing she hears the soldier say is something about the subject at the Austin zoo being neutralized. For the hundredth time today, Julie finds herself asking out loud, "What the fuck is going on?"

With all the soldiers back in the house, she has her chance. *This is it*, she thinks. *I either burn with the house, or get shot running into the woods.*

She takes a deep breath and runs like hell.

CHAPTER FOUR

1

Austin Zoo, Austin, TX

I was really hoping I could talk Fi into going home after the incident by the monkey cage, but she is a pretty stubborn girl and won't even hear of leaving before she gets her train ride and something from the gift shop.

"How about this, sweetie," I say, trying to bargain with her. "If we leave now, I'll get you two things from the gift shop."

"I wanna go on the train." Her mind is made up. At least the incident hadn't scared her. I am happy for that.

"Okay, sweetie, but after the train we need to leave." She is looking at me as if trying to figure out why I want to leave so badly. I don't want her to be afraid. "Daddy got home from work late last night and is really tired. I figured we could go home, relax, and watch *Dora* on TV." Fi looks at me the same way her mom does when I'm lying; as if I'm full of shit. I smile, hug her, and we walk to the train.

We make our way around the African Lion and Bengal Tiger cages quickly. It is already 10:50 and the train leaves on the hour. As we walk past the lion cage, I notice that there is only one lion in there. *Fucking hell. Why are there so many goddamn animals missing?* Thankfully, Fi is thinking about the train ride and doesn't notice the absent cats.

After the large cat displays, we dart past the Black Bear cage. The bear has a huge display with a lot of land, a fountain, and some large boulders to climb on. I glance over my shoulder as we walk by and noticed that the bear is also missing. There is another smaller cage up toward the northern end of the display where the zoo volunteers place the bear when they clean the larger display. It's possible he is in there, but with all the other absent animals, I'm doubtful that's where he is. Even in that smaller cage, it would be tough not to see him. I stop by the display to read the information. This one is male, weighs five-hundred pounds, and when standing reaches six feet tall. This animal is not one that I want to have a run in with. I just can't help but think where the hell the bear and all the other missing animals are.

"Come on, Daddy," Fi whines as she tries to pull me from the bear display. "We're gonna miss the train."

"Would I ever miss the train ride?" I ask. Damn. She's onto me. We leave the missing bear behind and finish the walk to the train. Along the way, we pass display after display of empty enclosures. The bobcats, cougars, and binturongs are all missing. Even the large corral they've set up for the petting zoo is looking pretty sparse. They usually have three llamas, a bunch of goats, and six deer, but today I notice only two goats and one deer. I'm starting to wonder if there is some virus or other kind of illness ripping through the animals at the zoo.

We finally get to the train depot with about three minutes to spare. It is getting warmer today. We sit on the bench and wait for the lady to set up the cash register. I reach into Fi's backpack to grab the water I packed and remember there is a marine-issued combat knife in the pack. I grab the water quickly, thinking everyone might see the knife.

After a minute, we see the train pulling up to the station. We stand in line for our tickets and I can't help but look around, scanning for anything out of the ordinary.

2

Most days we are two of maybe ten people on the train, but today, with the schools being closed due to a holiday, there are a lot more people around. I do a rough count. About twenty-five to thirty people are in line for the train ride.

As the train comes to a halt, I have to laugh a little bit. As much as Fi loves this train, it is pretty sad looking. The train is a pretty old clunker that looks as though every run is going to be its last. It runs on electricity and therefore has to be recharged every night. The head car, or locomotive, has a raised platform where the driver sits and controls the brake and speed of the train. There are no individual cars either. Instead, there are twenty-one rows of seats with the last row facing backwards. Every four rows of seats make up what would be a car on a larger train. The train is divided up like this, I assume, in order to make going around curves easier.

There's also a fiberglass ceiling that helps shade the riders from the sun, but there are no sides, so you didn't feel boxed in. It's an open design that is very kid-friendly. The seats are small and low to the ground and because there are no doors, it's easy for a child to climb in and out of the cars by themselves. It's hard to guess how old the train might be. The faded red paint makes it look pretty ancient, but riding the train is Fi's favorite part of our daddy-daughter days. In her mind, I'm sure this is a huge locomotive, freshly painted and capable of going across the country.

I look at the people in line before us. They are the typical bunch: some families, a few single parents with their kids, and the random grandparent and grandchild. Standing a few people ahead of us, I notice a young, single woman with no kids in tow. She has sunglasses and a wide-brimmed, floppy hat on. Almost as if she is trying to hide her face, and I swear she faintly smells like smoke. Not cigarette smoke, but almost like she has just ran out of a burning building.

What I don't notice, at first, is the young man standing about eight people behind us, staring intently at the woman in the floppy hat.

3

I don't need to ask Fi where she wants to sit, She walks straight to the back of the train. She loves sitting in the last row, the one that faces backwards. She's told me that when we sit in the last row, she feels like it's just the two of us all alone on the train. How can you not love a kid that sweet?

Before we sit down, I look at the other families seated on the train and notice the woman in the large floppy hat. She is sitting about three rows away from us, looking like she is anything but interested in this train ride. She catches me looking at her and quickly turned away. I sit down next to Fi and put my arm around her, thinking nothing else of the strange woman.

"Good morning, ladies and gentlemen," the conductor says on a microphone. "I'll be your conductor today and wanted to go over a few safety rules. Please make sure you are sitting down at all times when the train is in motion, and that you keep your hands and feet inside the train at all times. If for some reason the train does stall, please remain in your seats and do not leave the train. It'll be just another couple of minutes before the brakes are all charged up. Thanks and enjoy the ride."

I hug Fi closer. I'm glad she wanted to stay. The train ride is our "thing." I'm hoping that no matter where she goes in life, and no matter how old she gets, she'll always remember riding the train at the Austin Zoo with her old man.

My thoughts drift back to what happened by the monkey cages. Who was Sean, if that was even his real name? Was he really a domestic terrorist? I seriously doubt it. He looked about as threatening as a Disney character. But then again, it doesn't take a lot of strength if you have a bomb strapped around your waist. Ideals are always stronger than muscle. Nothing makes sense or adds up about what happened. He seemed more concerned about the animals. Didn't he even say something about liberating animals?

The even greater question, I think, was why the military was after that guy. Is he an ex-soldier? Is he really more dangerous than he looks? They said they worked for a private security firm. What the hell does that mean? I can't wrap my mind around it. Nothing about it makes sense. They came storming out of the trees, bound and gagged him, and then stormed off, all with at least twenty witnesses present. The soldiers, though, hadn't seemed to care.

The loud horn from the train interrupts my thoughts and jars me back to reality. "All aboard," the train conductor says. I turn to see how many people ended up on the train, and I catch the woman in the floppy hat staring at Fi and me. A shiver unexpectedly runs down my spine. *This is turning out to be one creepy and surreal day*, I think. So far, we've seen aggressive animals, unexplained blood in animal cages, seemingly-dead animals that suddenly disappear, and a man being forcefully taken by the military. It suddenly dawns on me how stupid I am being. Why the fuck are we sitting on this train? We should be halfway home by now. I stayed because Fi really wanted to ride the train. That's stupid. Things aren't right here today, and as a parent with a shred of common sense, I should have taken her away from this place immediately. So she'd be angry with me for an hour or two. So what? Something is definitely wrong here and I think I've realized it too late.

As the train pulls away from the platform, I have a bad feeling in the pit of my stomach. "Something's not right," I whisper out loud. "Something's definitely not right." I look down at Fi. She is kicking her legs and is all smiles. *If there is something wrong*, I think, *there's no way in hell I'm gonna let anything happen to Fi. No matter what.*

4

Jason sits five rows away from Julie. He is pretty sure she won't recognize him. They met only that one time when he came by with Sean to "donate" some animals to her shelter. He feels bad about giving her those animals without telling her where they came from. He's read a few articles on her and knows she is doing great work at that shelter. She never refuses any animal no matter how old or sick it might be and is known to take in just about anything. She was the only choice he and Sean had. He figured the animals in the lab were being fed some kind of steroid or experimental drug and that was why they were so aggressive. In time, he reasoned the drugs would pass through their systems and they'd return to normal. "They just needed to de-tox," he would say, trying to convince himself.

Jason sits on the train thinking about how he and Sean liberated the animals and had barely escaped with their lives. After the liberation, they'd regrouped at the Animal Rights First office. At first they'd just sat in silence, trying to make sense of what the fuck had just happened. The crushing reality of losing Vicktor and of seeing that soldier blow his brains out of the back of his head had only just started to sink in.

It's so fucking typical, Sean had said between sobs. *They pump those poor animals full of God-knows-what, they become violent, and then they send in a crew to kill them all. Fucking assholes.*

Dude, I don't know what they were testing in that lab, but those animals ... Jason's sentence had trailed off. *Those animals weren't right. Did we really save them from those men, or did those men start killing them because we let them out of their cages?*

Jason could tell by Sean's reaction that he hadn't thought about that. *You mean it wasn't a coincidence that those guys showed up?* he'd asked. *You think they were there to stop us and when they saw that we had already opened several cages just immediately started killing them to avoid them from escaping?*

Jason had started. *Look,* he'd reasoned. *That place had some pretty sophisticated state-of-the-art security, and it was all hidden. It's almost like they didn't want people to see just how secure that place really was.* By then, Sean had stopped crying. *I think we set off a silent alarm that was sent directly to that military-looking squad. They didn't want the police there or else they would have just had a regular alarm hard wired to the police department.*

But ... but what were they doing in that lab? Sean had asked.

How the fuck should I know? You were the one who was working there. Didn't you see anything?

I saw... I mean... I was there to get...

You got overwhelmed when you saw all those animals in cages and you lost your head. You fucked up, Sean. God only knows what we released into the neighborhood.

Do you think they're still dangerous?

Are you kidding me? How could you ask that? A fucking monkey took a chunk out of your leg and it sure looked like those animals were chewing their way through the soldiers.

They were scared and were panicking. You said it yourself that they were probably pumped full of steroids or something. Right?

We need to fix this. We need to go see if we can round up any of the animals we set loose. We at least need to round up the cats, dogs, and hamsters. Those are the animals that kids will try to approach. Sean had grown silent at the mention of kids. *Come on. We have some protective gear. Let's go round them up. I read about this shelter in Hyde Park that takes in animals, no questions asked.*

Sean hadn't move. Jason had responded by jumping up and hitting his shoulder. *We need to make this right,* he'd yelled. *If any kid gets hurt by one of those animals, I couldn't live with myself.*

They'd picked up a few drinks to calm their nerves and then went around the neighborhood looking for the animals they'd freed hours beforehand. At first they drove around looking for the liberated animals, but realized they were most likely hiding in shadows and cowering under porches and backyard decks. They were about to go back to the office to park the car so they could continue their search on foot when they found them. As they drove by a large field, they noticed in the moonlight that it was littered with bodies. Jason at first thought the worst, and that the animals had attacked and killed a rancher or farmer and a bunch of field workers? Upon closer inspection, they realized the animals themselves were what they saw scattered across the field. Not just some of them. *All* of them. And they looked dead.

They'd parked the car next to the field. Jason had just been about to get out when Sean asked: *What are you doing?*

I'm getting out of the fucking car so we can get these animals, Jason replied. Sean's arm had tightened around Jason's.

What? Look at them, they're dead, Sean had practically whined.

Are you fucking crazy? Those animals are nuts and pumped full of some kind of chemical. How do you know they're dead?

Just look at them. None of them are breathing.

Jason had hesitated before saying, *Stay there a second.*

He'd opened his door wide enough to get his arm through, then reached down and picked up a rock before tossing it into the field with the animals. It made a squishy, dull thud noise as it hit a dog and then bounced and hit a rabbit.

Sean and Jason had watched to see if any of the animals would move. They hadn't. They'd then looked at each other and, without saying a word, both decided to get their gear on, grab the cages, and collect the animals. *Man,* Sean had said, breaking the silence. *I kinda wish we had one of those flamethrowers.*

Jason had looked at him incredulously. *What?* Sean had then asked. *These animals are freaking me the hell out.*

Let's not forget that these animals are the victims. They may be violent now, but they need our help more than ever. Let's go collect them and take them over to that shelter.

Then what do we do?

"We go see Janet and get you checked out." Janet was a third-year medical student that was also a member of Animal Rights First. She was a great doctor who loved animals, and best of all, wouldn't report Sean's wounds to the police.

They'd gotten out of the car and had gone to the trunk to get the protective gear on. The whole time, they didn't take their eyes off the animals in the field. *By the way,* Jason had then asked. *How're you feeling?*

Ya know something, Sean had then replied, *it doesn't hurt at all. The only time it hurt was when the damn monkey was actually biting me, but like ten minutes later, it didn't hurt at all.*

They'd finished putting on their gear. They were both wearing the suits that attack dog trainers wear. They'd had thick pieces of rubber-covered foam protecting them from head to toe. Only their hands had been exposed. The protection the suit offered was too bulky for the work they needed to do. So after throwing a bunch of cages into the field, they'd walked toward the animals slowly. The field, it turned out, was actually a large piece of untouched land that the city hadn't yet developed. It was full of rocks, sand, wild flowers, and weeds. Jason had felt like an idiot for thinking it was part of a ranch.

They'd walked about twenty feet into the field before coming upon the first animal: a typical, run-of-the-mill house cat. It looked dead. Its eyes had been closed and hadn't looked like it was breathing. Sean and Jason had looked at each other before Sean nodded, prodding Jason on to take this first animal. Jason had been sweating like a fat man at a physical in that rubber protective suit. He'd swallowed hard and knelt down next to the cat, squinting while trying to see if the cat was breathing. Its chest hadn't move. He wasn't sure what would have been creepier: if the cat and all the other animals were playing dead, or if they actually were dead. If they were dead, what the fuck had killed them? Whatever it was, was it contagious? Jason had arranged the cage next to the cat before opening the door. He'd touched the cat quickly to see if it would react. When it hadn't, he'd scooped it up and threw it into the cage. He'd slammed the door, looked up at Sean, and then said: *You can breathe now, Sean.Man, they sure look and act fucking dead. You got the next one.I'm taking this one back to the truck.*

About six feet away from the cat, Jason had picked up a monkey: the same kind that had attacked Sean in the lab. He'd kicked it with his padded foot, thinking how fucked up this all was. Its eyes had then bolted opened as it jumped up and wrapped its arms around Sean's forearm. The monkey tore apart the protective padding on the sleeve and bit into his hand. Sean had screamed, but couldn't shake the monkey off of his arm. It sunk its teeth deeper into Sean's forearm and began to tear away chunks of his flesh.

Jason had ran over with a tree branch cocked back like a baseball bat. *Hold the fucker away from your body,* he'd yelled. Sean had thrust his arm away from his body and Jason had swung hard, connecting with the monkey's ribcage. They'd both heard the unmistakable crack of breaking ribs, but the monkey hadn't loosen its grip one bit. A few feet away was a tree. Sean had run over to it and started smacking the monkey against it. The first few smacks struck the monkey in the broken ribs, but again, it hadn't seemed to notice. Sean had then twisted his arm and started beating the monkey on the head. After a few hard knocks, he'd heard a large crack and looked to see that he had split the animal's head open. Jason had run over, grabbed the monkey, and threw it to the ground.

Jesus Christ, Sean had gasped, wincing through his teeth. *That mother fucker was fast.*

Let me see how bad it is, Jason had replied.

No way, dude. There's no way in hell I'm taking off any of this gear until we are outta this field. Besides, the pain is already going away.

Going away, Jason had answered. *How's that even possible? That fucker was on your arm not five-seconds ago. Is it numb? Is that why you don't feel anything?*

No, Sean had answered. *It's not numb at all. There's just no pain.*

Jason had managed to force a smile onto his face. He hadn't wanted to scare Sean, but that just wasn't normal. He should've be in excruciating pain. Just another fucked up piece of the puzzle. *Well, good,* he'd said. *Let's finish up here so we can get you to Janet.*

They'd both turned to collect more animals and noticed that the spot where they'd flung the monkey was empty. All that remained was a bloody wet spot. The monkey was gone. They'd just looked at each other and went to work.

One by one, they'd placed the unconscious/dead animals into the cages. There were no other incidents with another animal suddenly regaining consciousness. By the time they finished rounding up the animals, they counted twenty-two in total, and the sun had risen. They decided not to postpone the ordeal any longer and went straight to the animal rescue in Hyde Park. Jason had already had his story in place: they'd received the animals from a veterinarian's office that was closing and had vowed to find homes for them all Sean had liked the story, It was short, with little details to get confused.

The train jerks as it pulls away from the platform, jarring Jason back to reality. He again looks over at Julie and wonders why she is on this train. He is here because this is the last place he knows Sean visited. They were talking on the phone when the line went dead. Now Sean is missing. *This has been a really fucked up couple of days*, Jason thinks.

5

The kids are all giggling and excited as the train pulls away from the platform. Parents are smiling, talking on cell phones, and engaged in conversations with their kids. Fi sits close to me, looking around. We know every square inch of both the train and the path. The total ride spans about fifteen to twenty miles. After leaving the platform, the train passes by some large pens holding long horns, ostriches, and donkeys. After those animals, the trees begin to get thicker and we pass by the parking lot into a more remote and isolated area. A slight decline in the tracks reveal that the path was cut through a wall of rock. It's a very beautiful and serene ride and it's easy to forget you're in Texas. The train will take a rather sharp turn to the left to reveal the large, sprawling, green hills of the Hill Country in the following moments.

Fi loves looking around at the high rock walls, all the different kinds of wild flowers, and the old trees. There are also little wooden cutout displays of gnomes having afternoon tea, ladybugs playing checkers, and leftover scenes from Thanksgiving and Christmas that have since become another part of the ride.

"Look," I say, pointing to the parking lot as we slowly start to build up speed. "Van you see our car?"

"Yeah, Daddy." I know she isn't even looking. She is looking at the fake fossils that were placed alongside the tracks and hung up on the trees by the zoo staff.

The zoo staff, I think. I hadn't realized it until this moment, but there are usually around fifteen volunteers working at the zoo. They feed the animals, clean the cages, maintain the grounds, and do all the things required to keep the zoo open. Today, not including the volunteer driving the train, I've seen four, maybe five volunteers. *Just another mystery to add to this fucked up day.*

As the train passes the parking lot and further away from the more populated zoo grounds, I turn to notice the floppy-hatted girl feverishly texting away on her phone. I don't know what it is about her, but I feel there is a story to her.

"Look, Daddy," Fi says as she grabs my arm. I knew exactly what she is pointing at. A split second later, we drive past a fake coyote skull hanging on a tree. Fi looks at me with a big smile on her face, as if she's just seen it for the first time. "I love that thing, Daddy. What's it called again?"

"It's called a fos . . ." I notice something off to the left, out of the corner of my eye. My eyes grow wide when I am able to focus on the image about fifteen feet to the left of where we are. "Come here, sweetie," I say to Fi as I hug her close, making sure her head is pressed against my chest. She doesn't need to see what I am looking at.

Off to the left, in a little clearing, are about eight to ten animals. I assume they are laying down, just as I assume they are real.

What I am looking at are the missing tigers, the bear, and the monkeys , but they all look dead. The other parents on the train aren't as quick, and their kids start noticing the animals.

"Look at all the animals over there, Mommy," one little boy says. "Why are they all asleep?" His mom just stares, thinking what every other parent must be: *What the hell are tigers, a bear, and some monkeys doing all the way out here? Are they dead?*

When Fi hears the other kids asking questions, she looks up just in time to see the train passing the animals. "Is that a new display, Daddy?" she asks. "Why is it so far away that we can't see it better?"

A new display? That must be it. Austin is full of local artists and maybe one of them donated their time and skills to creating a realistic animal scene for the train ride.   Maybe it's just a coincidence that the artist re-created the exact animals that were missing from their cages and displays.

Artist my ass. Those animals sure looked real.

"Daddy," Fi says. "Are those animals injured?"

"No, sweetie. They probably got out of their cages when the volunteers were cleaning them. Then when the volunteers found them they shot them with a dart to make them fall asleep."

What bullshit. Those animals were real, and they looked dead.

About ten feet in front of us there is a small clearing, and if you look back at the right moment, you'd be able to see that clearing with all the animals littered about. I turn to Fi and, ask her what she wants to do after we leave the zoo to preoccupy her. It's my last chance to see into that clearing. Talking to Fi, I let my eyes drift to the clearing. A split second later, we are past it, but it's too late. All the hair stands on my arms. I could have sworn that the dead animals were all gone. That was impossible. I would have seen at least one or two volunteers dragging the bodies away.

Adrenaline starts pumping through my veins as panic kicks in. I look down at Fi and am positive that we aren't safe. I don't know what the threat is, but I know there is one. I want to get off this train and out of the zoo, but now we are stuck and there's an awful lot of weird shit going on. I turn around to look at the floppy-hatted girl. She is staring right at me, her cell phone five inches from her ear. She was making a phone call when she saw the exact same thing. The apparently-dead animals that, moments ago, were strewn all over the clearing, are now gone.

6

I'm glad Fi and I are facing backwards. I can hear the other parents behind us talking and wondering what exactly they saw in that clearing. I can tell that most of the families didn't walk around the zoo before the train ride. They probably arrived ten minutes to eleven o'clock and came straight to the train depot. They didn't know all the weird shit that was going on all morning long. The aggressive animals, the abduction of a zoo volunteer by the military, and all the missing animals. They only saw the one isolated incident of the animals lying dead-like out in that field.

The train continues.

The sun is strong and bright now. Much hotter out today than the news said it would be. Sunlight really isn't my friend anymore, not after my eye surgery. Even though I only had a corneal graft to treat keratoconus in my left eye, the procedure made both eyes extremely sensitive to light.

Fantastic, I think. *This is just what I need. Something bad is happening here and soon I won't be able to see a goddamn thing.*

I hold Fi close as the train continues on its way. We round another corner and I can see that everyone's eyes are focused on the landscape, trying to see if there are more dead animals out there.

We pass a thicket of bushes that I recognize from our many rides along this exact route. I know we were getting to the part of the ride where we begin to go down an incline. The incline lasts about fifty to sixty feet and ends in a rather sharp turn. The conductor will start braking the train at about thirty feet so when we hit the curve, we'll only be moving slightly faster than walking speed. The scenery at the end is breathtaking. We'll ride through this part full of bushes and trees only to see it open to a beautiful view of the Hill Country: large, green hills that reach up to touch the radiant blue, cloudless sky. It's a beautiful view and Fi's favorite part of the ride. There is also an antique-looking broken-down wagon where the curve begins. Fi always points to it and asks me what it is. She knows exactly what it is. It's just another one of our daddy-daughter things.

I feel Fi looking up at me and manage to put a smile on my face. She knows I'm worried about something. How can she not? It's written all over my face. My wife always tells me I wear my emotions on my sleeve and I try not to around Fi, especially if I'm worried about something. The last thing I want to do is make her as concerned as I am.

I turn just as the train begins to descend to look at the other passengers and the conductor. It seems the others are pretty content on writing off what they saw as some kind of "zoo event." I wish I could do the same, but I've seen too much weird shit today to convince myself everything is all right. I catch the conductor looking around at the landscape. I'm guessing she is trying to spot any more animals, alive or dead. At least there's another adult here on full alert. As she is looking off to the right, I see her squint, as if she sees something. She then freezes and, unconsciously, her jaw begin to drop. She saw something, and whatever it was, it saw her.

She reaches down for the walkie-talkie. I turn to see if I can get a glimpse of whatever scared her. As she brings the walkie-talkie to her mouth, I see a golden-yellowish flash sail over the conductor, but with the cloudiness building in my eye, I can't be absolutely sure of what I saw. One thing is certain: whatever that flash was, it took the conductor's head clean off her shoulder's and left behind a headless body with a walkie-talkie clutched in its hand. It happened so quickly that she didn't have time to utter one word of warning or even let out a scream. Blood spurts in geysers from her neck. The people sitting directly behind her, unaware of what has just happened, are being covered in her blood.

I look at the floppy-hatted girl quickly, and judging by the look on her face, I'd say she saw exactly what I did. She turns pale in front of me as the blood drained from her face. Another passenger catches my attention only because of his reaction. He is sitting behind the floppy-hatted girl and also saw the flash remove the conductor's head, but what catches my attention is that he doesn't seem shocked by it. Almost as if he expected something like this to happen. I begin to yell back at the man, but am distracted when a woman starts screaming. This sets off a myriad of screams and cries from adults and kids alike. Fi is trying to turn to see what has happened, but I hold her close, her face covered. "It's okay, sweetie," I lie. "Someone just cut themselves. They'll be okay."

"Did they stick their hand out of the moving train, Daddy?"

I can't help but smile. "Yes they did, sweetie."

"Are they going to be okay?" she asks.

"They're gonna be fine, sweetie."

The train continues to pick up speed as we descend the hill. I look over to see the curve about twenty feet away. There's no way we were going to make the bend going this fast in this piece of shit train.

My adrenaline continues to pump through my system. Now is the time to react and protect Fi and myself, or sit by and put us in harm's way. I can't worry about scaring Fi any longer. I turn to the people sitting in the front of the train. "Someone get up there and grab the brake. We're going too fast for that curve!" I yell, trying to be heard over the screaming woman in the first row of seats. *And someone slap that screaming bitch*, I think.

One older man about fifty years old doesn't exactly hear me, but sees me pointing to the curve ahead. He is able to put one and one together and realize we are going to derail unless someone grabbed the brakes. He is two rows behind the conductor's seat. He taps a man in front of him on the shoulder and I can see his mouth moving as he points to the curve. The younger man just stares blankly at him before turning his back. The older guy then grabs and shakes his shoulder.

We are thirty feet from the curve.

Finally, the older guy stands and climb over the seat to get closer to the conductor's car. He shoots the younger guy an icy stare as he moves past him. *Unbelievable*, I think. *That younger guy has two young kids and won't do a goddamn thing to help*. In times like this, you don't think about being a hero, and that is the furthest thing from my mind. I am thinking about surviving and protecting my little girl. I remember that day in Philadelphia in 1980 as I watched my best friend being mauled to death by a feral dog. I'd stood in terror that day and watched someone die, then swore I'd never let that happen again. Especially not with my own child. The screaming woman shakes me back to reality.

The older man has planted one foot onto the conductor's seat and tries to push the unfortunate woman's body off the train. Kids and adults alike are crying, but now have something positive to focus on. This older man was risking it all to help slow this train down. He pushes the headless corpse off the train and sits down. As he reaches for the brake lever, another flash, this time brownish-red, shoots across the conductor's seat. I don't even have time to blink. When I am finally able to process what has happened and focus through my deteriorating eye, I expect to see another headless body. Instead, I hear panicked, pained cries from the older man.

Whatever that flash was took off the man's arm at the shoulder. Even through my bad eye I can see the blood draining from his face. The younger man that ignored him before is now on his feet trying to help him. Too little too late. In another second, the brown flash finishes off the older man, but this time, instead of just his head missing, the entire top part of his body is gone. All that is left is an exposed ribcage on top of wobbling legs. Half of the man's heart is left behind, spewing forth its contents all over the already-bloodied first row passengers.

No one screams this time. Shock settles into both the kids and parents along the front row almost instantly. *What the fuck could do that to a human?* I ask. I look to see the floppy-hatted girl looking right at me. This time, she doesn't seem as shocked as when the conductor was decapitated. Either she is coming to terms with what is happening or she knows what is going on. I look past her to see what kind of expression the older, armless man has on his face this time. He is gone. I quickly scan outside the train to see if he has already bailed out. There is no trace of him.

We are twenty feet from the curve.

"Get ready! Brace yourself!" I yell to the girl and to any other passenger who can hear me. "We're gonna derail!"

The young guy that tried to help the older man goes to pick up the walkie-talkie. As soon as his hand touches it, the guy screams. He holds up as bloody stump where his hand used to be. There is no flash this time, so I stand , trying to see what removed the man's hand. Jumping off the left side of the conductor's seat is what looks like a monkey, but different. It has simian qualities, but the mouth and teeth are unlike anything I've seen on a primate. Right before it jumps off the train, it seems to look around at all the people on the train. I lock eyes with the monkey and it sends a shiver up my spine. It then jumps off the train with the man's hand still in its mouth. I turn to look back at the floppy-hatted girl and can tell she's seen what has just transpired.

We are fifteen feet away from the curve.

There is nothing left to do but prepare to crash. We are going about thirty miles an hour and the curve is right in front of us. I grab Fi's backpack and put it on her. Luckily, she still sleeps with her favorite blanket and I always bring it to the zoo just in case she wants to take a nap on the car ride home. In addition to the blanket, I always pack an extra set of clothes for her on our outings. You never know when you'll need them, and we needed them right now.

I pick her up and hold her, face first, against my chest. "Sweetie, we're gonna have to jump off the train. I need you to keep your head pressed tight against my chest, okay? The backpack has enough padding that will protect your back when we hit the ground. I'll be your padding for your front side." I try to smile. "Don't worry," I say, forcing a smile. "This'll be fun." I am scared to death. The ground surrounding this part of the tracks is covered in rocks and sand and old tree roots. I just have to make sure that when we hit the ground that my back lands first. No matter what.

"But the lady said we shouldn't leave the train no matter what." She is scared. We all are.

"It's okay, sweetie. We're going too fast to take this curve and the train is going to roll over. I'll protect you." I know I'm scaring her, but this is no time to try and come up with a convincing lie. I need to tell her what is going on so she knows just how serious our situation is. She doesn't question me any further. I kiss her nose. "Just make sure to press your head tightly against my chest."

SHIT, I think. *Fi has that knife in the backpack.* I can't help but think of the knife coming out of its sheath as we hit the ground and stabbing my little girl. I unzip her bag. Luckily, the knife is still resting on top of her blanket. I tuck the knife under the band of my pants.

"Get ready, sweetie. We're gonna jump pretty soon." I hold her tight. I look down the train to see a few of the other parents following my lead and using the backpacks to protect their kids. *This better fucking work*, I think. I look back and see the floppy-hatted girl getting ready to jump as well. Our eyes meet and an unsaid promise passes between us that we will find each other, if we live, after we jump off the train.

We are two feet away from the curve. so I figure the best thing to do is jump off the left side of the train. The train is going to roll, and if we jump off the right side, it will just roll on top of us. Unfortunately, most parents are gearing up to jump off the left side of the train. I try to yell to jump off the right side, but between the screams and prayers, no one hears me. Then I see something that stops me dead in my tracks. Some parents are doing nothing. They are still sitting in their seats, holding their kids on their laps tightly, hoping the train will be all right. Looking at those poor kids, my eyes tear up. They don't have a chance.

We approach the curve. I brace Fi against me and wrap my hand around her head, hoping it would give her a little protection. "Soon, honey," I yell.

As the train hits the curve, I see the conductor's car jerk violently and jump straight off the track. The cars behind it follow. I watch all the cars jerk and jump the tracks one by one. One of the families still sitting in their seats are ejected from their seats and tossed around. I can see blood spurting from the parents and kids' mouths and the look of horror on their faces as they realized they made the wrong choice to stay on the train. Then I hear the sound of bones snapping and breaking. I can't look at them any longer.

It is time. "Here we go, sweetie," I say as we jumped. We sail in the air as I hold Fi tighter than I ever have before. Behind us, I can hear the twist of metal and can only imagine what is happening to the people that decided to stay on the train. Passengers were screaming as they became part of the trains' structure. Broken steel, broken bones, blood, and torn flesh fused together in some Cronenbergian nightmare.

I twist in the air so I will land on my back. An instant later, we hit the ground hard. The air is violently knocked from my lungs as Fi's body slams into mine. I manage to keep my hand around Fi's head, holding her close to my chest. As soon as we hit the rocky earth, we start to roll toward the train, but at least we weren't in danger of it derailing. The backpack served its purpose of taking most of the impact off Fi. We roll six or seven times before we slam into a bush and come to a fierce stop.

Neither of us say anything. We just lay there. I am trying to assess how hurt I am, and I think Fi has lost consciousness. I know she hit her head because my hand is aching, but sense she's ok because I feel her heartbeat against my chest. It is a strong heartbeat, and she already seems to be breathing more clearly. I take a quick inventory: no broken bones or ribs. I did, however, feel something warm and sticky rolling down the back of my neck. I panic, thinking something has impaled me. I run my free hand around my head and find the cut on the back of my skull. *Not bad*, I think. *I'll take that over a broken bone.*

"Fi," I say. "Fi, are you okay?" She raises her head and smiled at me.

"That was kinda fun." I know she is trying to make me smile, and it works. I hug her tight.

"Are you okay, sweetie? Is anything broken? Are you bleeding?" I get her off me quickly and remove the backpack. There is a medium-sized branch impaled through the mesh. The clothing and her blanket are the only things that kept it from penetrating her. I shudder to think of what could have happened and shake it off. *No use worrying about what could have happened*, I think. *We're still in the shits here.* "Can you stand up for me?" I ask. She does. I turned her around, looking for cuts, or worse. Other than a lot of bruises on her legs and a small cut on her arm, she's fine.

I look around at the twisted wreckage of the train. Body parts and twisted metal are strewn all over. The train had come apart like a toy. There was nothing left that even remotely resembled the vehicle we'd been riding on for the last two years.

"Come on, sweetie," I say, taking her hand. "Let's go help the others."

7

You have to wake up... you need to open your eyes...

Frank's eyes shoot open. He is expecting to find darkness, but the brightness of the sun makes him jerk his head back as if he was slapped in the face. He tries again, this time gradually opening them so they can accept the sunlight. As he squints and tries to see around him, he realizes that he has very limited motion. He tries to lift his head, but his neck muscles are failing him. *What the fuck happened?* he thinks. He tries to wiggle his fingers and toes and has no idea if they are moving. He still can't lift his head to see. It's becoming pretty clear that he can't feel any part of his body. It's almost as if he is just a head laying on the ground with nothing else connected to it. Then he thinks about his sons, Jeff and Rick, and tries to move again, with no luck.

"Okay, okay," he says, trying to calm himself down. "I need to relax and think." He tries to focus on the last thing he could remember. "The train," he says in a raspy voice, "I remember the goddamn train was going too fast." He tries to wiggle his toes again. He also remembers seeing the guy with his daughter all the way at the back of train getting ready to jump. "Fucking idiot," he says out loud. At least he thinks he's talking out loud. Come to think of it, he can't hear his own voice.

"The best thing," he remembered telling his kids, "is to stay on the train."

Focus asshole, he thinks, trying to get back to his memories.

"Jeff and Rick were sitting next to me as we got closer to the curve." Frank still can't tell if he is talking out loud or not. "They wanted to jump, but I told them just to sit there and brace themselves. All trains have some kind of safety mechanism that prevents them from becoming a run-a-way train." Don't they? *Fuck.* His current situation kept interrupting his thoughts. *Why the fuck can't I feel my legs or arms, and where the fuck are my sons?*

Jeff and Rick are his seven-year-old twins. He doesn't get much time with them between his job and the divorce, but when they were together, they always had fun. He is still very close to them even though he only gets to see them every other weekend. They were good kids, and understood that Mommy and Daddy just couldn't live together anymore. He was glad to have a friendly divorce with no drama.

Yes, he thinks excitedly when he begins to feel the fingers on his right hand wiggling. He doesn't have much mobility, but it's a start.

He remembers hugging the boys close as the train turned into the curve. Everything jerked violently and he recalled Jeff almost being torn from his grasp. "Oh God," he says at the thought of Jeff being thrown from the train. Where is he? Did he hit a tree? Is he wandering around out there looking for him and Rick?

With his right hand, he begins to feel around. He feels something cold over his right thigh. *It must be part of the train.* He attempts to move it, but it may as well have weighed a ton. He then reasons that, since he can't lift his head, he could possibly roll his neck side to side. Slowly, he tilts his head to the left. His eyes still aren't focusing. He sees some people walking around and a lot of twisted metal. "Help," he tries to shout, but realizes the only noise he makes is a faint whisper. *Okay, they can't hear me but I can hear them. My senses are coming back to me.* This small victory brings a smile to his face.

He rolls his head to the right and gets excited when he sees Jeff's shirt. That bright red Spider-Man shirt gives him hope. His adrenaline kicks in and he is able to free his right arm from the wreckage. *Making progress. Stay focused and get to your kids.* He tries to prop himself on his right elbow, but his body still isn't responding. "Jeff... Jeff," he whispers through his still-raspy voice. Wait. His voice isn't raspy he realized. It's almost a gurgling noise. Frank panics.

Out of the corner of his eye, he can see that man and his kid walking around. He remembers them being the ones who jumped off the train before they hit the curve. He sees them look at the ground, at the wreckage, at the trees, and into the woods. *Why the fuck can't they see me? What are they doing over there? Sightseeing?* He assumes they were looking for other survivors, but also figures there aren't survivors up in the trees. It wasn't that bad of a train wreck. His voice fails him as he tries to call out.

"They don't see us," he says out loud. "No one's gonna rescue us. It's up to me."

He reaches out with his right arm toward Jeff. Bursts of searing pain shoot up and down his arm. He bites his lip. He needs to make contact with his son to let him know he isn't alone. His fingers are inches away from the red shirt. He finds the strength to roll his head more in the direction to where Jeff is. That's when he notices the odd angle at which Jeff's head is lying. *Come on, eyes. Focus.* Ignoring the pain shooting along his arm, he finally manages to make contact with Jeff. His fingers try to stroke Jeff's hair as best as they can. "Jeff," he whispers. "Jeff, it's Daddy. We're gonna be alright." *He's unconscious. I need to bring him back to me.* So Frank does the only thing he can think of: he gently pulls on some of Jeff's long hair. *Thank God his mom ignored me and didn't get his hair cut.* No response. So he pulls harder to try to shock him back into consciousness.

As he pulls that second time, he feels his son move. Frank smiles. *Everything's going to be al...* But he realizes Jeff hasn't moved because of his father's touch. As he pulls on his son's hair, he realizes Jeff's head is tilted back at an impossible angle. He needs to know. Frank keeps pulling only to find that Jeff's head is barely still attached to his body. A sheet of fiberglass from the roof of the train had torn off during the wreck and slammed into his son's throat, nearly decapitating him. All that is keeping his head attached is a thin flap of skin on the back of his neck.

Frank can't stop his hand and keeps pulling. Jeff's head continues to arch back until he sees his son's lifeless eyes staring at him upside down. The thin flesh-hinge gives way and Jeff's head rolls from his seven-year-old body, coming to rest inches from Frank's face.

Tears immediately well up as he looks deeply into his son's lifeless eyes. Flashes of Jeff as a baby come flooding into Frank's mind. His first steps, his first day of school, his fifth birthday party. He wants to sob, but can't find his voice. He feels the world beginning to spiral. He is suddenly having trouble breathing and starts gasping for air. He is losing it. He's never been in shock before, but imagines this is what it must feel like.

"No," he says. "You can't lose it. Rick is still out there and needs you." The thought of his other son alone gives him strength. He still can't feel his legs or left arm, but the mobility in his right arm and hand was growing by the minute. He knows it's the adrenaline and that it won't last forever, so he needs to take advantage of it right now.

He pushes himself up on his right elbow in order to get a better view of the scenery around him. His search for his other son, Rick, ends as quickly as it begins. Frank can't handle what he was seeing. It was too much for his eyes to process. He starts. There is a reason he can't: both had been severed during the crash. About six feet away lay his one mangled leg, separated right below the knee. It is so twisted and broken he can't even determine if it was his left or right. His other leg is nowhere to be found. He looks down to see the stump where his right leg used to be. There is only about two-thirds of his thigh there. He doesn't have time to panic. He figures he didn't have much time left to do anything.

There, on his back the whole time, is Rick, lying face up. He has a piece of unrecognizable metal embedded in the left side of his skull. Judging how far it is inside of him, Frank figured it must have slammed into his son at a tremendous force. Sinking deeper into shock, Frank realizes there is also a metal rod from one of the seats stuck through Rick's throat. *Wait*, Frank thinks through the haze in his mind. *His head is resting on my chest.* He reaches over with his only functioning hand to grab the rod through his son's throat. He doesn't want this to be the last image he has of his son. He tries to yank the rod free. When he does, he feels something pull inside himself.

Ignoring the pain in his chest, Frank is determined to pull that metal rod out of his son. He yanks harder and feels it give. He also feels something tear in his chest. *What the fuck was...* He realizes what he's just done. The rod hadn't just torn through his son's throat and pinned him to his chest: that rod had also gone straight through his own lung and created a seal, . By removing the rod, he's broken the suction that was keeping him alive. His lungs fill with blood. He smiles. *What the fuck do I have to live for now? My kids trusted and believed in me. I told them to stay in the train. They did. Now they're dead. Now we're all dead.*

His blood continues to pour into his lungs and he knows he is drowning in his own fluids slowly. He cries, hoping he will see his kids again in some afterlife that he know might not exist. He fucked up and his bad decision killed his kids. Jeff and Rick would never grow up and experience life, as theirs ended on a rundown train at the Austin Zoo one spring day. He looks at Rick's lifeless body lying on his chest one last time. He tries to reach over to give him one last hug, but his body failed him. He can't help himself and smiles.

He sees that man and his daughter walking around and finds himself angry at them, but knows it wasn't their fault. It was his.

"I should've jumped," Frank says between tears. "We should've jumped."

His smile fades as he lays his head down and stops crying.

8

"I can't believe this wreckage came from the train we've been riding once a week for the last two years," I mumble. I look down to see Fi looking up at me. I smile and bend down to give her another hug.

All around us are the twisted metal and shattered fiberglass remains of an object I once thought of as a symbol of Fi's childhood. Now, as I look around, I can't identify anything that used to resemble a train. Children and adults are both crying. They are lucky. If they're crying, it means they are alive. I see too many people who are now permanent parts of the twisted sculpture in front of me. *Why did they stay on the train? How could they possibly think they'd survive that crash? I know we were only going around thirty to forty miles-per-hour, but they had to know we weren't going to make that curve.*

I'm angry with the parents who kept their kids on the train. I know they were paralyzed with fear. I can understand that. But their kids... My thought trails off. Even among all this horror, part of me can't help but feel good. I looked fear in the face and took an action that saved our lives. I reacted quickly to a terrifying situation and lucked out. I hug Fi closer to my leg.

I hate the fact that she is seeing so much pain and suffering. I want to shield her from this grizzly scene, but what would she think of me if we just walked away and didn't try to help anyone? I wouldn't be able to live with myself or be able to look her in the eye.

The worst we see is a father and his two sons. I remember seeing them on the train and I would guess they were about six to ten years old. The father kept them on the train. I remember seeing the one boy's bright red Spider-Man shirt right before we left. His dad was hugging him and his brother tight. I couldn't imagine what was going through his head as that train tumbled and the cars rolled over their bodies. It was horrible. The one son was decapitated and the other had a hunk of metal in the side of his head, pinning him to his dad's chest by a metal rod through his neck. I can only hope and assume that they all died quickly. The odd thing is that the father's legs were severed, yet there is nothing lying around his body. It's almost as if…

"Daddy," Fi says. "I'm thirsty." She won't take her backpack off. She's told me she feels safer wearing it.

As I reach into the pack, I remember that I removed the knife right before we jumped. I quickly run my hand along my waistband. The knife is gone. "Fantastic," I accidentally say out loud.

"What's wrong, Daddy?" Fi doesn't miss a thing.

"Nothing, sweetie. I was just looking for something."

"Are you looking for that knife?" she asks. I roll my eyes and can't help but laugh a little. Nothing. She misses nothing.

There is no point lying to her. "Yes, sweetie. That knife." She joins me in my search for it. It could be anywhere, and the fact that my eye is slowly getting cloudier doesn't help in our search. We are wasting precious moments. Whatever it was that killed and maimed those people on the train is still out here. It isn't attacking us right now, but I have no doubt that it will be back. If it could take off a person's head while the train was moving, then God only knew what it could do to a group of people just standing around. "You know what, sweetie? Let's not worry about the knife right now. Let's go see if we can help anyone else."

About twenty feet from the main wreckage, I see a mother and daughter. They, too, jumped before the train hit the curve, but off the wrong side. They got lucky though. It looks as though one train car rolled and bounced right over them, missing them completely. As Fi and I walk closer, we see that the mother was knocked unconscious but her daughter is fine. We approached slowly, so as not to scare the daughter. The daughter is shaking her mom, trying to wake her up. She looks about a year or two older than Fi.

"Hi," Fi says as we get closer to the girl. "My name's Fiona, but everyone calls me Fi. What's your name?"

The girl looks up. She is scared and her eyes give away her sense of fear. "I'm Amber," she answers. "My mom..." Her words trail off as her gaze goes back to her mom.

"Hi, Amber," I say. "Why don't you come over here and keep Fi company while I help your mom." I can see her mom's chest moving. Thank God. The last thing I want is to have to tell this poor girl her mother died. As I kneel down beside her mother, I glance over and see Fi sharing her water with Amber.

I can see the bump on the woman's head, and though I'm no doctor, it doesn't look too bad. A discolored lump has formed, but it isn't too large of a injury. Further back toward the top of her head I notice that a lot of her hair is clumped together. I gently feel around her scalp until I found the source. She has a four-inch cut on the top of her head, but I am relieved to find it has already clotted on its own. She is going to be fine. She's lucky.

I ask Fi and Amber to bring over some water and gently pour some on the mother's forehead and hair. The coolness starts to bring her around.

"Come here, Amber," I say. "I want you to be the first person your mom sees." The woman slowly regains consciousness. She has trouble opening her eyes in the sunlight, but I can see her smile weakly as she makes out the silhouette of her daughter.

"Mommy," Amber almost screams as she throws her arms around her mother's neck. She looks disoriented. When she sees me kneeling beside her, she immediately starts grabbing at Amber and wildly swinging her arms in self-defense. I can't blame her. Not everyone saw those things attack the people on the train, but those who did knew we were in a lot more trouble than just this train derailing.

"It's okay, it's okay," I say. It is hard to get a good look at her. My eye is getting cloudier by the minute, but she looks to be in her mid-thirties

"Bullshit it's okay," she says in a raspy voice. She stops swinging around her arms when she realizes I am no threat. She quickly sits up and tries to scan around, but the blood she lost makes her dizzy. "Go slow, Be careful," I say. "Your daughter's right here with my little girl."

"How can you say that? Did you *see* what happened before the train wrecked?" It is amazing what adrenaline can do. She is regaining her strength by the second. She isn't panicking. She just knows we were all in a very fucked up and bad situation.

"Yeah," I respond, lowering my voice. "Did you get a good look at what it was?"

"No. All I know is that it's really fast and seems 'f-ing' pissed off." At this point, she realizes we aren't in any immediate danger and she focuses her attention of Amber. Mother and daughter are happy to see each other alive. "I'm Cassie, and this is Amber," she finally says.

"I'm John, and this is Fiona," I respond.

"But everyone calls me Fi," Fiona quickly adds.

"Thanks for the help." She holds her head as she looks around at the wreckage. "Now what the hell do we do?"

"Fi and I have already been around the wreckage. The survivors are gathered over there." I gesture behind me. "There's not too many of us. We should go join them. Can you stand yet?" I'm looking at the wounds on her head. "The cut's not too deep and has already stopped bleeding, and that bump on your head doesn't look too bad either. I'm sure you have a bitch of a headache, but at least you'll be all right. You probably rolled over a tree root or a rock."

As I help Cassie up, I whisper so only she can hear, "*Don't go over by the main wreckage. There's some pretty horrible things in there. A lot of people stayed on the train. They didn't make it.*" Cassie looks me in my eyes and I can feel her asking me how anyone could've remained on a train headed for doom. I have no answer for her.

We avoid the main wreckage so Amber and Fi won't be exposed to more of the aftermath. We join up with the other survivors. There is a mom with her kids (a son and daughter,) a mom and dad with their son, a father and grandfather with their son/grandson, and a single man. I realize I haven't see the girl in the floppy hat. I could have sworn I saw her jump off the train before we did, though can't remember from what side. I scan the main wreckage looking for her within the twisted metal, but my one eye is so cloudy that my vision has been reduced to about five to eight feet in front of me.

I turn to say something to everyone when I notice a figure sitting down next to a tree stump. I squint and realize it was her. The floppy-hatted girl alive and well.

Minus her floppy hat.

9

As the four of us walk over to join the others, I notice the floppy-hatted girl is holding something in her hands in an almost protective manner.

"Is everyone alright?" I ask, realizing it is a stupid question. I see one of the fathers begin to say something back and cut him off before he can get a word out. "I mean is anyone seriously hurt? Broken bones, bad cuts or bumps on the head?" Everyone just kind of mumbles that they are all right.

Their reactions make me angry, but I bite my lip and don't say anything. I am just glad that Fi and I are alive. Besides the train derailment, there is something, or some *things*, out there. What is really pissing me off was that the adults aren't being strong for their kids. The children are scared shitless, and you can see it in their eyes. They thought they were going on a nice outing to the zoo with Mom and Dad and, out of nowhere, are standing in the middle of a train wreck, surrounded by dead bodies and creatures who're hunting them down.

These parents need to get their shit together, I think, getting angrier.

"We need some kind of plan, and we need one fast," I say, trying to relay to the other adults the seriousness of the situation. "My name's John, and this is Fi."

Ignoring our introductions, one of the fathers quickly responds: "I think we should just stay here with the wreckage. I'm sure the conductor made a call back to the station that the train was out of control. They're gonna look for us where the wreckage is."

All the other parents look at each other in silence. Did this guy not see what happened on the train before it derailed? Did he not see something tear off the conductor's head? Finally, one of the mothers speak up. "I'm Susan, and these are my kids, Karen and Tom." Then, turning to the man, says, "Maybe you didn't see what happened before the train derailed, but there was no call to the station before the wreck. Something…" Her sentence trails off as she tries to find the right words. "Something disabled the conductor right before we crashed."

Nice choice of words, I think. We all look back at the father, waiting for his response.

"What're you talking about, 'disabled?'" he shoots back. "She was careless and got knocked off the train by a branch. So fine, if you don't think she got a call out before she fell off, I'll call the zoo right now." He pulls a cell phone out of his pants pocket. "I'm not just gonna stand by and hope someone comes looking for us."

I want to be angry with this idiot, but I can see just how scared he is. He is around forty-five years old and has the physique of someone who works behind a desk. He is there with his wife and two kids, all of whom appear calmer than their dad.

"Look," I say. "We all need to remain calm and work together on a plan of action."

"You guys can work on a plan of action. I'm calling the zoo right now to tell them what happened." He punches in the zoo's number and lifts the phone to his ear. "Hello," he says. "Hello? Is anyone there?"

I can see him getting red in the face through his frustration and fear. We are all watching him as he makes the call. Then the flash comes. It isn't as fast this time, but it is just as ferocious. An orange-brown streak appears out of nowhere and rips off the man's arm, most of his shoulder, and part of his neck in one vicious attack. The rest of us stand there, stunned. Half of the man's body is practically gone. The rest of his body remains standing upright.

Blood bubbles out of his torn neck and shoots out of the socket where his arm and shoulder used to be. His eyes are wide with fear, almost like he knows what happened.

His wife and kids and just about everyone else starts screaming. I grab Fi and run over to the tree. The girl-minus-the-floppy-hat still sits there. The color has drained from her face.

"Everyone get over here," I scream. Some of them run over immediately. Others are frozen in fear.

The man's body finally gives in to gravity and collapses to the ground. Then, in another flash, the orange-brown blur races in, grabs the lifeless body, and disappears. Everyone seems to stop making noise at the same time. The cries and panicking cease. Everyone is stunned and trying to make sense out of what they've just witnessed. We look at each other, silently affirming what everyone is thinking.

The orange-brown *thing* wasn't a thing at all. It was a tiger. One of the very same tigers housed in this very zoo.

10

"Did you see that fucking thing?" one of the fathers asks. "It ... it looked like a tiger, but it moved so fast." Then, turning to the rest of the group, asks, "Can tigers move that fast?"

We all just look at each other, waiting, and hoping that someone will offer up a plausible explanation. I have to break the silence. "I'm no expert, but I really don't think they can move that fast. I mean, maybe if they had a lot of open space where they can run and build up speed. But..." I gesture around us to finish my point. We are surrounded by dense woods. There isn't enough open space for an animal to build up the amount of speed that tiger had.

Everyone gets my point.

"Well, we all saw it. How the hell did it get so fast?" The father is looking for some kind of answer in order to retain his sanity. He needs some kind of anchor in reality, but right now, things seem to be very far from real. The older man he is with (I assumed it was his father) comes, stands behind him, and rests his hand on the man's shoulder. That seems to calm him down for now.

"Look, everyone," I say. "We need to face the facts. There are creatures out there hunting us down. They've killed three people so far and we have to assume they aren't done yet. Now I think..."

"Creatures... you mean there's more than one of those things? How they hell do you know that?" the same father asks.

"Look... what's your name?" I ask.

"Kyle," he responds.

"Kyle, right before we jumped, I saw a monkey running around on the train."

"What makes you think it killed anyone?" Kyle asks. I can see him trying to connect everything, but his brain won't let him.

"Right before the monkey jumped off the train, and I know this is gonna sound ridiculous, I could swear it turned around and stared at Fi and me." Before Kyle can say anything, I continue: "I know that you're thinking the stress of the situation is making me imagine things, but that monkey stopped and stared at us as if he was saying, 'I'll see ya later.'"

"Okay, so the monkey fucking looked at ya. So what? At least it didn't kill anyone like that goddamn tiger."

"That's not completely true. There's more."

"Oh yeah? What's that?" Kyle is beginning to piss me off.

"Remember the older guy on the train that tried to get to the breaks?" Mostly everyone nods. "Well, that monkey had his hand in its mouth. I think it was the monkey that dismembered and then killed that man, not the tiger."

"What are we going to do?" asks Kyle in a broken voice. He puts his hand on top of his son's head. I realize I shouldn't be angry at this man. He is scared like the rest of us and is worried about protecting his son against an enemy we know nothing about.

"I just wish we knew something more about these goddamn animals. I don't wanna scare anyone any more, but we have seen one tiger and one monkey so far. I'm gonna assume that there are more animals out there like them." That seems to make everyone stop and think. "I know some of you saw that clearing with all those apparently dead animals in it. I saw it too, and I saw a tiger in that clearing. I can't be a hundred percent sure it's the same tiger, but come on. What are the chances of there being two tigers?"

"It was the same tiger," says a previously unheard voice. It's the girl that used to have the floppy hat. She's still sitting at the base of the tree, but now seems more alert and in full survival mode. "I saw the animals in the clearing too. I think I may know what's happening here."

That definitely gets everyone's attention. We all step closer, ready to hear some kind of explanation for what is happening.

"I think I speak for us all," I say. "We're all ears."

The girl with the missing floppy hat begins to tell her story.

CHAPTER FIVE

1

Somewhere around Killeen, Texas

The van has been traveling for hours. It's stopped only once to get gas, and even then, no one but the driver had gotten out. He'd stared at the ground the entire time he filled the car, and had purposely made no eye contact with anyone else at the gas station. Yet he'd been completely aware of everything going on around him. When he finished, he'd returned to the van and drove away.

To anyone else, he is just an uptight soldier on his way back to base. To the other four people in the van and Colonel Butsko, this is the most important mission of their life, and possibly, the rest of the world's.

"We're about an hour-and-a-half away, Sir," the driver says into the intercom. The 'Sir,' Colonel Butsko, is at the base, anxiously waiting for the cargo to arrive. Anything that could possibly hinder this mission--a flat tire, a busted fan belt, an overheated engine--could put the entire world at risk.

"Roger that," Col. Butsko responds. "Keep me posted on your progress every fifteen to twenty minutes. Over."

"Will do, Sir." Then, to the back of the van, Wilder says, "We're almost there. How's the cargo?"

"Cargo is subdued and contained, Sir." This brings a silent sigh of relief to Wilder. No one in the van is wearing anything to divulge his or her rank, or even what branch of the military they belong too. That is on purpose. If a tire blows out or the engine overheats, they don't need any gawking bystanders asking a bunch of questions.

Wilder isn't sure about the exact contents of the cargo, but knows that it is extremely important to get back to the base. Check that; he knows what the cargo is, he just doesn't know the entire story of why it is so important. Having the highest rank in the van, Wilder was at least privy to some intel. He knows the cargo has the potential to be extremely deadly and can threaten the safety not just of America, but the entire world.

Wilder has seen a lot of combat and has been in a lot of life-threatening situations, most of which have never made it onto the evening news, but knows driving this van is the most important mission of his life.

"Sir," says an excited voice from the back of the van. "The cargo is moving around."

Fuck, Wilder thinks. *Just another forty-five minutes and we'll be there.* He was prepared for such a turn of events. From the outside, the vehicle looks like a regular blue panel van, but inside it was stocked with the latest biomedical equipment. The equipment has one sole purpose, and that is to keep the cargo subdued and alive until they reach their destination.

"Sir, his eyes are opening," the soldier in the back says calmly. Neither he nor any of the others in the back are worried. They are battlefield-tested soldiers, handpicked for this mission. With all their experience, they thought they were being shipped off to another undisclosed destination to take care of some problem that threatened the safety of America. They also figured the mission would never make the news. That part is true. Not even a whisper of this will make the news. Col. Butsko has made sure of that.

"His eyes are open, Sir, but it doesn't look as though he's aware of anything yet," Laning reports.

"Just let him be, Laning," Wilder responds. "We're gonna be there soon. We don't want him to wake up. We just need to get him to base and turn him over to Butsko. After that, our part of the mission is done. Understood?"

"Yes, Sir," says Laning. Then, after a couple of minutes, asks, "Permission to speak off the record, Sir?" Laning and Wilder had gone through basic training together and both entered Ranger school. They excelled well past the others in their class, but Wilder went to Officer Candidate School, while Laning proved himself on the battlefield. They met up again in the Middle East and found out they worked better together as a team. From then on, they were inseparable. The higher ups figured it would be pretty foolish to get ninety percent from each soldier working alone when they could get two-hundred percent when they worked together. Since then, they'd gone on the same missions and received the same time off.

Wilder looks into the rearview mirror and catches Laning's eye. Laning then turns to the others in the van and, at once, they all switch off their coms.

"What is it, Laning?" Wilder asks, already knowing the question.

"What the fuck is going on here?" Laning brashly asks. One of the reasons they work so well together is because they complement each other's talents. Wilder is the logical, rational thinker with a warrior's heart, while Laning is the more passionate 'let God sort 'em out' type. "I mean seriously, Dan--there's enough firepower and practical combat experience in this van to take over a small country, and we're just here to transport some guy to a Texas military base? It doesn't make sense."

Wilder looks around at the men. He knows he can talk freely. This is his squad, and they've been together for five years in and out of so many hot spots that he'd lost count. "You're goddamn right it doesn't make sense, but I can tell you that this is possibly the most dangerous mission we have ever been on." That comment makes everyone stare.

"You're joking, right?" says another soldier.

"I shit you not, Kane. You know I don't have the whole story either, but I can tell you that that guy," he nods in the direction of the man in the protective bio-gear, "could be the beginning of the end of the world."

The guys know Wilder is not one to exaggerate dangers. They all stop and look down at the man.

"What the fuck is wrong with him?" another soldier asks. "I mean, fuck. Are we safe back here? We don't even have one piece of protective gear on, and this 'thing' he's in looks about as thick as a condom."

"The Colonel wouldn't knowingly put us in harm's way. You know that. The cargo isn't contagious unless you come in contact with the subject's blood or saliva. Just keep your eyes on him. We're almost there." Wilder again looks at the men through the rearview mirror. He knows they have a million questions, and they also know that he has no more answers than what he's just told them.

They all switch on their coms, sit back, and keep their eyes on the cargo.

2

Jim's eyes feel like they have hundred pound weights on the eyelids. He is having an odd dream when he was jerks out of sleep. He tries to look around, but the light is bothering his eyes. He tries to relax and let his eyes adjust to the light. Slowly, the image of five men sitting around him comes into view. He can't make out anything specific. It is almost as if he is looking through a plastic bag. He starts to panic. *Am I dead? Do they think I'm dead?* He realizes that if he is questioning it, he can't be dead.

He tries to remember the last thing before he passed out. He was in the shelter with Julie. Julie... where the hell is she? Is she all right? *I was bitten by something*, he thinks. He makes a fist with his left hand, expecting to feel pain. Nothing. *Maybe it was my right hand.* He makes a fist with his right hand, but instead of experiencing a shooting pain, he feels nothing. *What the hell? No... I know it was my left hand.* Another fist and there's still no pain.

He attempts to raise his left hand only to find it bound to a gurney. He tries to lift his head and feels the leather strap across his forehead holding him firmly in place. He is also able to feel something on his temples and other parts of his head. When he moves, something tickles his cheeks. Looking down the bridge of his nose, he can see wires hanging from his head down past his cheeks. He realizes he is on some kind of monitor.

What the fuck is going on? Why are these men just sitting around me? he thinks. He then realizes he can see one of the men looking down at him. *Wait*, he thinks. *A second ago, I couldn't see anything. Am I still inside the plastic bag?* He is surprised he is remaining so calm. He was never one to keep his head in an emergency. He remembers the time when he was playing soccer with his brother and other friends in that league championship game. His brother had stepped into a hole and broken his ankle. When the paramedics arrived, they'd had to attend to Jim first because he was hyperventilating so badly. He didn't hear the end of that for months after it happened. *That's just the way you are, buddy,* his dad would tell him. *You really need to stop being so overly sensitive.*

Growing up in a small Texas town hadn't been easy. He'd hated football and most other sports, but most of all, he hated hunting. His dad would drag him out every season to try to "bag a deer." He'd always aimed too high or too far to the side. He might've been a good shot. Who would know? He'd sworn that he would never hurt or kill an animal.

A split second later, he can hear the monitor he is hooked up too. The steady beeping is, he assumes, his heartbeat. His senses are coming back. He figures the drugs are wearing off. He listens to the men talking and realizes they are military. He begins to panic, but the heart monitor keeps the same steady rate.

Just as Jim is beginning to make sense of his surroundings, he is hit with a tremendous hunger. *My God, I've never been so hungry in my life.* He looks at the men around him. *I really need to eat.*

He tries to ignore his hunger by focusing on what the soldiers are saying: "...not unless you come into contact with the subject's blood or saliva. Just keep your eyes on him. We're almost there," one of them says.

Almost where? he thinks. *Am I the cargo? What the fuck is happening?* He tries to say something, but no sound comes from his throat. He looks around and finds two large symbols along the mesh above his chest. One he easily recognizes as the biohazard warning sign. The other looks familiar, but he can't remember where he's seen it. It is a large circle with a black outer rim. The inside is shaded green. In the center lies a smaller red circle with three additional circles forming a broken triangle. Loosely connecting the broken triangle are three half arcs. *Damn*, he thinks. *I know I've seen that somewhere.*

Then it hits him like a truck: "Why the hell am I in a biohazard bag?" he asks. The men around all look down at him at the same time. *Looks like I got my speech back.* "Please, someone help me. Why am I in this bag? Where are we going?" The men all remain silent. He feels the vehicle they are in make a sharp turn and can tell by the change in sound that they have left the main paved road. "Where are we going? *Please!* Someone answer me!"

That gets a response. He sees the man sitting closest to him lower his hand to his side arm. *Not really the reaction I wanted.* As odd as the situation is, he can feel himself getting stronger with each passing minute. But not only is his body getting stronger. His hunger is as well. *This is the best I've ever felt*; he thinks. *I'm just so damn hungry ...*

3

"The cargo is waking up, Sir," Laning whispers into the intercom. Laning is sitting closest to the cargo and isn't taking any chances. His hand rests on his Glock.

"Fuck," Wilder says, "Nothing's simple." Then, to his men in the back, he whispers, "Maintain continual visual contact with the cargo and watch both the heart and EEG monitors for any spikes in activity." He looks at the clock and sees it is time to check in with Butsko.

"Well, that's just it, Sir," Laning reports. "The cargo is moving around, but there's nothing registering on either monitor."

Wilder stares out the windshield and drives in silence for a few minutes. "Maintain visual contact. We're almost there."

Wilder briefly thinks about the last mission he was on with Laning and his men. They were sent in to check out some abnormal activity in a group of caves picked up by one of the satellites over Afghanistan. It was supposed to be a simple recon mission. *Nothing's simple.* The first seven caves they'd checked were empty with no traces of anyone being in there for at least a week. They'd been about to check out one last cave when a rogue group of Taliban ambushed them. Those fuckers just came out of nowhere; inside the last cave, on top of the hills, and two came up out of a sand trap they had dug into the ground.

But Wilder and his men were good. Not only good, but the best. No one had hesitated or missed a beat. The two coming out of the sand trap were taken out first. Each got a double tap with one round in the chest and another in the head. Kane had taken care of three coming out of the cave. You could see the surprise on the Taliban's faces when their ambush did nothing to shock the Rangers. Instead of retreating, Kane had jumped forward and thrust his fist into a man's throat, immediately breaking his windpipe. As he suffocated, Kane had grabbed him and used him as a shield against his comrades' barrage of bullets.

The six that sprung from the hills were more difficult to deal with. They'd had the advantage of being in an elevated position. Wilder had fired as he dropped to the ground and rolled closer to the hill to get out of range. He'd looked over to see that Kane had taken out the Taliban in the cave and was positioned to get a fix on the ones on the hill. Wilder had signaled to Kane to hold his position. When he'd looked around for the others in his squad, he'd seen Mickey was down. His instincts had told him to get him out of harm's way, but then he saw the back of Mickey's head lying five feet away from his body.

That'd pissed Wilder off.

His men saw the look in his eyes and knew what was about to happen. Wilder didn't get like that often, but when he did, there was no way to stop whatever he was about to do. You could almost see the human part of him disappear as a more feral and animalistic nature gripped him. He'd become a warrior, a killing machine, and nothing would stop him until he was done. Laning dubbed that his "warrior mode," and had seen it in South America, where Wilder took two bullets in the shoulder and didn't even flinch.

Wilder had slung his rifle over his shoulder and grabbed two fragmentation grenades. He rolled out from where he was and threw the grenades onto the hilltop. Before they even exploded, he'd had his assault rifle in his hands, shooting at the targets. He'd taken out four Taliban before the others were able to jump in. It hadn't lasted long, but Laning was glad The Warrior showed up that day.

A bump in the road brings Wilder back to his current mission. He continues to drive in silence.

4

Why do they keep referring to me as 'cargo?'' Jim wonders , but if he's spoken out loud, the others don't acknowledge him at all. He feels all the eyes in the vehicle focus on him. Part of him is scared, but another distant place inside him is getting angry. That is a new feeling for Jim, as very rarely did he get angry. His old man would tell him, *If you don't start getting angry and standing up for yourself, people are gonna walk all over you your entire life.*

I guess he was right, thinks Jim.

He can feel his blood pressure rising as a million thoughts run through his head. Some are basic thoughts about survival and how he can get out of this situation. Other have him imagining tearing out of this plastic bag and ripping the throats out of the guys around him. He smiles as an image of how that would go down filled his head.

God, I'm so hungry.

Jim realized he didn't hear any noise coming from the heart monitor. *That's weird, isn't it?* He also realized he wasn't panicking. Jim's been a worrier all his life. A headache is always a brain tumor and a scrapped knee is always going to get infected and lead to an amputation. Here he is lying in this moving vehicle, strapped down on a gurney inside a biohazard containment bag, and is surrounded by a group of soldiers. Despite this, is oddly calm.

Calm and hungry. *Very* hungry.

The soldier's eyes and silence are broken by a loud voice over the intercom. "We're here." He feels the vehicle come to a stop. He still isn't panicking, but his heart is racing a mile a minute. There is still no sound coming from the monitors.

"The cargo is fully awake, Sir," the man closest to him reports.

"Are those fucking things on?" one man asks.

"They're hooked up and the battery is juiced. I don't know why they aren't working, Sir."

The side panel of the van slides open. Jim tries to turn his head, but the leather strap is firmly in place. Out his peripheral, he can see that there were at least eight to twelve other people waiting outside. Jim immediately notices that they are all dressed in those biological hazmat suits. The kind you might see in a movie about the outbreak of a virus or some other kind of disease.

Jim gives in and begins to panic. Without even thinking, he bolts upright and tears through the leather straps on his head and arms. Everyone around him scrambles and runs toward him and the van. The soldiers riding with him all have their pistols aimed at him with their fingers on the triggers. Someone in the back, also dressed in the containment suit, shouts, "Stand down, Rangers."

Jim feels something uncontrollable rising inside him. His hunger is turning into an urge that is quickly becoming a blood lust. He wants to leap out of the van and kill everyone around him. His fists are balled and he feels a kind of energy and strength he has never experienced before. He also feels the urge to sink his teeth into everyone in his way. He wants to taste flesh and blood. His mind is crystal clear and his reflexes are ready. He is a tightly wound-up spring ready to uncoil. The soldiers around him see his fists and someone comes running forward with a rifle. Without hesitating, the soldier shoots Jim in the chest with two rounds.

Stunned at first, Jim realizes they weren't bullets, but tranquilizers. *Big mistake*, he thinks. He jumps out of the van, ripping the bio-bag from his legs, and runs toward the closest person. He has never felt so alive. His senses are sharp and his speed and agility could rival any athlete. He grabs the soldier closest to him and tries to sink his teeth into him, but the thickness of the bag still over his head prevented him from penetrating the soft neck of the soldier.

He pushes the soldier away and begins tearing at the bio-bag around his head and upper body like a trapped animal. He sees the soldier with the tranquilizer gun aim and fire off another four rounds into his chest and stomach. Almost immediately, he feels its effects. He drops to his knees. He looks around and feels as though he is in some crazy movie.

A twisted smile comes over his face. *A movie*, he thinks. *That's where I know the other symbol from.* He remembers staying up late the other night watching a movie about some foreign government creating a biological weapon to use against the U.S. The foreign military base had a symbol all over the lab where the weapon was being manufactured. It was the same symbol on the outside of his containment bag.

The symbol designates him a bio-chemical weapon.

Jim is losing consciousness quickly, but he still smiles. He knows he is going to be kept alive, and when he regains consciousness, he will finish what he started. He is still hungry, and nothing will prevent him from satisfying his hunger.

Jim smiles as he sinks into darkness.

CHAPTER SIX

1

In the hills around the Austin Zoo

Everyone seems to grasp the weight of the situation fully. We're stranded in Hill Country after living through a train wreck with an unknown number of animals hunting us down. I still have to remind myself this is actually happening. Whenever I reach down and feel Fi hugging my leg, I realize just how real this is.

Everyone calms down after the last attack as best we could. Trying to take our minds off of what we just saw, we all go around and introduce ourselves. Besides Cassie, there is another solo mom, Susan, with her two kids, Karen and Tom. Next the dad who kind of lost it for a little bit introduces himself as Kyle, Then his son, Kevin, and his father, Willie. That just left Jessica, and her son, Bill Jr, whose father was slaughtered in front of us all.

We all try to console Jessica, but she seems unusually relaxed and calm. There's no telling when or if she will lose it. I make a mental note to keep my eye on her. I don't know why, but I feel as though it is up to me to lead this group. I've already stepped up. There's no way I'm going to put me and my daughter's fates in the hands of someone else. The only plan I have is to survive and get Fi out of this fucking mess. My mind keeps wandering back to that day when I was ten years old. There's no way I'm going to stand around frozen in fear and watch some rabid animal tear apart my little girl. No fucking way.

The girl whom I'd initially identified by her floppy hat stands and brings me back to earth. Before she says anything, Julie walks over and hands me my K-Bar combat knife that I lost when Fi and I jumped off the train.

"Where did you find this? How did you know it's mine?" I ask.

"I saw you putting something under your shirt right before you two jumped," she responds. "It flew off you before you even hit the ground. I saw it bounce under a bush."

"Thanks," I say reluctantly. "You really didn't have to do that." I can read her enough to tell she knows more about what is going on here than anyone else. I wonder why she would risk finding my knife instead of seeking safety. I ask her that exact question.

"When I saw what it was you dropped," she answers, "I assumed you were some kind of military guy or something."

I look at her inquisitively.

"You know, you had a combat knife, so I thought you might be some kind of trained soldier who could help us out." I can see the look of hope in her and now everyone's eyes.

"I'm sorry to disappoint you, but I'm not a soldier. I was never even a Boy Scout." Many of the hopeful eyes fade into defeated looks. "I'm a chef, out here like all of you to enjoy a day at the zoo with my kid."

"Why are you carrying around that knife?" the woman named Susan asks.

"I collect knives and I was getting this one sharpened at work. I left it in the back of my car by accident." Everyone looks let down. "Look everyone: we're out here alone and need to stick together. I may not have Special Forces training, but I'm going to make damn sure my little girl stays safe." That perks most of the people up.

"We don't even know what the hell we're up against," says Kyle.

"Well," I say as I look back over at Julie, "I think she can fill us in."

2

"Look," Julie starts, an edge of unease in her voice, "I'm gonna tell you right off the bat that I don't know everything that's happening here. I can only fill you in on what I know."

Trying to calm her down, I reply, "Anything, and I mean anything you can tell us about what is going on here, will be more info than what we have right now." I can see her relax a little. "We're all in this together."

"Are these animals rabid?" asks the grandfather, Willie, before Julie can start. "I've seen some rabid animals in my day, but never like this."

"I don't know if they're rabid ..." Julie's eyes become distant. "All I can tell you, and you've seen it with your own eyes, is that these animals are very aggressive."

"Okay, hold on," I interrupt. "I feel like we are skipping ahead. Let's start from the beginning; at least the beginning of the story for you." I look around to see many different expressions. Some look pissed off, as if this is all Julie's fault. The last thing we need is people in the group attacking each other. Others look at Julie as if she is going to reveal everything about what is happening and how we can get out of this.

Julie takes a deep breath and a swig from her water bottle before beginning her story. She tells us about the animal shelter she runs in Hyde Park and what happened there earlier this morning. She describes how the animals seemed almost catatonic one moment and then how they became extremely violent and aggressive the next.

"And then there was Jim." Julie's voice trails off. "Jim was with me from the beginning. He helped me with everything, from fixing the old house up to helping care for the animals every day." Tears start to form in her eyes.

"What happened to Jim?" I ask softly.

"He... he was attacked by the animals. He was opening the cages to feed the cats. They were just lying around. They looked dead, but as soon as he opened the cage they just attacked him. I never saw anything like it before and I've been around animals my entire life."

She takes a long pause. It seems as though she is trying to get the image out of her head. Before she can start again, I ask, "When you say 'attacked,' what exactly do you mean?" I feel everyone's eyes on me. They know what I am asking.

"Well," she continues. "They didn't just nibble on his hand. They..." She means to continue, but sees all the kids listening to her every word. She looks at me as if asking if it was is right to continue. I nod. We are in the shits. Everyone knows it including the kids. We need to hear her story.

"Those cats were tearing hunks of Jim's flesh away. I've never seen such a look in any animal's eyes. It was as if they weren't animals anymore. They had this look in their eyes, this... this hunger. They were completely focused on Jim's hand and they were feeding on him. Feeding!"

"What are you saying?" Kyle interrupts. "That those cats were possessed by something? That's freaking ridiculous."

"No, they weren't possessed, you idiot." I can't help but smile at Julie's response. "This isn't some B-movie we're in. All I'm saying is that those cats, who moments ago looked dead, suddenly jolted up and attacked Jim with a ferocity I have never seen before."

I have to ask the next question, fearing I already know the answer. "What happened to Jim?"

Julie then proceeds to tell us about her call to animal control and how the operator was useless until she mentioned that her friend was bitten. "Then this very no-nonsense man got on the line. I could hear the line switch over like I was transferred. I think his name was George. I could swear he was military." She must have seen all the looks on our faces. "My ex was in the military and he just had this manner about him, very rigid and focused all the time. That's the vibe I got from this guy."

She goes on to tell us about the conversation with George.

"He sure didn't sound like he was from animal control," Jessica chimes in. I was hoping she'd been listening. I was afraid she was in shock from just losing her husband.

"That's exactly what I thought," Julie throws back. "But it gets weirder." That definitely grabs our attention. "Not ten minutes later, five soldiers in full combat gear showed up, burst into my house, and torched the entire place. They put Jim in some kind of bag... it looked like a containment bag."

"They burned your house down?" asks Willie.

"They were burning the animals in the cages and the house was in the way," Julie replies bitterly.

"Where did they take Jim?" I ask.

"I have no idea. The only reason I'm not with Jim is because I escaped through a trap door in the house."

We are all stunned, all trying to process the information Julie has just told us. There seems to be some connection, but judging by the looks on everyone's faces, no one can make it.

Kyle breaks the silence. "So what the hell does that have to do with these animals attacking and killing us here? Are you saying those animals survived and followed you on some kind of odd vendetta?"

My eyebrows furrow as Kyle asks that question. My eyebrows are telling him, 'That's the stupidest question I've ever heard.' To everyone I say, "I don't know what it is, but there has to be some kind of connection between Hyde Park and here. There's no way there could be two separate instances of highly aggressive animals that far apart." Then, turning to Julie, I ask, "So what brought you to the Austin Zoo?"

"Yeah," says Kyle. "Did you just want a relaxing day at the zoo after almost being fried?" Willie whacks Kyle on the back of his head.

"Have some goddamn respect, son. This woman just lost her friend and home." Kyle is beet-red with a combination of anger and embarrassment. "It's a valid question," Willie continues. "What did bring you to the zoo?"

"Right before I ran off into the woods, I heard one of the soldiers say something about the Austin Zoo. I only heard one side of the conversation, so I have no idea what they were talking about." She pauses. "He said something about a subject at the zoo being neutralized."

"'Neutralized'," says Kyle. "What the hell does that mean?"

"That's what I wanted to find out," says Julie. "I wanted to see if there was an animal, or animals, at the zoo behaving aggressively."

Staring down at Fi, caressing her hair, I say, "They weren't talking about an animal." All eyes focus on me. "Jesus Christ. They were talking about a man."

3

"Story time's over," says Kyle. Julie is staring at me. I know she wants to hear my story that connects her to this mess. "It's time to get the fuck out of here." Willie again whacks Kyle upside his head. "What?" Kyle almost whines.

"There're kids around. Watch your language. I raised you better than that." I am starting to really like Willie. "You need to keep it together for Kevin and everyone else here. We're all scared, but the only difference is you're acting like a p-u-s-s-y," Willie snaps.

Kyle immediately turns bright red again and looks down at the ground.

"What do you think our next move should be, John?" Willie asks?.

Great, I think. *They* are *looking to me as the leader*.

"I think it's obvious that we need to get some help out here," Cassie answers. "I can't believe no one has come out here for us yet."

"They may not even know we had an accident," I add.

"Hold on!" Julie almost yells, then says, "You know another piece of this puzzle. I wanna know what's going on."

"You will, Julie," I reply. "But right now, I think Kyle's right." Kyle's eyes shoot in my direction. "We need to get some kind of plan together." Kyle nods in agreement. I am hoping that by agreeing with Kyle, I will give his ego a much needed boost, and make him feel he has a voice in the group. I need to get him into a group mentality because there's no room for cowboys going off on their own.

"First thing we need to do," Kyle says in a renewed, authoritative voice, "is to get some help out here." He kind of gives me a look as if he was waiting to see if I agree with his move. I nod my approval and Kyle takes out his cell phone.

"Wait a minute!" Amber yells. She finally looks like she is coming out of her haze. She lapsed a little after I helped her mom, Cassie, regain consciousness, but am glad to see her coming around.

Everyone's eyes dart in Amber's direction. "Don't use that!," she yells to Kyle, pointing at his cell phone.

"What are you talking about?" Kyle questions. "We need to get help out here, sweetie." I don't know if he intended it, but he stressed the word *sweetie* to the point that it sounded condescending. "We're all gonna be okay, you'll see. Help will be here in a couple of minutes after I call."

Kyle opens his phone and starts dialing 9-1-1. "Stop it!" screams Amber. "You're gonna get us all killed!" Amber is shaking violently as Kyle waits for a voice on the other end of the line. He puts his hand over the phone and loudly whispers, "Everything's gonna be alright, sweetie." No sarcasm on *sweetie* this time.

Amber turns chalk-white. She is looking over Kyle's shoulder. I see the bushes shaking about twenty feet behind Kyle. Everyone sees the same thing.

"Kyle," I say in a very level and calm voice. "Hang up the phone and put it down." He furrows his brow at me, not understanding.

"Hello... yes, I'm here!" Kyle almost screams on the phone. "We're at the zoo and there's been a horrible accident." The bushes are shaking violently now.

"Kyle," I say again, but this time he ignores me, focusing his attention to the person on the other end of the line.

"... the train derailed and there's something out here hunting us down. No this isn't a joke. Does it sound like I'm fucking joking? People are dead out here." Kyle is practically shouting into the phone. Then I hear it: a low, guttural growl that went goes through my bones.

"KYLE!" I shout. "Hang up the goddamn phone!" With that, I point behind him. He turns with the phone still on his ear. When he sees what we are all looking at, he freezes mid-sentence. I gesture with both hands to put the phone down, but Kyle is frozen with fear.

We can all hear the growling getting more frenzied. The animal, or whatever is in the bush, is getting ready to attack. I grab the knife and again yell to drop the phone. I can't be sure of what I am seeing, because my left eye is really beginning to deteriorate into a milky fog, but the sound of that beast is unmistakable.

I've had enough of the subtlety and scream, "For Christ's sake, drop the fucking phone!"

It is too late. The animal attacks. It leaps through the bushes so quickly that even if both of my eyes were functioning perfectly, I don't think I would have seen it. Whatever it is looks to be about as big as a medium-sized house dog, but the noise it makes is completely foreign.

Time suddenly freezes. For a moment I am ten years old again, playing street hockey in Philadelphia ...

Whatever that thing is, it's charging Kyle. He still hasn't dropped the cell phone.

My mind flashes down that hill in Philly where the dog jumped Dave...

I see Kyle's face change from shock to realization.

I stand there frozen in fear as Dave is torn apart. The dog thrashes and tears into Dave's abdomen ...

Kyle crouches down in slow motion and puts his arm over his face.

Dave is dead. The dog is still chewing. My best friend was killed in front of me and I didn't do anything. How could I just stand there and watch Dave die?

How could I just stand here and watch Kyle die?

I can't, I couldn't.

Time suddenly becomes real again.

Without thinking, I run toward Kyle. The animal has a good eight feet lead on me. *No way am I going to let this man get torn apart in front of his father and little boy. No way.* I have one chance. If I jump head-first at the charging beast. I might be able to grab its tail and at least slow it down.

I am running as fast as I can. The animal is like a cloudy blur in front on me. I can vaguely see a tail swinging, but my eyesight makes it doubtful that I'll be able to catch it. I have to try. With my knife in my left hand, I hurl myself head-first at the animal. We are about two feet away from Kyle when I feel something furry hit my right hand. I don't hesitate. I ball my first as fast and hard as I can until I feel the tail in my hand. The beast doesn't so much as yelp or growl. It keeps charging, but is slowed down with my added weight dragging behind it.

Kyle is now in a kneeling fetal position. Willie sees his opportunity and dives at Kyle, knocking him out of charging animal's path. I blink hard to try to get a clearer image of the animal. I can't believe this thing is dragging me behind it. I have to act fast or this thing will turn on me. I hold onto the tail and quickly lash out. The knife easily penetrates the animal's fleshy backside. The beast merely looks back at me as if I am little more than a fly on its ass. I pull out the knife and thrust again, this time further up its back, toward its spine. The resistance the knife encounters tells me I've hit something important. The animal's legs buckle and I let go of its tail. We both roll along the ground until we come to a stop.

I can still feel the knife in my hands and start to panic because I can't see anything or get my bearings. My eyes uselessly try to focus, but everything is a milky white. I curl into a ball just as Kyle had seconds ago.

"Daddy," I hear Fi scream. No... I don't want her running over here. *Please*, I think. *Someone stop her from coming over here.*

I hear the animal growl. I can't get an image of it, but it sounds close. I tuck tighter into my fetal position, trying to protect my vital parts. I hold my breath a little too long and feel myself lose consciousness.

4

I wake panicked and disoriented seconds later. My first thought is whether Fi is all right or not. I start to look around and feel someone holding my hand. Fi. *Thank God*, I think. I look up and can't make out the details of her face. My left eye is rapidly deteriorating. I need my eye drops. As if the situation isn't bad enough, now all I can make out are faint shapes with my left eye. My other eye is clear, but because I didn't get the corneal graft in that eye, I am legally blind in it. I feel helpless, but muster up the strength to stand for Fi's sake. Someone here has to protect her.

"That was incredibly brave," Cassie says.

"And stupid," Kyle adds with a partial smile on his face. "Thanks, man. If you hadn't grabbed that thing's tail, I'm pretty sure I wouldn't be standing here thanking you." He holds out his hand. It takes me a minute to realize he is trying to shake my hand. As we shake, I try to look him in the eyes. I am probably staring into his forehead.

I notice a bloodied, white towel wrapped around his arm. "Are you all right?" I ask.

"Yeah, yeah. The bastard managed to graze me with his teeth, but you slowed him down enough for my dad to pull me out of the way. Some hero I am, eh? My sixty-eight-year-old dad saved my bacon while I was curled up in a fetal position prepared to become doggy chow."

"This isn't about heroics," I answer. Then I realize the terminology he's used. "Doggy chow? You said 'doggy chow.'"

"Yeah," he responds. "That friggin' thing that attacked us was a dog, but I tell ya, I've never seen a dog move that fast. It was like a dog on steroids."

A dog? I think. *Any household dog would have surely slowed down after I grabbed its tail.* Then my mind wanders to earlier in the day. *I know that was a monkey on the train before it derailed, and I could have sworn I saw a tiger and something that resembled a bear. What the fuck is going on here?*

Then I remember something that happened before the dog attacked. I turn to Amber: "Amber, you seemed to sense the attack before it happened. How did you know that dog was going to attack?"

Amber looks at her mom. Cassie realizes that too. "Go ahead, honey," Cassie says. "How did you know?"

"Well," Amber starts. "I noticed that, on the train, the woman was killed, like, a second after she picked up the radio, and then I noticed that other man was attacked when he pulled out his cell phone to call for help." She looks around, waiting for someone to connect the same dots she has.

We all just stare. She rolls her eyes and continues: "Well, it seems that anyone who tried to call for help was getting attacked."

There is a collective intake of breath as we realize Amber is absolutely correct.

"Oh my God," gasps Jessica, the wife of the man who was killed while on his cell phone. "Bill was killed because he was on his cell phone?" She looks around, desperately trying to get someone to tell her how ridiculous that is.

No one disagrees with Amber's theory.

Even with my bad eye, I can see the blood drain from Willie's face. Squinting, I also notice that he's dropped the cell phone that was in his hand.

"Okay everyone," I chime in, trying to prevent a panic. "We know we are dealing with some very aggressive animals that seem to have some level of intelligence." To that, everyone looks at me. I continue before anyone can cut me off. "How else would they know what a cell phone does?" I look around and no one offers a counter theory. "I don't know this for certain, but these animals may have come from a circus or something."

Now I am getting some pretty strange looks. "Why do you think that?" Julie asks.

"Well, there are so many different kinds of animals. You saw it yourself in that open field. There was at least one tiger and something that I swore looked like a bear." Susan and Cassie shake their heads in silent agreement. "I know I saw a monkey on the train right before it derailed."

"So you think these animals were trained to be aggressive?" Kyle asks.

"I don't think they were trained that way..." I take a long pause. "I think, and remember that I have no proof of this, that maybe some kind of virus spread through the circus animals. Maybe some form of rabies." I've been thinking that for a while, and after saying it out loud, am convinced that it's not such a bad theory after all. Judging by the looks on everyone's faces, they all believe it's a viable theory too.

"Oh great," Kyle whines. "What about my arm?" He holds up his bandaged arm.

"Are you going to be all right, Daddy?" Kevin asks as he hugs his dad's leg.

I can see Kyle take in a deep breath. "Of course I am, Kevin. As soon as we get out of this, we'll go to the doctor and he'll fix me right up."

As blind as I am becoming, I can see the fear and doubt in his eyes. *That*, I think, *is the bravest thing I've seen so far.*

"So what's our next move?" Cassie asks. "We can't use cell phones to call for help, so no one probably even knows there's anything wrong with the train yet."

"Well, I think we should get back on the tracks and back track to the station," I say.

"Walk back?" Jessica asks. "You want us all simply to walk back and just let these rabid animals pick us off one by one?" Jessica is slowly losing it. Given the circumstance, I can sympathize, but I don't want anyone breaking down endangering the safety of anyone. Her son, Bill Jr., looks up at her, scared.

"I know you're scared, Jessica," Julie chimes in. "We're all scared. This is a screwed up and surreal situation, but there's no cavalry on their way in to save the day." She looks around at the rest of the group. "We need to stick together and find a way to save ourselves and our children." She pauses long enough to see if anyone is going to offer an alternate plan. When none is offered, she continues: "I think following the train tracks is as good a plan as any. I've never been out here before and I'd hate to get lost in these woods."

"The tracks are over that way," Willie says, pointing behind us. "I agree, and I think we should get started."

We gather up all the bottled water we can find and set out toward the train tracks. Julie walks beside Fi and myself. "Is this the right thing to do?" she whispers.

"I have no idea," I honestly answer. "But I do know that if we stand around here, those animals are just going to chew their way through us." Then I add: "You're around animals all the time. What do you think about my rabies theory?"

She thinks for a moment and then answers: "Rabies does answer some questions here, but I've never seen animals infected with rabies being so focused. Is it even possible for rabies to make an animal behave in such a way?" she asked. I let her think it through. "Later stages of rabies results in violent and uncontrollable movements, then mania before coma and respiratory failure." She looks up at me. "Rabies can explain some of the more aggressive behavior, but as a comprehensive explanation, it leaves too many holes."

"Do you think it could be some new form of rabies?" I ask.

"I don't know," she answers. "I do know that we better get help fast." Then, nodding over to Kyle, she says, "If this is a new strain, then the clock is ticking for him."

Ten miles outside Fort Hood, Killeen, TX

"Sir," Wilder salutes as he approaches Col. Butsko. Butsko is very preoccupied, hardly noticing Wilder and his team. *"SIR,"* Wilder almost yells. That seems to jump Butsko back to the here and now.

"Yes, Wilder." Butsko salutes back. "Good job on securing and bringing in the cargo. You and your men should head to Fort Hood and get some rest." Butsko doesn't even wait for a response before turning his back.

"George," Wilder says as he puts his hand on Butsko's shoulder. "That's it?"

"I don't know what else you're expecting," Butsko says as he stares icicles into Wilder's eyes.

"Sir," Wilder says as he straightens his back and stands at attention. "We've been working together a long time now. I've run a lot of successful missions for you, most of them completely off the radar. All I'm asking you for is five minutes of your time."

Butsko inhales deeply and looks around. The hallway is alive with soldiers and researchers running around. Some are dressed in the typical plain white lab coats, while others are decked out in high-tech hazmat suits. The stress is starting to show in his eyes. Butsko has just entered his sixties, but the dark circles under his eyes have him looking like he is in his late seventies. He keeps himself in great shape, though, at six-feet-two and with a solid one-hundred-and-eighty-pound frame.

Butsko has seen a lot in his career. He fought in the 1969 Tet Counteroffensive in 'Nam and saw action in Panama, Afghanistan, and Iraq. Being in charge of a cutting edge research facility is new to him. *This facility doesn't even exist. It doesn't even have a name.* He was chosen to overlook the new project and to make sure it stayed on track. His medical background and spotless mission record were what led to this promotion.

It was Butsko's idea to use a combination of military and civilian lab resources. The military side was supposed to work on the more cutting-edge aspect of the project. Who could have foreseen the breakthrough the project was waiting for? He knew the researchers in the Austin civilian lab were good, but he underestimated just how good they were. When he approached them with a government grant to further their research, they were practically crying with joy. Grant money had been hard to come by in the civilian sector.

Then those kids had to fuck everything up. Butsko felt his face getting red with anger just thinking about those three who broke into the lab and freed all those animals. They were still cleaning up that mess. They tracked most of them down to an animal shelter in Hyde Park, but he knew his men hadn't tracked, trapped, and cleaned them all. When that panicked woman called from the shelter, he knew he'd lucked out. Of course, they'd had all the animals tagged with tiny computer chips, but every single one had malfunctioned.

"Okay, soldier," he says to Wilder. "You have five minutes. What's on your mind?"

They walk to one of the lesser chaotic corners of the corridor. "Colonel," Wilder starts. "That man in the van ..."

"What about him, Dan?"

"Sir, he was dead for over half the trip." Wilder and Butsko's eyes lock into a fierce stare. "The monitors," Wilder continues, "were completely silent, and even after his eyes opened and he started regaining consciousness, the monitors still had no activity. One minute he was dead, and the next he wasn't."

Butsko stares at Wilder. "You find this odd?" Butsko finally asks. "You've had your chance to walk away from here, Dan. If you really want to know the answers, then you are mine from here on out."

"What the fuck is going on here... Sir?"

"Effective immediately: you, Laning, and Reynolds now work exclusively for this facility, its security, and for The Project." Wilder doesn't blink or budge. "Dan," Butsko continues, "you have to stop thinking in terms of black and white. Technology has developed to the point where we can manipulate the black and white, so there's an indefinite amount of shaded areas. We have stumbled upon one such shaded area and that's what this project is about. We're here to save lives."

"Save lives?" Wilder asks. "That man in the van was dead."

"'*Was*'," Butsko corrects, "is the keyword."

5

The group has been walking along the railroad tracks for about twenty minutes. John could feel the eyes of the predators on them. John knew the animals were out there, but he didn't say anything. John suspected the others were feeling the same way.

I look around and see that Willie and some of the kids are starting to lag behind. We need to stay together. "How about we take a couple minutes break everyone?" I ask. Everyone immediately stops and finds a place to sit down. Looking around, I think this probably isn't the best place to stop. We've settled into the gorge cut through the rock. The only way out is to keep moving forward. If the animals attacked us here, we'd be trapped. Just as I'm about to tell the group we should move out of the gorge, Julie breaks the silence.

"John, I think now would be a good time to fill us all in on what you know. I told you what happened at my shelter and what led me here. Now it's your turn." The others in the group all agree.

I know it's useless to argue, so I take a drink of water before beginning. "I don't know what the hell is going on any more than you all do. All I know is one more piece of the puzzle. It may not even be connected to what's happening out here."

"I don't know if you've noticed," Susan says, "but there's a lot of very weird shit going on around here."

"Did anyone hear about or witness what happened over at the monkey cages about an hour and a half ago?" Everyone shakes their heads. "Well, we noticed that a lot of the animals were missing." I put my hand on Fi's head. "There's usually four lemurs in the cage, and today there were only two. The Colobus monkey and a few tigers are also missing."

"Well, I think we found all the missing animals," Kyle says.

I continue: "We also saw what looked like pools of blood in most of the cages, and when we were at the Patas monkey cage, we ran into this guy who was acting really strange. He seemed to notice all the aggressive behavior and missing animals as well."

"Who was he?" Julie asks.

"He wore the same uniforms the zoo volunteers wear. His name tag read 'Sean.'" I wait to see if anyone has anything to offer. Silence.

"This is your story?" Kyle asks. "This is what you didn't want to tell us?" Willie gives him another quick smack upside his head.

"Just listen, Kyle," Willie tells him. That brings a small smile to everyone's face.

"When I told him that we noticed the odd behavior of the animals as well, he started asking us a ton of questions. He was kind of babbling and he looked really scared."

"Is that it?" Kyle asks, flinching as if expecting another smack from his dad.

"No. Then, as we were talking, three men dressed in full combat gear rushed out of the woods and contained him." Julie's eyes spark up as soon as I mention the soldiers.

"There were soldiers in full combat gear?" Julie asks. "That... can't be a coincidence."

"I know. These guys said they were a private security firm, but I'd bet my last dollar they were military."

"What did they do to that man?" Susan asks with a shaky voice.

"They cuffed him and said to the growing crowd that he was wanted for acts of domestic terrorism." Everyone's eyes stay on me. "Look," I continue, "I only met that guy for, like, ten minutes, and nothing about him screamed out that he was dangerous. In fact, right before those men arrested him, he was saying something about 'saving them' and 'liberating them.'" Looking at Julie, I see her turn pale white again.

"Could he have been talking about animals?" she asks to no one in particular. Then she looks straight at me and asks "That man...could he have been talking about liberating animals?"

Before I have a chance to answer, everyone turns as we hear a loud growl coming from behind us. Everyone stands and bunches together. I put Fi behind me quickly. I try to see where the growl is coming from, but my eye is too cloudy to see anything.

"What the fuck was that?" Jessica screams.

No one answers because no one has an answer. We are all staring into the trees. I knew we shouldn't have stopped here. It suddenly feels like we are in a trap. The path behind us is blocked some growling monster, and in front of us the trees are beginning to shake violently. These fucking animals have us trapped.

6

My adrenaline dumps into my system as I look around. The animals have surrounded us, and the sight in my left eye -my *good* eye- has deteriorated to the point where all I can see are vague shapes. Julie is huddled up next to Fi and me. I have to take precautions.

"Julie," I whisper. "I need you to do something for me."

Not breaking her surveillance, she whispers back, "What is it?"

"If something happens to me, I need you to take care of Fi and make sure she gets out of here safely."

"Look," she replies. "We'll all be fine as long as we stick together. No more heroics from you, okay," she says, forcing a smile.

"No... look... it goes beyond our situation. I can barely see out of my left eye. All I can see are rough shapes of things. Everything is cloudy." She is about to question me, but I cut her off. "I'll explain it later. Right now, just please promise me you'll take care of Fi if something happens."

"Of course I will, but let's not let it come down to that. Stick close to me and I'll be our eyes." Julie is something. Here I am asking her to take care of my little girl in case something happens, and she offers to put herself in harm's way just to get us through this. I nod my approval of the plan.

Without warning, an ear-piercing howl shakes the trees and draws all of us closer together.

I can't help myself. I have to say something to the group. "Look, everyone. We're trapped by these things. They're up on high ground and have our only two possible escape routes cut off." I let that sink in. When no one said anything, I continue, "We need to stay together. Grab anything you can use as a weapon. A branch, pointy rocks, anything, and if you have the opportunity to hurt one of these things, take it. Don't hesitate."

"I work in a goddamn bank," whines Kyle, "I'm not Rambo. We've all seen how fast these things can kill. How the fuck are we supposed to kill them with sticks and rocks?" Willie doesn't smack him this time.

"Get it together!" Jessica shouts. "I already lost my husband to these things. I'm not gonna lose my son too."

"Let's not lose it guys," I say. "Remem…" The rest of that word gets caught in my throat. That all-too-familiar orange-brown flash comes shooting out of the bushes above us. I can see its cloudy shape as it rockets toward the group. "Here it comes everyone!" I shout. "Get the kids in the middle of us."

It is too late. That son of a bitch tiger doesn't slow down for a second as it tears through our tight group, slashing its way through Susan and Willie. It is almost as if it is specifically going for…

"Protect the kids!" I shout too late. In one fluid motion, the tiger carves a path through the adults, like a hot knife through butter, to get to the kids. I have a death grip on Fi and she is grabbing my leg so tight that I think she is going to cut off my circulation.

We all hear a muffled cry as Tom, Susan's eight-year-old son, is snatched up by the tiger. Susan doesn't even realize her son is gone. She is still reeling from having her arm flayed open to the bone.

"Jesus Christ!" Kyle is screaming in a high-pitched voice. "That thing just cut right through us!"

I can see Julie still looking around at the trees and bushes. "I don't think they're done yet."

"Where's Tommy?" Susan starts screaming. "Where the fuck is my son? Oh my God… *no!*" she screams. She was hitting her breaking point and I can't blame her. Her son, who was standing right next to her, was taken from her without her even realizing it. "Someone please help me!" She is becoming hysterical. "I need to get my son." She starts to break away from the group, and that's when she realizes her arm is stripped to the bone.

"Susan," Willie says. "You need to stay with the group. I don't think they're done yet."

As if on cue, three animals burst through the bushes, rushing toward us. They aren't as fast as the tiger. One looks like the monkey I saw on the train, a bear, and... a goat. I can't help myself. I actually laugh out loud as the absurdity of the situation hits me like a shovel to the face. We are being attacked by a fucking goat. Last week, Fi fed a little fucker just like it from her own hands.

Julie elbows me in the ribs and shoots me a look. "Only one person per attack is allowed to crack up. Are you with me?"

"Yeah, yeah, I'm with you. Damn you have a boney elbow."

The monkey is almost upon us. We've been coming to this zoo a long time. The biggest species of monkey they have is called the Capuchin. On average, they stand about two feet tall and weigh about five pounds. "Fuck me," I whisper. "That monkey is at least three times bigger than any of the ones in the zoo." It is fast. Too fast. "What the fuck is happening here?" I ask.

I notice the same thing about the goat. They normally aren't known for their grace and speed, but the one charging us is fast. Real fast. *Could the rabies virus make an animal faster?* I ask. *Since when do goats have sharp teeth?* The goat is charging, teeth bared, as if it is ready to sink them into the first thing, or person, it gets to.

Then, behind the goat, comes the black bear. I've seen on nature specials that bears can run pretty fast, but this one is more agile than a gymnast. It is leaping over fallen trees and large rocks, the whole time its icy gaze focused on us. It seems to purposely stay behind the monkey and goat, almost as if it is letting the other two animals get to us first.

And they do.

We all huddle tightly together. A few of us hold sticks in front of us, hoping one of those animals will impale itself. I don't see that happening. These animals are too smart and agile for that, and now seem to have a purpose. It no longer appears that they are randomly attacking us. Thinking back, the first person they killed was the train conductor, and then they systematically attacked anyone who tried to call for help. Now... no. I can't start thinking like this. My mind is searching to make sense out this situation and is beginning to create connections that just aren't there. Next thing I know I'll be creating some big, elaborate conspiracy theory.

I shake my head, re-focusing on the situation. The monkey reaches the group first. With no hesitation, it lunges after Cassie. Cassie is hunched closer to the ground with Amber tightly between her arms. Cassie looks up to see the monkey airborne and coming straight at her. She doesn't have time to react.

The last thing Cassie will ever see is the monkey coming straight at her, teeth bared and claws ready to kill. She tries to duck, but the monkey slams against her, its claws immediately sinking into her skull as it wraps its arms around her head. Willie is standing closest to Cassie and tries to help. He sees his opportunity and in one fluid motion, he grabs the monkey by its tail.

To Willie's horror, he tears the tail right off the monkey, and it neither stops nor screams out in pain. It is focused on Cassie, and nothing is going to alter its twisted plan. Willie just stands there, a bloody tail in his hands. Blood shoots out of the stump and covers his grandson, Kevin. Willie grabs the boy and pushes him back into the group.

Cassie's screams are muffled and the monkey's body covers her entire face. When it realizes its tail is gone, it looks over at the rest of us, as if to acknowledge its mutilation, but also to show us that it doesn't care. Then as it returns its attention to Cassie, opens its jaws and clamps down on her nose. For a split second, Cassie thrashes. Then, in one horrible tearing motion, the monkey bites through bone and cartilage and tears her nose off her face.

Blood shoots from the gaping hole on Cassie's face. She screams as the monkey goes in again, this time tearing chunks of flesh off her cheeks. In less than two bites, you can see into her bloody mouth. Cassie's screams are muffled by the blood flowing down her throat.

After it is done working on her cheeks, the crazed monkey starts on her eyes. It pulls one of its claws out of her skull just long enough to push it deep into her right eye. Cassie stops screaming. She is past the point of pain. Her body immediately goes into shock as the monkey's finger digs deeper into her brain. It finally pulls its finger out with her eyeball in its hand.

"Give me your knife!" Julie yells at me.

I hand her the sheathed knife and see her throw it to someone. I can see Willie catch the knife and remove it from its leather sheath. Willie moves closer to Cassie and the monkey. Without hesitating, Willie plunges the knife into the monkey as it is pushing its bloodied finger into Cassie's left eye socket. He twists the knife and tries to fling the monkey off Cassie. By any other standards, that money should have been dead. Willie thrusts the knife in a second time, this time going straight through the monkey's rib cage and into its heart. It just turns and looks at us as it chews on a piece of Cassie's cheek.

Willie looks over, horrified, like he has no idea what to do next. Then he grabs the monkey with both hands and pulls it off Cassie. Its claws, still deep inside Cassie, drag across her bloodied head. Willie shudders as its claws scrape across the bones in her face and skull.

"Over here!" I scream. Willie sees his opportunity and quickly throws the monkey over to where we were standing. It hits the ground hard. I don't wait to see if it is going to get back up. Julie and I both look at each other and, in a flash, begin stomping on the monkey. We hear its ribs snap like dried twigs. My foot connects with the monkey's head. I don't think twice and press down with all my strength. The monkey lets out a small whine as my foot caves in its skull. It twitches a few times and then lays there motionless.

The goat is on us next with bared teeth and hunger in its eyes. Willie throws the knife back and, luckily, Julie is there to catch it. She hands it to me and I quickly take it out of the sheath. I run to where Willie is and see that Kyle is huddled down, trying to protect his son. The goat goes in to attack Kyle, but right when it is about to sink its teeth into him, it stops. I can vaguely see it sniff Kyle and, at the last moment, decide not to bite him. *What the fuck*? As quickly as it's decided not attack, it turns and sinks its teeth onto Willie's hand.

Willie howls in pain as the goat takes off four of his fingers. I see the goat chewing on Willie's digits and take my chance. I lunge, aiming for the goat's ribcage, but it turns and instead I sink the knife right through its forehead. Luckily for me, I had picked up some speed behind my assault, and my momentum helps push the blade through its skull. The goat goes wide-eyed as the blade sink into its brain. The goat slumps, dead, before hitting the ground.

Everyone turns in what feels like slow motion. We are all expecting to see the bear charging after us, but, in fact, there is no bear in sight. I haven't realized I've been holding my breath, and slowly exhale in relief. I run back to where Fi and Julie are and pick Fi.

Then I hear a panicked voice: "Where the hell is Kevin?" Kyle shouts. "Kevin!" he yells, calling out to his son.

"Oh my God!" another voice yells out. "Amber is gone too."

Now I know why we didn't have to fight off the bear. The monkey and goat attacked the adults while the bear swooped in and took the kids.

7

We all sit around, stunned by what has just happened. The animals, it seems, are attacking for a specific purpose. They're killing the adults and taking the children. For what? Why would they have been taking away the kids?

Fi, Julie, and I huddle, together creating a tight circle. It keeps Fi feeling safe, but deep down, I know when those animals target Fi that she's as good as taken. I'm not going to sit around and wait for that to happen.

Right after the attack, I was able to get everyone to move out of that location and onto more open ground. We are no longer bottlenecked in, but the animals now have more options for attacking. We are in the semi-dense part of the woods. There were enough trees and bushes and dried twigs on the ground that we should be able to hear if any of the animals approach. I focus on the word *should*.

I look around at everyone. Susan laid about fifteen feet away with a t-shirt wrapped around her flayed arm. She is in shock, more from losing her son than her wounds. Close to her, Willie is doubled over, holding his hand. He removed his jacket and wrapped it around the stubs where his fingers used to be. He's managed to stop most of the heavy blood flow, but my guess is that his hand is still slowly bleeding into his shirt. After we all realized the bear had taken Amber and Kevin, Jessica had discovered that Cassie's body was gone. I couldn't help but feel that was a mixed blessing. Her face and head had looked as if it were tossed into a meat grinder. There would've been nothing left to identify her as a female, let alone as "Cassie." It would've been worse if we had to keep her body around us. She would have been a constant reminder of the fate awaiting us all.

What is truly terrifying is that, with Cassie and Amber gone, there is nothing left to show they were even here. This weird, empty feeling sits in the bottom of my stomach. I'm not sure if Cassie was married, divorced, or widowed, but if she was a widower, then there is nothing left in the world to prove she and her little girl had ever existed. A slow, cold chill runs up my spine.

It is time for action. There are only three kids left in the group. Chances are, Fi will be gone after the next attack. *Over my dead body*, I think. Bad choice of words.

"Listen up everyone," I say, trying to sound in control. "I don't know what the hell's happening any more than you do, but I can *see* what's happening. These goddamn animals are taking our children and killing the adults." I pause to let that sink in. Everyone knows it, but I am the first to verbalize our situation.

"How is this possible?" Kyle asks in a broken voice. "How the hell can these animals be organized to the point where they have a plan? Just saying it out loud... it sounds fucking ridiculous."

Julie cuts in before I can respond. "I don't know how this is happening," she offers, "but it *is* happening. These animals are more aggressive, intelligent, and organized than is naturally possible." Kyle starts to say something, but Julie won't let him get a word out. "But we all have to agree that whether it's possible or not, it's happening." Kyle exhales and drops his head so his chin rests against his chest. He is beaten down and obviously defeated. I can't blame him. Those animals took his son and are doing God knows what to him. I'd be devastated if I was Kyle, but right now, I need to get everyone motivated to action. I need to get everyone fired up and ready to fight back, and by doing so, protect my little girl.

"Maybe... maybe they aren't dead," a shaky voice suggests. We all look over and see Susan sitting up with a glimmer of hope in her eye. I know her fragile mind depends on this absurd sliver of hope.

Kyle is about to say something, but I can't take the chance that he'll crush her with the reality of the situation. Cutting him off, I say, "Susan." I hesitate, trying to pick my words carefully. "I don't know what those animals could possibly want with our kids," I can feel Julie shoot Kyle an icy stare, "but ... but." My mind abandons my train of thought.

"What he's trying to say is that, most likely, our kids are dead," Willie takes over, trying to talk through the pain and clenched teeth. "But," he continues before I can jump back in, "I think we'd all agree that since we don't know for sure, we need to assume they're still alive." He winces. "That was my grandson those fucking animals took, and I'm not running away or dying until I see a body and know for sure he is gone."

Willie sure knows how to get to the point. We all look at each other. "If we're going to look for our kids," I say, "then we're going to need everyone, injured or not." It is my intention to lead everyone out of these goddamn woods, even if I have to dangle the hope of finding their missing kids. I'm not trying to run away; I'm trying to save my daughter. If I have to, I will endanger the lives of every last person here to ensure her safety. Including mine. I know how cold and calculating it sounds, even in my own head, but it is the truth.

Everyone stands and tries to prepare themselves for what is about to happen. I can see it in their faces; they all know that, by looking for the kids, we may never get out of the Hill Country foot hills alive.

I let Julie lead the way and follow her. For the time being, I can still see the vague outlines of shapes, but pretty soon the cloudiness will completely overtake my eye and render it useless. Well, more useless. We gather together, forming a tight outer ring made of the adults in case they try to attack again

We move in the last direction we saw the attacking animals run. I know we are going to find some bodies, one way or another.

CHAPTER SEVEN

1

10 miles outside Fort Hood
Wilder's head is still swimming from what Butsko was implying. *'Was' dead? How is that possible? This isn't science fiction. A dead body is a dead body. Right?* There's always been a rumor in the pipeline about scientists experimenting on how to reanimate dead tissue in order to create a platoon of super soldiers who don't require much sleep or food, and who can't be killed by conventional weapons, but those are just stories. Right? He's read books about how the Nazis dabbled in the occult in an attempt to gain some kind of upper hand against the Allies, but this is America. *We don't do that, right?*

But reanimating the dead? Wilder shakes his head and thinks, *Bullshit. Butsko is a genius at psychological manipulation. He knows I was freaked out by that guy in the van, so he planted some bullshit sci-fi story in my head to let my imagination run wild.* He laughed. *I haven't survived this long by giving in to superstition.*

He goes to look for Butsko. He has some explaining to do.

2

The woods around the Austin Zoo
Jason limps through the dense woods. He has no idea where he is. The last thing he remembers is the train picking up speed and heading for that sharp curve. He jumped long before anyone else did. He assumed everyone else jumped as well. Who the fuck would be dumb enough to stay on a runaway train headed for a hairpin turn?

As he jumped, he remembers seeing the girl from the animal shelter also getting ready to do the same. He didn't think she remembered him. They'd met only briefly that one time when he and Sean had dropped off the 'liberated' animals. He remembered those beautiful eyes though. As soon as he'd seen her standing in line to board the train, he knew he'd made the right decision to visit to the zoo.

He hadn't followed her. Hell, he'd thought he'd never see her again. He'd come to the zoo looking for Sean. He'd been worried about him. After they'd rounded up as many of the animals they could that night, they'd grabbed a couple hours of sleep and then drove to the animal shelter. Sean hadn't looked too good. He'd been slightly pale and sweating. At the time, Jason had chalked it up to nerves as a result of the situation.

Then he'd started thinking about the animals from the lab they'd broken into. *For fuck's sake*, Jason had thought. *We saw a monkey take a flamethrower blast in the chest and just sit there.* What if they'd been trying to develop some kind of cure for rabies and those animals were infected in order to test it? Fuck. That meant Sean was walking around carrying the rabies virus.

Jason was pissed at himself for not thinking about that at the time, but so much had happened that his mind had been reeling. Vicktor had been shot in the head point blank by some crazy Rambo fucker and Sean was bitten. The animals they'd been trying to liberate had attacked them, and now they are on the run. *I did* not *think this one through*, Jason had thought. So he'd decided to go to the zoo and see how Sean was and try to convince him to go the hospital. Then he'd seen the girl again. That very same girl to whom they'd 'donated' the liberated animals. That was more than a coincidence. She was there for a reason, and he'd bet dollars to donuts that her being at the zoo was connected to those fucking animals.

He'd followed her to the train and had been planning on questioning her, but then the conductor had lost her head and everything had gone to shit. Now he is out in the woods with what felt like a broken ankle, trying to find either the train station or the others from the train. *And let's not forget*, he thinks, *that whatever killed the conductor is still out here as well.*

This has not been a good week.

Sean usually volunteered at the Austin Zoo a few times a week. He would feed the animals, help clean the cages, and do anything else to help out. He loved to be around the animals. Jason had arrived at the zoo just as they were opening. The girl in the gift shop had told him that Sean was working and that she was surprised because he "looked like death." That hadn't put Jason's mind at ease. Not at all. He'd walked around for a good hour looking for Sean, but he'd been nowhere to be found. Around eleven o'clock, he'd figured he'd get on the train because it went right past the tool and supply sheds that you couldn't reach on foot.

That's when he'd seen her: the girl with the beautiful eyes. But love at first sight had been the furthest thing from his mind. He'd known that he, Sean, and Vicktor had something bad the other night. It was more than just breaking and entering. They'd thought it was a civilian lab doing cosmetic testing, but all the high-tech and hidden security painted a different story.

He passes into a clearing and sees the unmistakable aftermath of the train wreck. There is twisted metal, broken wood and shattered fiberglass everywhere. As he looks around, he smiles. His suspicions were right that no one stayed on the train. Everyone jumped before it derailed. He is sure there were some broken bones and cuts and a concussion or two, but at least they are all alive. *If people didn't jump off the train,* he reasons, *there'd be dead bodies left behind.*

No dead bodies pepper the wreckage.

He looks down by the base of a tree and sees the floppy hat the girl was wearing. He tries to determine which direction they went. He sees a lot of footprints in the dirt about ten feet away, and figures they are heading to the tracks that lead back to the station. "Not a bad plan," he says out loud. He moves some branches out of his way and heads in the direction of the tracks.

3

10 miles outside Fort Hood

Wilder finds Butsko walking down a sterile hallway. Butsko doesn't hear Wilder come up behind him.

"We need to talk," Wilder says as he puts his hand on Butsko's shoulder. Butsko twists around in a flash and has Wilder pinned against the wall with his arm locked behind his back. One small twist and Butsko could break Wilder's wrist. "I see you haven't lost your reflexes, Sir," Wilder hisses through his teeth.

"Sorry, Dan," Butsko apologizes, releasing his arm. "You need to be high-strung and on constant alert around here. Trust me," he says, staring into Wilder's eyes. "It'll save your life."

"Against what?" Wilder asks, seeing his opportunity. "What's going on in here that could kill us?"

Butsko stands about a foot away from Wilder and eyes him up. "I've already put in the request to give you complete security access. It'll probably still take a few hours to get." He motions for Wilder to follow him through the door that they are next to. Butsko punches in a code and a metal panel slides up, revealing a retinal scan. After looking into the scanner, the thick metal door slides open. It makes no sound other than a 'whoosh' as it opens into a darkened room.

The door closes behind them. "You don't have official clearing yet, but you will."

"How can you be so sure?" Wilder asks. "My combat record is flawless, but my 'following orders' record is spotty at best."

"Because I get what I want now." Wilder starts to smile, but sees that Butsko is dead serious.

"What exactly is this facility for, Sir?" he asks. He notices the lights haven't come on yet.

"Cut the bullshit formalities, Dan. 'George' is fine."

"Lights on. Butsko," George says loudly in the room. At his command, the room gradually get brightens, allowing their eyes to become accustomed to the light.

Wilder doesn't know what to expect. He could have sworn from talking to Butsko that the room was empty. There doesn't seem to be anything in the room to absorb their voices. As he looks around, he realizes he is right.

The room is absolutely empty.

"Sir... uh, George," Wilder says while looking around. "What the fuck is going on here?" He looks Butsko right in the eyes. "We've known each other for a long time. We are both no-nonsense, no-bullshit soldiers. Sure, I've had my problems following orders in the past, but whenever I'm out in the field, I'm the best there is, and now," Wilder says with his arms stretched out, pointing to the empty room, "we're standing in an obviously top-secret facility that's not part of a military base but is close by to one. We're in a very secure room that's completely empty, and you tell me I am getting a top-level security clearance." He pauses to see if Butsko has anything to add.

"Don't forget," Butsko adds, "the man in the van you transported here."

"Freedom to speak, Sir?"

"I already told you to forget the formalities."

"What the fuck is going on? What's with all the cloak and dagger bullshit? What is this facility, and what's being done in it?" Wilder can feel his anger rising. He has been a pawn in the past, being sent into dangerous situations with no intel or clear direction. He is starting to feel that way again. "Either tell me what the fuck is going on here, or you can take your top-level security clearance and shove it up your ass."

Without moving his eyes from Wilder's, Butsko says, "Open viewing windows. Butsko." With that simple command, twenty-five sliding doors all around the room silently open to reveal viewing panels inlaid in the steel walls.

Wilder remains still and looks around. "You thought this room was empty right?" Butsko asks. Wilder just nods. "Well, if you are going to be a part of this team, you better stop assuming you know what's going on." Wilder looks at Butsko again. "You thought," Butsko continues, "that the guy in the van was dead. You *thought* this room was empty. Forget everything you think you know about science, about death. We live in a different world now than what existed ten years ago, or hell, five years ago." He pauses for a second to let those words sink in.

Wilder looks around the room, but still can't see into any of the viewing panels. He looks at Butsko: "'About death?' You're not making any sense, George."

"The man you brought to this facility was indeed dead." Wilder stares in disbelief. "When we picked him up, he was bitten and was in the first stages of the infection. He was feverish, sweating, and cold to the touch Right before you and your men picked him up, he died. He had no vital signs at all, and then halfway here, he... well, you know what happened."

Wilder can't even think of the next question to ask. "What... what bit him?" he finally manages to ask.

"He was bit by an animal," Butsko says, matter-of-factly.

"What kind of animal?" His mind starts categorizing various animals and whether they were capable of attacking a human being.

"We're not sure," Butsko replies. "When we were ready to question the subject, he had already slipped into a coma."

"What do you mean you're not sure? What the fuck are you talking about? Are we dealing with some kind of new life form?" Wilder's head is spinning. *This really is sci-fi,* he thinks.

"No, no," Butsko says. "It could be any of them," he says, nodding into the room. "Behind these panes of glass are animals. Infected animals."

Wilder is still wrapping his mind around this. "What are they infected with?"

"That," Butsko responds, "is the million dollar question." They start walking toward one of the viewing panels. "Let's start from the beginning, Dan."

"Yeah," Wilder echoes, his eyes already fixed on the nearest viewing pane. He breaks his stare to look over at Butsko. "The beginning."

They walk over and look through the closest viewing window.

4
The woods around the Austin Zoo

We journey deeper into the woods hoping we are on the right trail, but deep down, I think every one of us is secretly hoping we won't run into the animals. Let's face it: we are a group of tired, scared, thirsty (and in my case, half-blind) individuals being hunted by creatures that have taken our children for who knew what reason.

Willie decided to take the lead. He hasn't mentioned anything, but something tells me he has seen combat before. He is walking through the woods and barely making a sound, constantly scanning everywhere, including the trees, looking for danger. Add to that the fact that his grandson, Kevin, was taken, and I for one am glad he is with us. He is walking about fifteen to twenty feet ahead, guiding us along. No matter how good he may be, though, something tells me if one of those animals wants to take him out they, will take him out. Quickly.

I want to take the lead, but my eye has gotten progressively worse. The milky fog is thickening as my body rejects the graft. I can barely make out shapes now. I'm not in a good place. I feel weak and of no help to the group. Worst of all, I feel like I'm letting Fi down. How can I possibly protect her if I can't see the danger coming? Right before we set off on our search for the bodies, I pulled Julie aside to tell her how bad my eye had gotten. She said nothing, but the way she'd held my hand let me know she would help me protect Fi. That's all I care about right now.

"How you holding up, Fi?" I ask. I just want to hear her voice to know for sure that she is still behind me.

"I'm okay, Daddy." Then, after a few minutes, she asks, "How is your eye?" Fucking hell. She doesn't miss a thing.

"My eye is great, sweetie," I lie. "Don't worry about my eye. I need you to look around constantly, and if you see any trees or bushes moving, you need to tell Julie or me. Okay?" Using my daughter as my eyes, I officially feel completely useless.

Willie signals and the group stops. No one is talking. There really isn't anything to say. He walks back to the group, scanning the area. "I thought this would be a good place to catch a rest," he says as he sits on a fallen down tree. He is barely winded. My first impression of him as the older, frail grandfather was grossly mistaken. If not for his injuries, he would be the man I'd bet on to survive this mess, but his weakness is starting to show.

Willie is pale, and I know he lost a lot of blood after that animal took off his four fingers. This guy is a survivor, and if it is at all possible, I am going to help him find his grandson. Kyle, on the other hand, has no survival instincts. For the first ten minutes of our search, he'd complained about it being useless and that the only thing we were going to find were the animals, and then we'd all be dead. Willie had looked back at him and finally said, *If you can live with yourself after this is over knowing you didn't even attempt to find your son, I obviously don't know who you are.*

Kyle had looked like he was slapped in the face. Willie then finished his thought by saying, *I know I raised you better than what you are right now.* After that, Kyle had shut up and followed along with the group. I was sure that, after he repaired his ego, he would come around and help out.

"Do you think it's safe to stop and rest?" asks Jessica, obviously scared at becoming a sitting target.

I look over at Julie. She scans the area and sees that we have plenty of escape options. "I think this is as good a place as any," she replies. We all sit down. I rub my eye, hoping that when I take my hand away, I will be able to see clearly. No such luck.

"We've been walking around for almost an hour," Kyle says. He isn't complaining; he's simply stating a fact. "How far could those animals have gotten with our chil..." He chokes back a tear before he can finish his sentence. He's been in denial since Kevin was taken, and now the reality of the situation hits him like a truck. Willie sits down next to him and puts his arm around his shoulders. We all sit there in silence. There is nothing to say.

"We're going to find them, son," Willie says. He surprises me by how sure of himself he sounds. He then turns to everyone and says, "We're not in a good situation here. I'm not gonna lie to you all. None of us have any kind of training, we have no weapons other than one combat knife, and most of us are injured." Everyone's eyes are fixed on Willie. "We're up against something that is unexplainable. I grew up on a farm and have been around animals all my life and I've never before seen any behave so aggressively. We can sit around and speculate based on the little bit of information from these two--" he points at Julie and me, "--but the bottom line is that we're in danger, but they also have our kids and my grandson. For that, I won't stop looking until I know what happened to Kevin and all our kids."

Willie's motivational speech was well needed. I can almost feel everyone straighten their backs and push their shoulders back, but the positive energy among the group is short lived. One moment Willie is getting everyone pumped up to search for the children and then, in a flash, the tiger comes tearing out of the woods, viciously taking him down. The arm Willie has around Kyle remains on Kyle's shoulder as the tiger separates man from limb and pins him to the ground. It happens so fast that no one has time to react.

I hear Julie scream as she pulls Fi and me to the ground. All I see is a large mass on top of Willie. The tiger has opened its massive jaws and sunken its teeth deep into Willie's throat. A wet, tearing sound echoes through the woods as the tiger rips deeper into his throat. Willie lets out a couple of painful gurgling sounds before the tiger thrashes its head and rips away Willie's throat along with most of his lower chin.

Willie dies immediately, but the tiger stands there as if taunting us to attack. Black blood drips from its mouth as it chews on part of Willie's throat. It lets the other parts of Willie drop from its mouth as it stares at the rest of us standing there in absolute terror. It feels like it is sizing us all up to see who'll be next.

I can hear the beast breathing heavily through its nose. From what I can make out, this thing resembles a tiger in form only. I'm no animal expert, but this is a fucking gigantic tiger for such a small zoo. I've been here with Fi a thousand times and we've never seen a cat this big. What kind of infection could possibly alter the size of an animal? Could it be the stress of staring straight at death that is making the animal look bigger? Possibly. Fear and stress can really screw with you, but even its fur is different. There are spots all over the tiger where large patches of fur are absent. Its flesh has a bluish-gray color to it and looks diseased, like how I'd expect a corpse to look. Its eyes are the most disturbing thing. They are unlike anything I've ever seen on either beast or man. There is nothing behind the eyes. They have the cold, icy stare of a pure predator that knows no fear and feels no remorse. This tiger was altered by something, though whether it was by a virus or natural selection, we don't have time to figure it out.

One thing we all understand is that this tiger wants to kill all of us, and there may be nothing we can do about it.

I jump when I feel something brush against my leg. I look down to see Kyle reaching for my knife. I grab his hand and stop him. Kyle, in the last few hours, has watched these things take his son and tear apart his father. He wants to kill it, but what the fuck is a seven-inch blade going to do against this beast in front of us?

I look Kyle in the eyes. As bad as my eye has gotten, I can still see his desperation and pain at everything he's lost. I shake my head back and forth and mouth the words, "Don't do this." He looks at me and then over at Fi and quietly responds, "I have nothing left." My hand falls away from the knife as he takes it.

I can't let this man go on a suicide mission. I jump up, waving my hands frantically. The tiger's head jerks violently in my direction and rests on me. I can feel Julie's hands on my ankles trying to pull me back to the ground. I take a step forward. The tiger stares at me as I slowly walk away from Julie and Fi. I need to distract this monster so Kyle at least has a fighting chance. Deep down, I know he doesn't have a plan. He is just going to attack and try to get one or two lethal blows in.

The tiger starts to crouch lower to the ground. *Jesus Christ,* I think. *What the fuck am I doing?* Just as I see the tiger's back legs dig into the dirt, readying itself to pounce, a rock comes sailing out of nowhere and hits the tiger in the head. I look around, trying to find the source of the rock, but only see the fog in my vision. Just then, a barrage of rocks start pelting the tiger. In the movies, this is usually the part where the cavalry comes rushing in to save the day.

But this is no movie and there was no cavalry.

The rocks are coming from Jessica, Julie, and even Susan. Susan's throwing arm was sliced open, so she is using her other arm. I look back at the tiger. It just stands there, allowing itself to be pelted with rocks. Quite a few hit it in the head and face, but it doesn't flinch once. "What the fuck is wrong with this thing?" I shout. Even on a rudimentary level, any animal would flinch. Then, behind the beast, I see the faint outline of a head peeking over a fallen tree. I realize it is Kyle. He'd taken the opportunity to go around the tiger as it was being hit with the rocks. It hasn't seemed to notice Kyle behind it. In a clumsy attempt, the man jumps up, screaming and running full speed toward it. I see Julie grab Fi and cover her eyes. We all know we are about to see a slaughter.

The tiger never takes its eyes off of me. It knows someone is coming up behind it. Hell, *everyone* can see it, but it just stands there. This thing has lost its natural survival instinct. It no longer lives according to the 'fight or flight' programming it was born with. It is now a pure killing predator that feels no pain and knows no fear.

Kyle is about five feet away from the beast, the knife raised over his head. It looks as though he is going to go for the ribs. He never gets a chance to find out.

Two feet away from the tiger and seconds before he is going to plunge in the knife, a wolf comes charging out of the woods and runs head-first into Kyle. The impact throws him back about ten feet. The knife in his hand is gone, lost on impact. I could hear Kyle trying to breathe. It sounds like blood is already starting to pool in his lungs. He painfully sits up, leaning against a fallen tree. The wolf is ten feet away from him and slowly approaching. "Fuck you!" Kyle screams. Blood is already dripping from the corner of his mouth. He turns his gaze and then shouts, "Leave my dad alone!" We all turn to see that the tiger has gone back to Willie's body. It' clamps its powerful jaws around his abdomen, picks the body up effortlessly, and walks back into the woods.

Kyle is crying and coughing up blood. "Why are you doing this to us? What the fuck is wrong with you things?" The wolf jumps into the air and lands on Kyle's chest, knocking him flat on the ground. It immediately rips his throat out with a loud, wet, ripping sound. Before Kyle dies, it turns and opens his belly with its claws. Kyle's eyes widen in fear and horror as he realizes he was being gutted alive. The wolf is chewing on part of Kyle as its claws dig deeper into his body. He dies shortly thereafter.

Something drops from the branches above Kyle's body and lands on the wolf. I rub my eyes to try to see what it is. It doesn't look like an animal, and no one else in the group is screaming. A man had jumped onto the wolf as it was eating Kyle and broke its neck. Time seemed to stand still as we processed the scene in front of us. Thoughts flooded through my head; was there another survivor from the train wreck? Those soldiers who arrested Sean, did they come back?

The man gets off the wolf and looks over at us and shouts, "Quick! Someone help me!" Without thinking, I rush over to where he stands. He never takes his eyes off the wolf. "Stand on the wolf's body," he says in a panic. When I don't move, he grabs my arm and shouts, "Hurry! We don't have much time!"

"Time for what?" I ask, confused.

"Time before this fucker gets up and attacks us again," he says as he nods at the fallen wolf.

"What are you talking about?" I question. "Are you crazy? You broke its neck. We all heard the bone snap."

"Listen to me, asshole," he yells, more out of fear than anger. "We have about seven more minutes before this thing wakes up and tries to finish the job it started with your friend over there." I don't know what to say. From what I can see of his face, he doesn't seem to be crazy. I put my foot on the wolf's chest.

"Step down," he orders. "Step down *hard.*" I press more of my weight onto the wolf. "Don't move, and don't take your foot off it. I gotta find something." He runs around, frantically looking for something on the ground. I look down at the wolf and jump slightly as I feel a twitch under my foot. Was it my leg? It twitches again, this time more violently.

"Hey!" I shout to the guy. "This thing is starting to move again!" I can feel all the blood drain from my face as I realize this beast isn't dead yet. Worse is that I have my foot on it. I know damn well that, no matter how much pressure I put on it, if this wolf wants to stand, it's going to stand. "Hurry up!" I shout

He comes running back with something in his hand. He apparently found what he was looking for. "Is it moving?" he asks.

"It started twitching a few seconds ago." I feel foolish. It was probably the wolf's death spasms as the rest of its life faded from consciousness.

"Okay, don't take your foot off of it," he says as he looks me square in the face. "No matter what happens, *do not* take your foot off this thing." I then see what he was looking for: my combat knife. He drops to his knees. "I can't believe how fast reanimation is occurring."

"What the fuck did you just say?" I ask, practically yelling. "Did you just say '*reanimation*?'" He looks up for a second and then returns to the task before him.

Without hesitation, he thrusts the knife into the side of the wolf's throat. The wolf jerks violently and lets out a high-pitched shriek. I am almost thrown off the beast. "Keep your goddamn foot on its chest!" the man yells. He begins to saw the knife back and forth inside the wolf's neck. The wolf is fighting back. My eyes may have been failing me, but I can see clear as day that this thing wasn't dead. Unfortunately, the Ka-Bar knife doesn't have a serrated side. Both sides, as sharp as they are, are smooth edges. I now regret not getting the knife sharpened last week.

Blood is spurting everywhere as he puts pressure on the animal's throat. I can't see what exactly he is trying to do exactly, but he needs a better plan. The wolf is getting more and more aggressive.

"Almost... got... it ..." he says through clenched teeth. Then I hear one last high-pitched squeal from the wolf. The man holds up his arm and in his hand is the wolf's head. I can feel all of us staring at him.

He grunts and threw the head back into the woods. He stands and hands me back the knife. Blood covers it from tip to hilt and I slide it back into its leather sheath. The man is breathing heavy as he walks back to the group. "Come on," he says. "We can't stay here any longer. We're sitting ducks."

I look around and ask, "Where's Kyle's body?"

The man doesn't even look . "I'm sure the other animals came in and took it while we were killing the wolf."

"Why didn't they try to stop you from killing one of their own?" Julia asks.

"They aren't working as a pack. They could care less if one or two of their ranks was thinned out."

"How do you know so much about these things?" Jessica asks.

"Because he used to work in the lab that created these things," another new person to the group says as he approached us.

"Look," the wolf killer says. "I'll be glad to tell you everything I know, but first we need to get moving. These things are getting stronger and faster and smarter by the minute. We need to move ... *now*."

None of us argue.

"Lead the way," I say to our new group member. Without a word, we head in the same direction that the tiger attacked us from. No one says a word. We all just follow.

5

We walk in silence through the woods. By now, our original plans to follow the train tracks back to the station are forgotten. We follow this newcomer hoping he has the answers to what the hell is going on and how we can kill these things.

"This should be good," the wolf-killer says as he looks around. We have been climbing up a hill for the last forty minutes. From where we are, we can see about a ten-mile radius of the woods around us. He's taken us to higher ground. Brilliant idea. I'm mad at myself for not thinking about that.

"I think it's time for introductions," I finally say as everyone sits. Our group has been cut in half (bad choice of words.) Of us that remain, only Julie and I have introduced ourselves. The rest have either had gone silent or are huddled over their surviving child.

"Now you know who we are," I say after a few minutes. "The big question is: who the hell are you guys? Where did you come from? It sure seems like you both know what's going on here." I pause for a second and then, "Is there any way we're getting out of this alive?"

"My name's Jason," he said before the wolf-killer could speak. "I'm a student and I belong to an animal rights group. I... I don't know how to say this," Jason stutters, looking for the right words, "but I think I caused this." Jason suddenly has eight icy eyes staring through him. Jessica stands, but before she can say anything, Jason continues. "Let me explain. I didn't make these animals what they are, but I helped liberate them."

"That's where I know you from!" Julie almost shouts. "You came by my shelter a few days ago and gave me a bunch of these fucked up animals. Do you have *any* idea what those animals did to my shelter? They killed my partner, slaughtered all the other animals in my shelter, and then the military came and burned it to the ground." She stares him straight in the eyes, not blinking.

"I'm so sorry," Jason almost whispers. "If I had known what was wrong with those animals, I would have destroyed them myself. I… I didn't know." He looks around at the group. No one is cutting him any slack. "Look, our… my intentions were good. We wanted to liberate a bunch of animals that were enduring God knows what kind of testing in that lab. We knew they were aggressive…" his voice trails off. Looking back up, he says, "They bit my friend and I saw them attack the soldiers."

"Soldiers?" Julie asks. "You saw soldiers too?"

"Yes," he answers. "These soldiers showed up and started torching the place. When they saw that Vicktor was bitten, they shot him point blank in the head. Those sons of bitches didn't hesitate for a second. They just blew him away. They were going to kill Sean and me as well, but the animals started attacking them. Those animals… they just tore those soldiers apart. I never saw anything like it."

"Yeah. We know," Julie says. "We've been getting attacked for the last four hours."

"Wait a minute," I interrupt. "Sean? Your other buddy's name was Sean?" Jason nods. When I describe Sean, Jason's eyes get wide.

"Yeah that's Sean," he says excitedly. "Where is he? Is he all right?"

"No, he's not all right," I answer. "Our soldier friends whisked in and grabbed him in front of about twenty witnesses."

Jason pales. "Where the hell did they take him?"

I don't respond. I just stare with a *you're serious* look on my face. I give Jason the shortened version of what happened to Sean.

No one says anything. I looked around at the group. Everyone looks beaten down and defeated.

"Come on everyone," I say, trying to sound positive. "We have another piece of the puzzle, and we now know where these animals are from. Some messed up lab was experimenting on them." I hesitate long enough for my reason to catch up to my racing thoughts.

"So what the fuck were they testing on those animals?" Julie asks. "What could they possibly be doing to them to make them this aggressive? For Christ's sake, we saw a goat tear apart a man… a *goat*."

"That's the same question I've been asking myself since we liberated the animals," Jason responds. "I'm thinking it was some kind of steroid." We all look at him questioningly. "I know it sounds weird, but I figured they were testing some new kind of steroids on those animals." Then, turning to Julie, he continues, "That's the only reason I brought the animals over to your shelter. I read about you and your work and figured these animals just needed to let the drugs run their course. After they got through their systems, the animals would be back to normal." He looks at everyone. "They just needed refuge." Jason stops talking and stares at the ground. "I'm a fucking idiot," he concludes.

Then, Jason suddenly looks up. "But," he says excitedly, "we *do* have one more piece of the puzzle that needs to explain himself." All eyes turn to the wolf-killer sitting about fifteen feet away from the group.

"My name's Brice," he says without looking up, "Brice Allen. I worked in that lab that Jason over there broke into." He pauses to let that sink in. Before anyone can ask a question, he says, "You're right, Jason. We were experimenting on those... *these* animals," he says as he stretches his arms and points to the woods around us. "You are way off on what we were doing in that lab."

"Well, how about you clear that up for us, Brice," I say angrily. I hug Fi closer to me. My eye is all but useless now and I need to know Fi is next to me.

Turning to Jason, Brice continues: "Go ahead, Jason. I know you're thinking it. You're the one who broke into the lab." Their eyes.

"How about one of you assholes fill the rest of us in!" Susan yells.

"Oh my God," Jason whispers.

"That's right," Brice says with no humor in his voice. "That wasn't some civilian lab you broke into, testing lipstick and eye shadow." Jason looks. "You," Brice says slowly, "broke into a private lab funded by the military and other interested defense contractors." Jason's eyes go wide. Brice is shaking his head back and forth.

"You have no idea what you released."

6

10 miles outside Fort Hood

Wilder's knuckles are turning bright red as he grips the edge of the viewing window he and Butsko are looking through. He is gripping that edge as if it is the only thing grounding him in reality, this reality. What Butsko just told him about the animals and the current situation has his head swimming. Admittedly, Butsko doesn't know the entire story. They weren't absolutely sure what they were dealing with. That's what the installation was for: to isolate, understand, and destroy the as-of-yet unknown threat.

The installation, nicknamed Sils, was built five years ago in order to research and develop more cutting-edge science, and implement the findings into practical military uses. They have everything at Sils: from weapon development to biochemical testing labs.

The facility was modeled after the Vector Institute in Koltsovo, Russia. The Vector Institute was, and some say still is, one of the most sophisticated biological research facilities in the world. The CDC and the U.S. Army Chemical and Biological Defense Command were both modeled after the Vector Institute. Vector was part of the Soviet Union's *Biopreparat*, which was that country's biological warfare agency initiated in the 1970s. *Biopreparat* was a sprawling network of secret laboratories, each one focusing on a different deadly hazard. At its height of operation, it employed 30,000 workers and developed bio-weapons such as anthrax, Ebola, the Marburg virus, Q fever, and small pox. At least those were the ones that the U.S. discovered.

What was most interesting about *Biopreparat* was that the research labs, scattered all around Russia, were mainly civilian research labs that, along with developing deadly bio-weapons, also did research into other harmless areas. All of this right in the backyards of communities and neighborhoods. This is how the Soviets were able to escape detection and continue developing destructive weapons all the way up to 1992.

The U.S. government liked this. *Hiding in plain sight,* one General had said. *This way, we can dive further into cutting-edge science and weapon development while working on genetically engineered corn in the same facility.*

Sils has the capabilities for all levels of biological hazard, CDC levels 1-4. Over the years since its initial construction, it has been upgraded with the latest security equipment, biohazard containment systems, and cutting-edge technology. Two years ago, the facility also got its own security team to guard it. When Wilder asks Butsko what outfit guards Sils, Butsko says it is so above top-secret that they don't have a name.

"Technically, they don't exist," Butsko says. "We could both be court marshaled just talking about them." He moves in closer to Wilder. "This is no bullshit, Dan. This facility is the real deal. You no longer exist in the everyday channels of the military. You belong to Sils now, as we all do."

Wilder stares at Butsko, trying to process everything he was just told. His world hasn't just turned inside out--it's imploded. There are alleys and dark corridors of the military complex he can't even begin to believe exist. Now he is part of that shadow world. "What about my team?" he finally asks.

"They've already been briefed and told what they need to know about this place. They don't know a tenth of what I've told you, and even you only know about two percent of what's going on here. They don't seem too happy to be a part of all this, but they won't leave your side, Dan."

Wilder looks back into the viewing window. The house cat is just sitting in the middle of the room, staring up at the same window Wilder is looking through. It doesn't move, it doesn't lick itself, and it barely looks to be breathing. A chill runs up Wilder's spine. It is almost surreal. This tiny house cat that can't weigh more than six pounds is being held in a state-of-the-art biohazard containment lab. No one is allowed into the room with the cat unless the cat is knocked out first.

Butsko and Wilder walk around and peer into the various viewing windows. Each contained one animal. There are about twenty-five containment cells holding all kinds of species, from house cats and dogs, to snakes, goats, chickens, and in a few rooms, cows and horses. The eeriest of all the animals are the predatory ones. There are two wolves and a tiger at the far end of the room. When Wilder looks through the window, he can feel those predatory eyes burning holes right through his head. He is glad there was twelve inches of reinforced steel separating him from those wolves and tiger.

"So," Wilder asks, trying to digest this info. "All these animals were released from one of the civilian labs outside of Austin a few days ago?"

"Yes. Some kids who volunteer at an animal liberation group broke in and 'liberated' them." Butsko says "liberated" in a low, deep voice, making it sound like a curse word.

"I'm having a hard time understanding how a bunch of kids could break into one of these labs," Wilder says.

"You have to understand that these are different times we live in," Butsko offers. "There'd be no point in using this civilian lab if we decked out the perimeter with all the most recent, state-of-the-art security and surveillance equipment. That would have eventually tipped someone off that there was more than just make-up being tested on those animals."

"Okay," Wilder says. "I can understand that, but why would such lethal research be conducted at that lab then?"

"Up until two days before those kids released those animals, that lab was one of our least productive." Butsko can't take his eyes off the wolves behind the glass. Shaking his head, he continues, "That lab was, in fact, a week away from being shut down. Then they had a breakthrough." Wilder notices those last words sound bitter.

"What kind of breakthrough?" Wilder asks.

Butsko turns to meet Wilder's gaze. "I've already told you too much. Your security hasn't officially cleared yet, and even then, I'm already telling you more than your clearance allows for."

Wilder's blood is beginning to rise. "You want my help, George?" he asks coldly. "If so, then I need to know what the fuck I've gotten myself and my men into." Their eyes are locked in a showdown. "This facility is just about the scariest place I've ever seen. Part of me doesn't even wanna know what the fuck is being tested and researched in here." Butsko starts to turn his head. "But," Wilder almost shouts, "if you need my help like I think you do, then you have to level with me. What kind of threat are we dealing with here?"

Butsko removes his hat and runs his scarred hand through his thinning hair. "We don't know yet, Dan. That's the problem. We just don't know yet."

"That's not a good enough answer, George," Wilder says.

"This project, Project Overman, started off with one goal, and then that goddamn lab outside of Austin hit a breakthrough. Now it seems as though the project has its own goal and we're playing fucking catch up trying to find out what that goal is." Butsko suddenly looks very old and tired. "We've been destroying these animals," he says as his hand sweeps around the room, "and studying them to find that goal."

"Have all the animals from that lab been neutralized?" Wilder asks, afraid of what the answer might be.

After a long pause, Butsko looks up. "No, Dan," he says. "All the animals have not been neutralized." A heavy silence falls between them. "There are still an undisclosed amount of animals out there. They could be dead. or they could be roaming around in some neighborhood." He exhales a long sigh. "Or even worse." "Let me guess," Wilder asks, trying to fill in the gaps of information. "Those animals are what attacked that guy in the van? That guy who seemed to come alive halfway through the trip?"

"Yes, Dan," Butsko answers. "Those animals which are still out there are capable of attacking and killing anyone they come into contact with."

"Then why the fuck are we just standing here? We need to be out there knocking on doors and putting up posters about some bullshit rabies outbreak. At the very least, we can warn people about not picking up stray animals."

"The rabies story has been running on the news for the last day and a half," Butsko says. "We're here because we need to determine what the hell those animals are carrying."

"Fucking hell," was all Wilder can come up with.

"Yeah, Dan," Butsko echoes. "Fucking hell."

"Let's get to work," Wilder says as he starts walking to the door.

7

The woods around the Austin Zoo

We are all still staring at Brice and Jason. We all want to ask him the same question, but I don't think anyone really wants to know the answer. Finally, Julie breaks the silence.

"So what exactly did Jason release?" Julie asks, barely above a whisper.

"It's not that easy of an answer," Brice starts. "You have to understand that the original parameters of the study were completely shattered with the breakthrough we experienced at the Hudson Research Lab." He looks around and sees he has the attention of every single one of us. Even Fi seems to be hanging on his every word. "We were set with the task of how to save lives, lives of wounded soldiers on the battlefield. With the technology we have today, we were doing an okay job of saving them in the theater, but we were losing a large percentage of our soldiers when they were sent back home. The long journey was just too much for gravely-injured soldiers, and they were dying from their injuries before their planes even touched down on U.S. soil." Brice seems very genuine in his emotions as he tells his story. I am starting to believe that this mess we are in was caused by good intentions.

"So," Brice continues, "we came up with the theory that if we could somehow put the mortally-injured soldiers into an immediate state of stasis on the battlefield, then transport them back to the U.S. to get treatment, we could save a whole lotta lives."

"What do you mean by 'stasis'?" Jason asks.

Brice looks around. We all hear noises from the trees. "Do you really think now is the best time for stories?" he asks nervously.

"This may be the only time we have left," I reply, purposely sounding overly dramatic. "Look," I continue. "Any info you can give us about these things could help us kill them."

"Kill them?" Brice almost laughs. "You want to kill them? No, no, no. We need to figure out where they are and then run in the opposite fucking direction, and fast."

"You fucking coward!" Susan screams. "We need to find our children!"

"Find your kids?" Brice's words fade away. "You mean they took your kids?"

"Yes," Julie answers. "These animals have been attacking and killing the adults. It's like they're killing us in order to distract us while other animals slip in and steal the kids."

"That's..." Brice is at a loss for words. "That's amazing."

Wrong choice of words, I think.

"Amazing? Amazing?" Susan stands now and begins walking toward Brice. "You think it's *amazing* that these fucked up animals are taking our children away and doing God knows what to them?"

"No, no... I'm sorry," Brice apologizes. "I don't mean it like that. It just seems their behavior and intelligence is growing and evolving beyond the level of basic survival."

"Hold on," I interrupt. "Why don't you go back a step. Tell us what you meant by 'putting the soldiers in a state of stasis.'"

Brice's eyes are constantly scanning the woods around us. "Okay, let me put it in basic terms. Shrimp boats go out to sea for weeks at a time, right?" We all nod. "Now, how do you think they keep the shrimp they catch on the first day as fresh as the shrimp they catch on the last day? I'll tell ya. They have this huge machine that individually freezes the shrimp as soon as they're caught." He pauses to see if anyone is going to make the connection, but when no one does, he goes on. "The shrimp are glazed with a thin layer of water and then individually flash frozen when they're still alive in order to preserve the maximum amount of freshness."

"Oh my God," I say out loud as I realize where this is going. "You were trying to freeze injured soldiers on the battlefield, weren't you?"

"Not quite," he replies. He seems to be getting excited at explaining and talking about his research. "We couldn't freeze them. There was too much irreversible damage on the cellular level. Instead, we theorized we could put them in a state of chemical stasis; one analogous to flash-freezing the shrimp." He looks around. "Now, before you get this image of the mad scientists locked away in their mad scientist labs, I can tell you that this was successfully being done on animals." He purposely looks at Jason when he says this last part. "Dogs were placed in this state of chemical stasis and then revived hours later. Just think about how many lives we could save if we could translate this to humans. A soldier steps on a land mine and gets half his body blown apart. Up until now, he's a dead man. But if we could immediately place him in that state of stasis, his heart rate would all but stop, thereby preventing him from bleeding to death. He wouldn't be in pain, thereby eliminating his body from going into shock, and he would be revived back in the U.S. at a state-of-the-art hospital already fixed up. He wouldn't have to experience any of the surgeries and his body could repair itself."

We all just stand in silence. "That's fucking crazy," Jason finally says. "You're talking science fiction."

"No," Brice cuts him off. "We're talking about real, cutting-edge science being used to save lives."

"So what happened during those experiments that resulted in these messed up animals?" I ask, trying to get to the part of the story that can possibly save us.

Brice's eyes take on a vacant stare. "We had a breakthrough. At least, we thought it was a breakthrough." No one says anything. "We decided to take it a step further and attempt to heal the soldiers while they were in stasis and on their way back to the U.S."

"Okay," I say hesitantly. "Why not?"

"I'll tell ya why," Brice's voice becomes dark. "Because that's when everything got fucked up and out of control."

"We're listening," Julie says calmly. We all sense it. It feels like we are starting to lose Brice. He's giving us good information, but he's really not giving us anything that we can use to fight these things off.

Brice looks at Julie: "We went too far. We were only trying to save lives, but we took it too far."

"Took *what* too far?" Julie asks, getting angrier. "What did you do in that lab?"

Brice has no time to answer. No one sees it coming, not even Brice. The tiger comes tearing out of the trees just to the right of where Brice is sitting. That fucker is moving so fast it looks like it is flying through the air. Brice's eyes are still fixed on Julie when the tiger slams into him. Its powerful jaws clamp down around Brice's chest. We can all hear Brice's ribs cracking as the tiger's jaw snaps shut. In one fluid motion, it picks Brice up and sweeps him off into the woods. It happened so quickly that Brice didn't even have time to react, but as the tiger disappears into the woods, we all hear the panicked and pained screams coming from Brice.

"Everyone protect the kids!" I scream as I grab Fi and hug her to my side.

The woods around us come alive. Sounds of shaking trees and breaking twigs and branches tell us the tiger isn't alone. I can only imagine that we are all thinking the same thing – that they've come back to get the rest of the kids. I think our search is over. We aren't going to find the kids. It's beginning to feel as if no one is going to find any of *our* bodies.

A deer comes racing out of a thicket of bushes to our right. At least, it looks like a deer. It has saucer-sized eyes that are full of death and hunger. It races by where Susan and her last child are. Susan's daughter, Karen, starts screaming. As the deer gets closer, one of the Patas monkeys from the zoo drops out of the tree and lands on Susan's head. It appears the animals were working together: the monkey running interference to distract the adults while the deer goes for the kids.

The monkey's claws sink into Susan's head and neck as she tries to throw it off. She screams and thrashes around. Thick rivers of blood run down her cheeks and neck.

Meanwhile, the deer races towards Karen. Karen is frozen in fear. She is watching this crazed deer racing toward her and as that monkey is tearing apart her mother's head. As Susan reaches up to try to grab the monkey's tail, the beast sees her injured arm and, in a calculated move, reaches out and runs its claws down it. Susan screams as her arm is flayed open a second time. The pain makes her weak in her knees and she drops to the ground. The monkey has started tearing out clumps of her hair and scalp. It almost seems to be do this to warn the rest of us away.

Jason stands, shocked like the rest of us at the ferocity of the attack, but runs to Karen when he sees the deer knock her over and sink its teeth into her leg. Jason picks up a large rock and begins beating the deer in the ribcage. The deer doesn't even seem to notice Jason's assault. Its attention is focused on Karen. It bends down and bites Karen again, this time in the other leg.

Jason is beating the deer with all his strength. Surely he should have cracked a rib or two by now. Then, out of nowhere, a grey streak races towards him. He turns with the rock in his hand to confront the new threat, but the wolf rams straight into his chest, knocking him to the ground.

"Stay with Fi!" I shout to Julie as I race over to try to help Jason.

"No Daddy!" Fi screams.

I run to the spot where I thought I saw Jason and the wolf tumble. My eye is all but useless now, but I can still see that the wolf is on Jason's chest. I take the knife out from its sheath, still bloody from the wolf Brice killed. Seeing that blood gives me hope. We saw one of these fuckers die, and that means we can kill another one.

I lunge forth with the knife leading the way.

About eight feet away, Jessica is huddled over her son, Bill Jr., afraid to leave his side. The tiger that just took away Brice is back. She knows it is the same tiger because its mouth and fur are covered in blood and it still has pieces of Brice's clothing in its mouth. Jessica starts to panic, but her survival mode kicks in and tells her that if she doesn't get it together, she can kiss her son and her own ass goodbye.

She grabs Bill Jr. and runs to the nearest tree. "Get in the tree, Billy!" she screams. She lifts him up and pushes him onto the first thick branch. "Climb as high as you can, Billy, and don't come down until I tell you it's safe." Billy reluctantly starts climbing the tree. Jessica knows the tiger could scale after him, but she has to do something. She can't just leave her son sitting around on the ground and wait for him to be picked off.

Jessica turns to see the tiger crouched low to the ground in an attack pose. She looks around and finds nothing she can use as a weapon. She closes her eyes, waiting for the beast to leap on her. She sees her husband behind her eyes. "No!" she screams. "I can't let this thing take my baby." Her hand is resting on the same branch she put Billy on seconds ago. She looks up and sees Billy has gotten pretty far up the tree. She grabs the branch and, with the strength of a mother fighting for her son's life, tears the branch from the tree. She closes her eyes and holds it in front of her like a jousting pole.

The tiger is digging its back paws into the dirt. It jumps forward just as Jessica is raising the branch. She hears a loud roar that shakes the leaves on the tree behind her. Jessica bends her knees and grips the branch tightly as the tiger charges. Right before the moment of impact, Jessica closes her eyes and bellows out a ferocious scream. The tiger slams into her and she is thrown backwards and rolls across the ground.

After a few moments, Jessica slowly opens her eyes. The tiger has impaled itself on the thick tree branch right through its heart. Blood is draining quickly from the beast. "I got you, asshole," Jessica whispers.

As she speaks, she feels something dribble down from the corner of her mouth. She tastes it with her tongue. Blood. She smiles as she thinks about how violently the tiger must have impaled itself to splatter its blood on her face. Jessica looks up the tree to find her son staring down at her in horror. "It's okay, Billy," she tries to say. "Mommy killed the monster."

"Mommy?" Bill Jr. says quietly.

"It's gonna be okay, sweetie." Again, she is having trouble catching her breath. Finally, she sees her son point to her chest. Slowly, she lowers her head. Tears well up in her eyes.

The tiger ran into her with such force that it not only impaled itself, but thrust the branch into Jessica's chest as well. Now that she's seen what her son was pointing to, the pain and shock begin to wash through her body. She is dying in front of her son.

Billy Jr. climbs down the tree, but he isn't fast enough. When he gets to his mom, she's already dead. The last image he has of her is a tear rolling down her cheek and mingling with the blood from her mouth. He sits down and cries.

John didn't reach Jason soon enough and the wolf's fangs sank into Jason's shoulder. My lack of eyesight forced me into being more cautious and unfortunately slower. Jason was screaming and trying to get the wolf off of him. Watching the wolf, I noticed it acting differently. Up until now, the animals were attacking, killing, and dragging the bodies away, but this time the wolf bit Jason and didn't thrash its head around and tear him apart. The wolf remained motionless with its teeth buried in Jason's shoulder.

I was close enough to make out what was going on and I didn't hesitate. Plunging the seven-inch combat knife deep between the wolf's shoulder blades, I was hoping to ease the wolf's hold on Jason. But going by Jason's screams, my attack did nothing to help Jason; the wolf bit down harder and deeper onto Jason, severing the ligaments and tendons that connect the bones. Releasing Jason from the beast's jaws was my primary concern as I pushed the knife deeper into the wolf, but that bastard had a tight grip on Jason. The wolf bit down harder and I heard Jason's collarbone snap between its teeth. For the first time today, I am glad I couldn't see out of my eye, and glad I couldn't see the look on Jason's face as his collarbone shattered.

Ten feet away I heard Jessica screaming and knew she needed our help. Killing this wolf became my only focus. Jumping off the attacking beast, I kept my hands on the knife. I started kicking the wolf in the ribs and could feel its bones cracking with every blow. I gained some leverage as I stood next to it, and I began to slide the knife deep in the wolf's back, alongside its spine. Nothing should be able to withstand the pain and injury I was dishing out on this creature. Half way down its back blood was pouring out of the beast in rivers, but the wolf still had its jaw clamped on Jason's shoulder.

I feel something brush by my legs. When I turn to look, it was another goat. This was starting to feel like the animals were conducting an organized attack. They were coming in waves as if to distract and disorient us. Keeping my hands on the knife inside the wolf's back, I kicked at the goat. I hit it twice in the head but that did nothing to stop it. I could feel the goat trying to bite my legs and almost let go of the knife that was still inside the wolf. Something from the corner of my eye distracted me and I could see another cloudy shape racing towards me. I immediately thought the worst: the bear was coming straight at me. As it was getting closer, my survival instinct kicked in and I dropped to the ground in the fetal position to try to protect myself.

"What the fuck are you doing?" I heard a hoarse voice screaming at me. "Get the fuck up."

I blinked hard to try to get a clearer vision of what was coming at me. Standing there crooked as his arm was wrapped around his upper chest was Brice. He had gotten away from the tiger and was coming to help Jason and I. Standing up as fast as I could I reached for the knife sticking out of the wolf. Pulling my foot back, I was about to kick the goat again when I saw Brice jump on top of it. Grabbing the goat, Brice wrapped one hand around its throat while the other wrapped around its lower jaw. Brice twisted violently, snapping the goat's neck and dropping it to the ground. Through clenched teeth Brice winced in pain as he tried to straighten up. I was staring at the goat lying motionless on the ground.

"Get with it man," Brice yelled at me, "or we're all dead."

Returning my focus to the wolf, I saw it had finally released Jason from its jaws. Jason was trying to crawl away but the pain from his shattered collarbone slowed him down. The wolf violently turned in my direction and knocked me to the ground.

"How the fuck is this thing still standing?" I shouted out to no one in particular. The wolf was looking at me with its dead eyes. If I didn't act quickly I knew this would be it for me. Before the wolf finished turning around to face me, I saw its balls hanging down. And knew this was my chance. Grabbing the wolf's balls, I starting squeezing and twisting them as hard as I could. I was experiencing the same blood lust as these animals as I was tearing the wolf's balls off. I felt the spongy flesh squish between my fingers as I tightened my grip. The feeling was like squeezing a panna cotta that had too much gelatin in it. The wolf was howling as I tore and squeezed its balls with more ferocity.

The wolf collapsed to the ground in pain confirming to me that these bastards did indeed feel pain.

"Watch out," Brice was yelling over to me. Releasing the wolf's shattered balls from my hand, I stood up. Brice fell on top of the wolf and plunged his hands into the wound on the wolf's back that I made with the knife. Grabbing the flesh on each side of the wound, Brice began pulling the wolf apart. The wolf was howling as Brice tore its back open, exposing bone, cartilage, and its spinal cord. Brice kept tearing the wolf apart until it stopped moving. When he was done, the wolf looked like it had been turned inside out.

For the second time today, I was glad I couldn't see.

Turning away from the remains of the wolf, I was screaming for Fi. I was looking around like a madman trying to locate Fi and Julie. I knew Julie would still be with her … unless of course something happened to her.

"Fi … Fi," I shouted as I started running around looking for them. I searched the area where I left them before running off to help Jason, but they weren't there. The only sign that they were there was a small pool of blood.

I looked over to where I left Jessica and saw a body lying on the ground with what looked like a dead tiger a few feet away from it.

Julie hugs Fi close, not wanting to let her out of her sight. Julie can sense the animals surrounding them, almost taunting them.

"Stay close to me, Fi," she says. "We'll be okay as long as we stay together and out of the way." Julie doesn't believe her words for a second.

"I want Daddy," Fi says, close to crying.

"Your daddy is helping Jason over there. He's going to be okay, and as soon as he saves him, he'll be back with us." Julie's never had any experience dealing with kids and isn't sure how to talk to them, but knows that Fi has seen everything, beginning with the first attack on the train. *Fi isn't stupid*, Julie thinks. *She knows we are in deep shit here*. Julie decides to tell her the truth. The truth, in these circumstances, can only save her life.

They huddle behind a fallen tree trunk where Julie feels they are relatively out of the way. All kinds of animals were running around--a tiger, some monkeys, some goats, the wolf John is trying to kill and some deer. She also remembers seeing that bear a while ago. Plus, the zoo is full of all kinds of animals. She has no idea how far this… this what… *infection?*… has spread. She watches John plunge that knife deep into the wolf's back. She can't believe that it doesn't faze the animal one bit.

She looks over at Susan, who's finally succumbed to her injuries. A deer and a llama stand over her.

"What are those animals doing?" Julie says, barely over a whisper. Fi look to see where Julie is looking. "Oh my God," Julie says as she realizes what is happening. She grabs Fi, covers her eyes, and hugs her close. The deer and llama are eating Susan's dead body. Now that her brain has accepted that two herbivores are eating a human being, she is able to process the animals tearing chunks of flesh from Susan's body. The deer is eating from Susan's bloodied head, tearing away chunks from her face and cheeks. Julie can see that Susan's lips and tongue are already gone.

The llama is eating away at Susan's stomach. Susan's intestines are spilled over the ground like some morbid bowl of spaghetti. The llama has already stripped Susan's left thigh of flesh.

Julie turns away from Fi as she feels the acid in her stomach working its way up her throat. She throws up three times before the bile starts to recede. She has seen a lot of very fucked up things these last couple hours, but watching a deer and a llama tear apart a human being is too much. She knows they were in a hopeless situation.

"Julie," Fi says as she tugs at her shirt. "Julie!" she says a second time, screaming.

Julie looks up, the sour taste of vomit still in her nose, to see an ostrich had come up behind them. It isn't a full-grown ostrich, but is big enough to kill them both. She grabs Fi's hand. "Run!" she screams, but the ostrich has already started its attack and is lowering its head, going in for the kill. Julie throws Fi over the fallen tree that was seconds ago their protection. The ostrich bites Julie's ear off as she tries to jump over the tree. Blood pours into her ear as she tries to fight through the pain.

"Don't wait for me, Fi! Just run!" she screams. Julie is able to get over the tree before the ostrich strikes again, but she is running spastically, not quite regaining her balance. Julie catches up to Fi. Before Fi can ask, Julie says. "I'm okay, sweetie. Let's get somewhere safe." She looks to her right just in time to see the tiger impale itself and Jessica on the branch. A scream sneaks out of Julie's mouth as she watches the life drain out of Jessica's body.

"Billy!" she screams. "Billy! Over here!" They run over to the boy who is crouched on the ground crying. "Come on, Billy! We need to get out of here!." She looks over her shoulder to see that the deer and llama have finished feasting on Susan. They are looking straight at Julie and the kids. "*Now*, Billy!" she screams.

Julie is too late. A lemur drops out of the tree and onto Billy's head. He screams and runs off in a panic. The last thing she sees is the Lemur's claws sinking into Billy's eyes. Billy runs into the llama and falls to the ground. The lemur's claws tear out his left eye. Julie watches knowing there is nothing she could do to help Billy Jr. The llama lowers its long neck and rips out Billy's throat. The lemur jumps off his head and disappears into the trees. By this time, the deer and a donkey have joined the llama and the three beasts begin tearing Billy apart.

Julie feels all hope drain from her. She realizes that looking for the kids is useless. The kids who were earlier dragged away are dead, torn apart by these animals. She hears a scream as she sees Brice come limping out of the woods. He is running toward John and Jason, who are still fighting off the wolf that has been joined by a goat. In an instant, everything becomes dream-like for Julie. It just isn't possible in the world she lived in for animals like llamas and goats to attack and kill people. The world shifts into slow motion.

Jessica's body pinned up against a tree by a branch, a tiger on the other end.

Susan's body lying a few feet away, torn apart by a deer and llama.

Six-year-old Billy's throat torn out by a llama.

Brice tearing apart a wolf.

An ostrich tearing off an ear.

Julie's brain can't process the images around her. She's worked with animals her entire life and has never seen anything like this. Even animals with rabies aren't this aggressive. She looks around to see the ostrich coming straight toward her and Fi.

She faints. Her body hits the ground and the last thought she has is, *I'm never going to wake up again.*

"Wake up, Julie, please wake up." Julie faintly hears the frightened voice as her body shakes back and forth. It is Fi. She opens her eyes. Next to her lays the ostrich. *The ostrich*, she thinks as she bolts up.

"Fi," she screams as she hugs the girl close. "I'm so sorry, Fi." She then pushes Fi at arm's length and inspects her for any injuries. "Are you okay?" she asks. Just then, a pain rips through her head as she remembers the animal tearing off her ear. "What happened, Fi?" she asks. "Who killed this ostrich?" She looks around and sees John with the knife back in his hand.

"John?"

"We got back here just in time," John says. Jason is sitting on a large rock, huddled over in pain. Brice is between them, bracing his arm across his chest. He is having trouble breathing. John then bends over the ostrich and, with a few jagged sawing motions, removes the ostrich's head from its body. He doesn't even try to hide the grizzly scene from Fi. He knows she's seen worse.

"Are the animals ..." Julie asks, letting her sentence fade away.

"They aren't done yet," Brice answers. She can hear the pain he is in every time he inhales through clenched teeth. "They may have stopped for the time being, but we need to get out of here."

They are all looking around. Not one animal can be seen, but all around them the trees and bushes are shaking.

"What's our next move?" Julie asks.

CHAPTER EIGHT

1

Sils Military Research Facility

Butsko and Wilder meet back at the lab that houses all the animals. They took a break two hours ago to wait for the official security clearance to come through so Wilder could brief his men on what was going on.

Mac Laning and Kane Reynolds stared at Wilder the entire time he told them what he knew. Finally, Wilder told them they were meeting Butsko at the lab, and there, everything would become clear. Or as clear as it could be.

"I'm sure Wilder has filled you guys in on what we are dealing with," Butsko says as he approaches the men standing at the thick steel and concrete door. Their hesitating answers confirm to Butsko that they don't believe a word of it. Part of him is happy about that. If he was told the story that he told Wilder, he would think the other person was full of shit and somehow testing him. *I'm glad these guys think for themselves. That's what we need here*, Butsko thinks.

"Your skepticism is well understood, men," Butsko continues. "But make no mistakes. What Wilder told you is exactly what is going on here." He spreads his arms and sweeps them about the facility. "Yes, there are other projects going on in here, but this project, the one you are all exclusively on now, has top priority." He looks them all in the eyes and emphasizes, "We've never been involved in a more important project than this." Butsko steps toward the door and punches in the code to reveal the retinal scanner. As the laser scans his retina, he says, "What's in this room could very well be the biggest threat not just to our country, but to the entire world."

The thick metal door slides open, but this time, the metal viewing windows are open and the men can see all the animals. Kane and Mac just look at each other.

"This is what we know so far," Butsko starts. "These animals were all being tested on for one reason: to save the lives of soldiers gravely injured on the battlefield." He doesn't wait for a response. "We were losing so many lives during their transport home that something had to be done. We hired a researcher who was doing cutting-edge experiments and successfully reanimating animals."

"Reanimating, Sir?" Kane repeats. The look on his face says it all.

"Yes soldier, reanimation." Butsko's voice is steady and very serious. "The dogs in the experiment were put down and then immediately placed in a state of stasis. You can call it 'suspended animation,' but what they were doing went well beyond that dated practice. A couple hours later, the dogs were brought out of stasis successfully, and there was no damage done on either a cellular or physical level. Those dogs, in fact, are still alive up in Pittsburgh."

Wilder, Laning, and Reynolds all look at him stone-faced. "Yes," Butsko says, "in Pittsburgh. They were doing reanimation studies in Pittsburgh."

"So," Wilder finally interrupts. "If those dogs are still alive, then I assume they are healthy and not aggressive?"

"Play the footage!" Butsko yells to no one in particular. A hidden screen drops from the ceiling and they watch three dogs running around and playing with small children. "This footage was taken last week. Those dogs have never so much as taken a nip at the children, let alone attack them."

"Okay," Kane says. "Then obviously it wasn't the stasis that made these animals so aggressive." He pauses for a second. "So what was done different to these animals than those dogs? "he asks as he nodded up to the screen.

"We have some theories," Butsko offers. "Unfortunately, the lab these animals were stolen from was completely destroyed." Butsko places great emphasis on the word 'stolen.' "Most of the computers were one-hundred-percent destroyed. We have two hard drives that we're trying to reconstruct in order to extract the last weeks' worth of research."

He takes the men over to one of the viewing windows. Inside is what looked to be a house cat, but this cat looks more sleek and predatory than the pet. Its teeth are longer, and even though its claws aren't extended, you can see the long, sharp tips sticking out. This animal looks like a hunter. Actually, it looks like a killer.

"We do know that the lab outside of Austin, where these animals are from, stumbled upon a breakthrough. They weren't just killing and then putting these animals into stasis. The researchers there knew that would do nothing to save the lives of soldiers." He looks at the enclosed cell with the house cat. "They conducted another procedure on these animals once they were in stasis. They engineered a virus that would start to repair damaged brain tissue, fix broken bones, and restore deteriorating muscles." He knew by the others' silence that he has their complete attention.

"The preliminary findings were amazing," Butsko continues. "After a few days, the animals were being revived better than when they were put down. Then the experiments went further. They were inducing brain damage in some of the animals before they were put into stasis. Other animals had bones broken, were burned, maimed, and various other injuries that soldiers might sustain in battle. In every case, the animals were coming out of stasis a few days later completely healthy." He turns to look at the others, and then, stone-faced, says, "Gentlemen, it was fucking amazing, and one hell of a breakthrough."

"We don't know what the new procedure was?" Wilder asks.

"Not completely," Butsko answers. "The breakthrough and the break-in of the lab were only days apart. They didn't even have time to brief us fully on what it was before the lab was torched. When we find the 'breakthrough,' we find the cause of these animals' aggressive behavior."

"Permission to speak, Sir?" Kane asks.

"You'll find that we don't follow all the protocols you are used to Kane. Speak freely," Butsko replies.

"Since we've been in here," Kane says as he looks around, "I haven't seen one of these animals do anything even remotely aggressive."

"Then you better pay attention," Butsko says as he nods at the house cat before them.

At the back of the enclosed cage, a metal door slides open with a "whoosh." A hand, protected by a level-four hazmat suit, drops a small mouse into the cage. Before the mouse even hits the ground the house cat pounces and cuts it in half. It then slowly eats the two halves.

"Jesus Christ," Mac says. "Now I know where the term 'cat-like reflexes' comes from."

"Keep watching," Butsko says.

A slightly larger door slides open and the same hazmat hands drop a larger cat into the cage. This one actually makes it to the floor. It runs to the opposite corner and arches its back, hissing and screaming. The altered house cat slowly stands on all fours and sniffs the air. Without hesitation, it pounces onto the new, larger cat, sinking its teeth into its throat and killing it in seconds. They watch, stunned, as it then guts the dead cat and begins eating its insides.

"What the fuck was that?" Kane almost shouts. "That thing just killed in less than a second."

After another minute, an even bigger metal slot slides open in the cage. This time a wolf-dog hybrid is placed inside. The wolf sniffs the air and is noticeably scared. The house cat slowly walks around the wolf as if it is sizing it up. It then darts behind the wolf-dog hybrid and bites on one of its hind legs. After it bites the wolf, it walks to the other corner and continues to eat the larger cat it had just killed.

"Again, what the fuck was that?" Kane repeats.

"You're starting to sound like a broken record, Kane," Wilder says.

"What do you make of this little demonstration, men?" Butsko asks as he turns to them.

"Whatever these things have inside them," Laning starts, "makes them fast as hell. I've never seen a faster, more accurate kill. That cat wasted no energy killing the mouse and larger cat."

"That's good," Butsko says. "We've been studying other infected animals here and their kill rate and accuracy is off the charts, but what else did you notice?"

Wilder doesn't give anyone the chance to answer. "It's not just instinctively killing," he says. "It's like it's assessing each situation to determine the best course of action."

"Go on, Dan," Butsko urges.

"Well, when the mouse was put in the cage, the cat barely even acknowledged its existence. It attacked and killed it before it even hit the ground," Wilder pauses. "But when the larger cat was put in the cage, it sniffed the air and looked like it was trying to determine what kind of threat it was."

"Obviously," Laning cuts in, "it didn't see it as a big threat."

"Right," Wilder says to no one in particular. "The same with the wolf. It sized it up and determined that in a fight, the wolf would most likely win." Wilder stands there looking inside the cage. "No wait. That doesn't add up. If it thought the wolf was a threat, then why did it sneak behind it and bite it? There's something else..." Wilder smacks his hands together. "It wasn't just determining if the wolf was a threat," he says, clearly excitedly at his own breakthrough. "It was sniffing to see if the wolf was already infected by our mystery virus."

"Bingo," says Butsko. "Infected animals don't attack and kill other infected animals. The mouse, a 'lower' life form, is immediately killed and eaten. The larger cat was judged to be the same and uninfected, and therefore, of no use. But the wolf," Butsko says, sounding excited, "the wolf was determined to be a slightly 'higher' animal. Believe me, that house cat could kill that wolf. But instead, it wanted to infect it, and that's exactly what it did by biting it."

The men are staring at the wolf, who is lying down on the floor now. "Wait," Wilder says. "That would mean..."

"That would mean," Butsko cuts in, "that the virus, or whatever the hell is inside these things, has its own survival instincts, and wants to propagate itself in higher life forms." He pauses a second and then, "In about two hours, give or take, the wolf is going to die, and then another hour after that, it will reanimate."

"Is this what happened to that poor bastard we transported here?" Reynolds asks.

"It is," Butsko answers. "It seems that the higher the life form, the slower the transformation. A bite like the wolf got would take about four to five hours to kill a human being." He looks at the soldiers closely. "The transformation would take about eight to nine hours."

"Transformation?" Wilder asks.

"Yes. That's the nice way of describing the process when the person dies and then wakes up again."

The men all look at the wolf on the ground and the house cat still eating the other mangled cat. Their silence tells Butsko that the gravity of the situation is sinking in.

"That's right, guys. We have some strange virus out there trying to climb the food chain, and we all know what's at the top of the food chain, don't we?"

Shivers ran up both men's spines.

After a long pause, Butsko finally breaks the silence. "Your silence tells me you understand the severity of what we are dealing with here. There's one more thing you need to see."

2

The train is a distant memory now. It seems like the crash happened years ago, but we all know better than that. The group that survived the wreck is down just to Brice, Jason, Julie, Fi, and myself.

We are heading back to the zoo. We found the train tracks and are following them. This time, though, we don't walk on them. That seemed to be a bad idea last time. Now we walk parallel to the tracks, keeping them about fifteen away but in sight all the while.

It is slow traveling. Jason has a shattered collarbone, and with every step he takes his pain becomes all the more evident. Brice is just as messed up. He is in so much pain it is impossible to tell what exactly that tiger broke. That bothers me, and I think everyone is thinking the same thing: how is it possible that the tiger didn't kill him? We have seen less powerful animals swoop in and kill, seen monkeys and goats tear apart people.

"Why isn't Brice dead?" I ask Julie in her remaining ear. "Judging the strength of the other animals, that tiger could have bit right through him and left him in two pieces."

Julie has wrapped a t-shirt around her head to stop the bleeding from where her ear used to be. She is silent and doesn't answer me right away. Then finally, she asks, "Do you really wanna know what I think?"

I just look at her through my cloudy eye. "Of course I do. The more I try and wrap my mind around what the hell is going on, the more confused I get. Nothing makes sense anymore. I can almost understand a wolf, a tiger, and a bear attacking, but when deer and goats start tearing people apart... Why the fuck didn't that tiger kill him?"

Julie inhales deeply. She seems to have an answer, but also appears reluctant to tell me.

"Because it didn't want to kill him," she finally says. She looks around, likely making sure Brice and Jason haven't heard her. She can see the look on my face and offers her own explanation before I could say anything. "Look, these animals have been displaying not only increased levels of aggression. They are also showing higher intelligence. They've been hunting us down all day. If they were going on instinct alone, they would've attacked and killed us all at one shot."

"But..." I start to say, and get cut off.

"But nothing," she says, almost shouting. "You heard Brice. These animals have been altered both physically and intellectually by God knows what. If that tiger wanted to kill Brice, then Brice would be dead."

I'm having trouble accepting what she is saying, but deep down, I know it is true. These animals have been in control since before we even got on the train. At first, it seemed all they wanted to do was kill us. The conductor and a few of the passengers on the train were slaughtered outright, but then, gradually, their plan seemed to change. Instead of just killing us, there seemed to be a larger purpose. Almost as if they wanted us for something. I let that thought pass as a shudder runs through me.

Soon after our discussion, Julie and I help Brice and Jason to their feet and we continue to follow the tracks.

Fi has been unusually quiet the last few hours. I know that everything that's happened is going to result in years of therapy. Before today, the concept of Death was something she never even considered, but now it's been shoved in her face in the most graphic and primal ways. I'm worried about her, but realize that my primary focus has to be on getting her out of here alive. So far, I've been very lucky. Thanks to Julie's help, we've kept Fi safe and away from those animals. Nut again, there is that thought in the back of my head: *If they wanted to take or kill her, they could've at any time. So why didn't they?* I shake these thoughts out of my head. There would be plenty of time to ponder the 'what-ifs.' Right now, we need to get out of these fucking woods.

I help carry Brice. He has his arm around my shoulders and we walk carefully. It doesn't help, and with every step we take he inhales through his teeth in pain.

Julie helps Jason and finds a tree branch that he can use as a makeshift cane. Jason is nearly doubled over in pain from his broken ribs. Neither one still have any idea that I am pretty much blind. Julie stays only a couple feet in front of me and I make sure to match her step by step every inch of the way. Fi walks between us. I'm hoping at least Fi feels, but Julie and I both know that if those animals really wanted her...

I'm amazed that both Jason and Brice can even stand, let alone walk. They are in a lot of pain, but their injuries should have rendered them immobile. Jason had even mentioned that he was in pain, but that he felt like it was subsiding with every step he took. Either he was going numb due to massive infection, or whatever the animals had passed along to him was starting to affect him. Neither scenario was good.

Since we started walking after the last attack, we have been aware that the animals are all around us. The trees are shaking, bushes are rustling, and the occasional animal screams out. If not for Fi, my will may have been broken by now. Fi keeps me going, and I need to protect her and bring her home safely. I was unable to do that all those years ago with my friend Dave, frozen in fear and watching him get butchered by that dog. All these years I've been so focused on whether or not I was brave that summer day. Walking through these woods, I understand now that 'bravery' isn't what it's all about. 'Bravery' is a meaningless and hollow word. Back then, I was a ten-year-old-kid who didn't realize how fucking cruel and violent the world was. That summer day opened my eyes and shattered my innocence just to show how ugly and brutal life can be. It's not that I didn't act bravely that day; it's that I didn't act at all. Life requires action, and on that day, I had stood there completely paralyzed. Unfortunately, Fi is coming to understand that same realization.

"What's that?" Brice says through clenched teeth. I can tell he's looking at something in front of us, but all I can see is that fucking milky fog of my eye. I instinctively drop to the ground. Brice screams out in pain. "I… I think it's a car," Julie says.

"A car?" I say with some excitement, standing. "Is it the parking lot?"

"Hey, yeah," Brice weakly says. "He's right. I see a bunch of cars."

I almost cry. Fi and I have been on that train so many times that I thought I recognized some of the landmarks. I was pretty sure we were going in the right direction, but with my eye, I wasn't going to get everyone's hopes up.

Jason starts to scream for help, but he can't inhale deeply enough to scream. Julie counts out nineteen cars in the parking lot. You have to figure that there are at least two people per car, so there should be at least thirty-eight people walking around. The Austin zoo isn't that large. Someone is bound to spot us.

"Hey, if the parking lot was back there," I say, "then the train platform should be up this way another fifty feet." No one says anything. "I'm sure there's gonna be a ton of people at the platform waiting for the train. It's only a few hours late," I say, trying to inject some humor.

"Don't you find that odd?" Brice winces. "That fucking train crashed hours ago. Why the hell hasn't anyone looked for us?"

Then a little voice says, "Maybe they tried, but the animals found them first."

We all look down at Fi. She's right. There's no chance a search party isn't out there looking for us. Either they gave up, which I doubted, or they were slaughtered by the animals.

"Jesus Christ," is all I could say.

Fi tugs on my shirt to get my attention.

"What is it, Fi?" I ask.

"I can see the train platform in front of us."

I can see the others' eyes light up as they spot the platform. I don't even bother looking for it, but I do notice one thing right away: the entire area is silent. There is no one waiting at the platform.

The others start getting excited as we approach the platform. "Keep it down everyone," I hiss loudly. Everyone stops and looks at me. "Don't you all feel how wrong this is?" I finally ask. "Look around. There's no one here. The train's first run is at eleven o'clock and then it runs every hour on the hour until closing time. This is usually the busiest spot in the zoo. So where the fuck is everyone?"

"They probably closed the train ride down and told people it was broken," Jason offers. No one appears to buy it.

"Jesus," Julie almost whispered. "What if the animals attacked people here too?"

We walking on the tracks until we finally make our way to the platform. The others are looking around. There are no signs of an attack. It just looks deserted.

Julie jumps onto the platform first. She and I help get the others up onto the old wooden planks. Jason screams as he rolls himself up. The others are looking around for any signs of people or animals.

Once on the platform, we see a large cage to our left. Julie asks what that usually houses and I tell her it is home to a very large turkey vulture from South America.

The cage is empty.

We walk off the platform and away from the train depot. In front of us are picnic tables where people would sit waiting for the train to arrive. There doesn't seem to be any signs of a struggle. Then Jason points out a woman's tennis shoe along the back fence behind the tables. The hair is starting to stand up on my arms.

Behind the row of picnic tables and the fence are four small cages. I remember looking into them once and saw a porcupine in one and an iguana in another. Again, they are empty. Part of the porcupine's cage has a huge hole in it. Either something broke out of the cage, or something broke into it. We walk past the empty cages. This is only a small part of the zoo, but I continue to get the eerie feeling that there is no one around. There is no laughter from children or the sounds of angry parents yelling at their kids.

There is just an uneasy stillness in the air.

Brice breaks the silence. "Look, we're all thinking the same thing. We shouldn't jump to any conclusions. Maybe they evacuated the zoo in time."

"If they evacuated the zoo, then why are all those cars still in the parking lot?" Julie asks.

Brice ignores the question. "I think the smartest thing we can do is make our way to the gift shop," he finally says. "There's some food and water and most importantly, phones." We all silently agree that is the best plan we can come up with.

We start walking toward the gift shop and I can't help but think, *Has our situation gotten better, or worse?*

3

Wilder and his men have no idea what to expect as they follow Butsko down the hallway. All along the corridor are metal panels that Wilder assumes are the same kind of retinal security scanners that Butsko used to get into the lab with the infected animals.

He shudders just imagining what kind of horrors are behind these thick steel and concrete doors.

Wilder has been in too many combat scenarios than he cares to remember, but none of them could've prepared him for the things he has seen here today. Infected animals clinically dead and then reanimated as aggressive predators, with the apparent goal of self-propagating the infection. That scares the shit out of him. He is used to the kind of enemy who is well-defined, easily recognizable, and easily killed.

Butsko had briefed him on the entire history of the project that led to this disaster, and he admitted that it started with the intention of saving the lives of soldiers mortally wounded on the battlefield. But like everything else, the military brass weren't happy with the original results. The stasis phase of the experiments had been a huge success. Causality rates on the battlefield had dropped thirty-eight percent among soldiers immediately put in stasis after being wounded. Researchers had set up experimental sites in parts of Afghanistan and Iraq where American forces were taking heavy casualties. In those facilities were special containers large enough to fit an adult male, filled with an oxygen-rich liquid in which injured soldiers could be submerged. The liquid would fill the lungs, thereby making breathing easier. This immediately reduced the amount of deaths due to post-injury cardiac and pulmonary arrest. Soldiers who had collapsed lungs and internal injuries could breathe without having to gasp for breath.

They had also discovered another benefit of this procedure. The oxygen-rich liquid also helped to cool the brain, thereby slowing the metabolic rate and bringing on a state of stasis. The soldiers were basically placed in a state of deep hibernation and completely stabilized for the long journey home. Once home, they were brought out of stasis in state-of-the-art hospitals. The rate of success for bringing the men out of stasis was one-hundred percent, but it still wasn't a perfect process.

Being in stasis did nothing to help repair the injured soldiers. They woke up with the same injuries sustained on the battlefield, and one of the side effects of the oxygen-rich liquid was the appearance of flu-like symptoms. This proved to be very detrimental to the soldier's recovery. So the researchers pushed to try and solve these problems. They hypothesized injecting the soldiers with some kind of virus to help repair the body during transportation back to America, but this led to a dead end. Every virus the scientists engineered did exactly what viruses do: they tried to take over the host. Attempt after failed attempt was made to engineer something that could help repair damaged organs, tissue, and bone.

Then a small lab outside of Austin, TX had a breakthrough that would change the face of the program.

The tech experts at Sils are still repairing the damaged hard drives from the destroyed lab. As of now, what exactly was injected into those animals while in stasis is unknown. The answer lies in that damaged equipment.

Butsko, Wilder, Laning, and Reynolds stop in front of a metal panel. They are at the last room in the corridor, almost as if they are trying to hide this lab from the rest of the facility. Butsko punches in his code, submits the retinal scan, and the doors open with a silent "whoosh."

Stepping inside the lab, it looks exactly the same as every other housing the animals. Wilder guesses that every lab on this floor looks alike. The lights come on and just as he's guessed, there are viewing windows situated along the perimeter of the entire room. However, there aren't any infected animals.

In the middle of the room is a large cage with thick, transparent glass, and no visible door. There are indentations all along the outside for scientists to insert their hands and be able to work on what was inside. In the middle of the enclosed cage is a lab table.

Wilder takes a step closer.

On the table is an adult human. It is difficult at first to tell if it is a male or female. There are tons of wires hooked to the subject's body, face, and head, leading to a dozen different machines. Each machine records different bodily functions, including brain waves, pulse rate, and breathing. Scientists work in checking the information coming from the machines. By every indication, the subject on the table is dead.

Everyone in the room is wearing a level-four containment suit. Everyone, that is, except Butsko, Wilder, Laning, and Reynolds.

"It's okay," Butsko says, almost reading Wilder's mind. "This is as close as we're gonna get to the subject."

Then Wilder suddenly recognizes the individual on the table. It is the same man that he and his men transported to this facility.

A thousand questions fill Wilder's mind. He finally settles on, "Who is he?"

"This," Butsko replies, sounding like a proud father, "might just be patient zero."

"Patient zero'?" Wilder repeats. "That implies..."

"That implies that there is some kind of outbreak," Butsko cuts in. "I told you men that this was more serious than any other threat we've ever faced. This goes beyond an American problem. This could threaten the world. We think the subject before you might be the first human to be infected from an animal bite." He lets that sink in before continuing. "This just might be the man where the virus mutated into attacking human beings."

"What's wrong with him?" Wilder asks.

"He worked at an animal shelter that ended up housing many of the infected animals released from the lab outside Austin. We're assuming that the guys who took the animals didn't know what to do with them, and so they dropped them off at a shelter in Hyde Park." Butsko hasn't taken his eyes off patient zero since they entered the room. "The poor bastard was attacked by one of the animals, and it practically took his hand off."

"Is he... dead?" Laning asks.

"He was," Butsko says bluntly.

"Was?" Reynolds asks.

"He's experienced and went through exactly what that wolf is about to go through down the hall," Butsko says. "He had a very high fever and flu-like symptoms for about four hours and then he died. Then, about eight hours after he died, and believe me when I tell you this man was dead, he woke up."

"Is he dangerous?" Laning asks.

"Considering we have no idea what is going on inside that man, I'd say he is the most dangerous man in the world right now." Wilder can tell that Butsko isn't exaggerating. "What scares me the most," Butsko says as his voice gets lower, "is that whatever we're dealing with can infect almost anything on earth." The men stare. "We don't yet know if this can infect plants, but we know for sure that both animals and human beings are in danger."

After a few minutes, Wilder nods to patient zero and asks, "So what are you going to do with him?"

"Watch, study, and monitor him until something happens," Butsko says calmly.

"What if nothing happens?" Reynolds asks.

"Something'll happen," Butsko replies. "Something *always* happens."

4

We are exhausted. The stress of the day is finally taking its toll. What's worse is that safety should have been around the corner, literally. The walk from the train depot to the gift shop only takes seven minutes even if you're taking your time, but right now, it feels like a thousand-mile hike.

We aren't walking slowly just because we are tired. Something just isn't right. We've seen a lot of cars in the parking lot, yet no people. I imagine we are all thinking the same thing. No one needs to verbalize our collective fear.

Passing by the reptile house, I can't help but take a look in. There are usually two very large iguanas inside. It is hard to see anything through my cloudy eye, but even I can see that the reptile house is empty. I'd have been more surprised if the iguanas were actually there. I put my hands out to signal to the others to stop, and like a well-trained combat squad, everyone stops at the same time without question.

"Look," Jason says as he points to the dirt ground around the reptile house. There are footprints going in every direction. "Hard to tell how many people were around here, but one thing's for sure: it looks like there was a panic. Maybe even a struggle."

"Christ," Brice says, breathless. . "It looks as though these people were dragged off."

"Yeah," Julie adds, "but it doesn't look like they were struggling as they were dragged off. See." She points to the long lines in the dirt. "If they were struggling, then the lines wouldn't be perfectly straight."

I again am glad I can't see what everyone else is looking at, but in my mind's eye I paint a vision of hell that even Dante himself couldn't have imagined. "What could have dragged these people away?" I ask, already knowing the answer.

"The real question," Julie asks, "is where did they drag them off too, and why were they dragged away?"

"Look, guys," Brice says through clenched teeth. He's in a lot of pain. His breathing is worsening and he's beginning to look as though he might fade on us. "We need to get to where we are going. I'm not gonna last too much longer."

We all start walking again in silence. The silence is more frightening than when we were in the woods and heard the constant shaking of trees and bushes. At least then we knew they were following and watching us. Now we are walking in stone-cold silence. The air is calm, and what little trees and bushes are around us remain eerily still as well.

We fall into the pattern of all taking steps at the same time. Everyone is looking in different directions. No one but Julie knows how badly my sight has deteriorated, so I pretend to look straight ahead. I have a visual range of about ten feet, which scares the crap out of me. There could be a fucking bear twenty feet away and I would never see it. Julie and I have agreed that we don't want to scare the others by telling them a newborn baby has better eyesight than I do right now.

We move forward, Julie helping me scan in front of us.

We are about fifteen feet past the reptile house, walking toward the petting zoo corral, when I suddenly feel tiny claws digging into my leg. I look down and see that Fi has grabbed on. I can feel her tears running down my leg. I bend to pick her up and hear Brice.

"Jesus Christ. Look," he says as he turns his head violently away from the petting corral. "God, I'm gonna be fucking sick."

I walked closer to what she had been looking at. I may not have been able to see anything, but then the coppery stench of blood mingled with the smell of shit from torn open intestinal tracts, told me that the people at my feet were torn apart and eaten by the animals.

It is a massacre, plain and simple. A fucking massacre. The bodies of children and adults litter the corral. I push Fi's face into my shoulder so she doesn't see any of this grizzly scene. Most of the bodies are children, innocent children who thought they were going in to pet some baby goats. Some kids had their faces chewed off, while others were torn limb from limb. In the center of the corral are two arms removed at the elbow revealing jagged bone. The fingers on both hands are intertwined. You can see that one hand belonged to an adult and the other to a child. It was their final embrace.

"I'm gonna be sick!" Julie yells as she runs to get away from us.

"Oh my God," I say, hugging Fi closer. I never believed in God and always thought praying was the equivalent to throwing money down a sewer grate. Neither action was sane, and both actions left you broke. Words escape me at this moment, and that phrase seemed as good as any. There are eleven bodies in the petting corral.

After Julie throws up a few times, she rejoins us and helps me count the corpses. Seven children and four adults. Although it looks like a hell of a lot more due to all the parts strewn all over the place.

My next thought terrifies me. I look up quickly and try to focus on the red barn in front of us. I think at any second that a horde of these animals will charge us.

"Did you see something, John?" Julie asks nervously.

"No. No, nothing," is all I can say. "That barn could hold a shit load of animals. They could just be sitting in there, waiting for us."

Everyone is now staring at the barn.

"What should we do?" Brice winces. We're losing him fast. He needs help immediately. I suspect something may have pierced his lung.

"I don't think there are any animals in there," Jason says nodding towards the barn. "Besides, if there were, what the fuck could we do about it?" Point well taken. These animals could take us at any moment, and the sooner we realize that, the better off we'll be. We need to get the fuck out of this zoo and get to our cars. The faster we do it, the better.

We leave behind the carnage at the petting corral. There is absolutely nothing we can do and those poor kids and their parents were dead long before we got there. We step off the main trail and veer to the left. This path leads up a semi-steep hill that will take us straight back to the gift shop and out of this hell. Once to the gift shop, there's only about another thirty feet to the parking lot. We are all gaining a renewed vigor and can see the exit as we approach it cautiously.

We climb the hill carefully. I have Brice's arm around my shoulder and Fi still holds my other hand. After the scene in the petting corral, she's had enough. She is starting to shut down, so I keep her close. Brice's breathing is becoming more labored the higher we climb. I start to hear a wheezing sound as he exhales. Not a good sign.

I think about all the times Fi and I have walked this exact path. It had to be at least a hundred times. We'd be talking about the train ride and all the animals from the petting corral that slobbered over Fi's hands as she pet and fed them. Remembering her smile and laughs brings a tear to my eye. So far, Fi has remained safe and untouched, but it will only take a split second of not paying attention to lose her forever. I let the tear roll down my cheek. I hug her closer with my free arm and feel a new strength flow through me.

I'm not ten years old and this is not my best friend, I think. *This is my little girl, and there's no way I'm going to let anything happen to her.*

As we come to the top of the small hill, I know what is up there. On all the zoo maps it's labeled as a "Retention Pond," and for as long as we've been coming to the zoo there has never been so much as a foot of water in that so called 'pond.' I've always thought it looked like a large crater from a meteor. Fi and I had our own elaborate story of how a rock from space slamming into the earth at this precise location, and then thousands of years later, the zoo was built around it. I can't help but smile thinking about all the good times Fi and I have had in this place.

We are getting closer to the top of the small hill when I hear everyone breathe in at the same time. I am behind everyone with Brice and Fi and can't see what they are looking at. I don't think I want to see.

"What the fu…" Brice starts, but he is silenced before he can get his final word out. A small donkey comes from our left and rams into Brice. He tries to scream, but the pain is too intense. He drops to the ground, gasping for breath.

I let him fall. I know I can't save both him and Fi. I make my choice and don't think Brice will fault me on it. I run to the top of the hill and see what everyone is looking at. Even through my deteriorating eye, I can see that at the bottom of the retention pond are what lay the bodies of, I am guessing, all the people that were at the zoo. There are children, parents, and grandparents piled on each other in some bizarre picture taken straight from Saint John Bosco's, "The Road to Hell." I squint, but can't tell if they are alive or dead. I am assuming the worst. This explains the trails we saw by the reptile house. This also explains where all the animals were.

They are here, and they are protecting their kills.

I swear I see one of the bodies move in that crater, but know better. My eyes are showing me what my brain wants to believe.

I immediately drop to try to get my bearings. I can see the animals all around us, but can't tell exactly how many there are. So far, Brice was the only one who was attacked, but judging by the sounds coming from behind me, the animals are still hungry. I can't stop myself. I scream at them as they tear apart Brice, "What's wrong? Eating children isn't filling you fuckers?" They don't pause for even a second, but keep chewing on Brice. His stomach cavity has already been emptied buy the ravenous animals. Only his left arm remains attached to his torso, and I can see a lion five feet away from Brice's body, chewing on one of his legs.

Jason starts to yell "run," but stops as some of the animals start to circle us. I can't exactly see the gift shop, but I know it is only about forty feet away from where we stand. "No way," I say to no one in particular. "We are too close for it to end here."

I curl Fi up and hold her closer to my body. I don't want her arms or legs to dangle behind me. Julie sees what I am gearing up for. "We can't!" she yells. "They're all around us!"

"Then find us a gap in their perimeter!," I yell back. "The exit is right there!" I frantically point in the direction of the gift shop. "Fi," I say, whispering into her ear. "I need you to do something for me. We're gonna make a run for the gift shop." She starts to cry as she buries her head harder against my chest. "It's okay, sweetie. We're so close. I know we can make it, but I need you to do something."

She lifts her head and looks me in the eyes.

"I need you to get on my back and wrap your arms around my neck and hook your feet around my stomach. Can you do that?" She buries her face back in my chest. I can see the animals moving in closer. They are fucking taunting us. They know they have us surrounded and don't even have to break a sweat to take us down.

"Fi," I almost shout, "we're running out of time. I know you're scared, we're all scared, but I need you to get on my back. I need both my arms." She looks up at me again. "I got you, sweetie. I got this."

Without having to put her on the ground, Fi crawls onto my back. She has an iron grip with her fingers locked around my neck. It is a stupid thing to say, but the 'dad' in me has to say it: "Hold on tight, sweetie."

I look over at Julie. "Which way?"

She nods to our left, and I know she is looking at the picnic area. There are at least thirty tables set up to accommodate big groups that come to the zoo. It isn't a bad idea. The tables will give us some room to run through the animals, and if we need too, we can jump from table to table until we reach the gift shop.

"You ready for this?" I ask.

"No, not even remotely," Julie says back, not joking.

"Me neither." Time is running out. "Jason, can you run?" I yell over to him.

"Do I have a fucking choice?" he asks, panic building in his every word. I can't even imagine how much pain he must be in. The collarbone is one of the thickest bones in the body, and to have it snapped in half like a twig by an animal's jaws… I shudder thinking about it.

"Just try to keep up behind us," I tell him. "We'll help you, Jason. We aren't leaving any of us behind."

The first picnic table is about five feet in front of us. I figure that if we can reach that table before one of the animals gets to us, we can get to higher ground. Then that negative, pessimistic voice in the back of my mind rears its ugly head. *There's no way in Hell you can reach that table. These animals are faster than you could ever hope to be. They've killed everyone and we're next.*

I grit my teeth and unsheathed my combat knife. "Let's go!" I scream to Julie and Jason. I run ahead, not looking back to see if they are moving. I have no peripheral vision and my 'regular' vision is fucked. I have no idea if there are any animals coming at us, and if they are, I sure as hell won't know from what direction.

I run forward, seeing the picnic table getting closer and closer. I hear a scream and turn my head to see Jason falling to the ground. I know he didn't trip, and that only happens in shitty, clichéd horror movies. My adrenaline is pumping at one-hundred percent. Jason was taken down. He is screaming for help, but Julie keeps running. I can't blame her. There is a five-hundred-

and-fifty-pound African lion taking Jason down. His screams are quickly muffled as the lion tears out his throat.

"Run, Julie!" I scream to her as I jump up on the picnic table.

Julie lowers her head and focuses on the table. She jumps about two feet away and land right on top of it. Adrenaline is a wonderful thing.

"Don't stop!" I shout. "Keep moving towards the gift shop."

We immediately start hopping from table to table as we make our way toward the exit. My mind wanders to when I was a kid playing 'don't-touch-the-ground-it's-made-of-lava.' Now it's not lava, and it's certainly not a game.

Some of the tables are so close enough together that we can just run across them, and others are separated enough that we need to jump. I am looking for the close tables, as the extra weight of Fi on my back really reduces my jumping. I hear Julie scream as she falls jumping from one table to the next.

"*Julie!*" I scream. I stop and contemplate leaving her. I can't do it. I run back to find her.

I can see that the animals have been following us the entire time. They have a look in their eyes that tell me they know they could take us whenever they wanted too. I continue looking for Julie.

"Julie … Julie!" I scream "Goddamnit!" I yell. Then, from the corner of my eye, I see the foggy outline of something crawling onto the table to my left. I don't hesitate. I stab into the air with the combat knife not even knowing how far away the animal is. I am either going to hit air or flesh.

I feel the knife sink into the target and I smile. Luck is on my side, but then my entire body freezes as I hear a gasp of air escape from the target I have just stabbed.

It was Julie.

I feel her blood begin to pool and leak out around the groove of the K-Bar knife. It is warm as it flows over my hand. I turn to her. Our eyes meet, and she has a look of surprise and pain. I look down to see that I had thrust the knife right below the ribcage.

"I'm… I'm," words escape me.

Julie's face scrunches up as the pain finally spreads out to every inch of her body. She starts to cry. She puts her hands on my shoulders and in a whisper, says, "Run. You can still make it." She then pushes herself off the knife and falls to the ground. She is immediately attacked by a deer and a pig.

I stand there in shock as the world around me runs in slow motion. I just killed a human being. Every heroic illusion I had of today's events has just melted away. I killed a human being who did nothing but help me protect my daughter and serve as my eyes.

I killed her.

I feel the same paralysis I had when I was ten years old watching my best friend being mauled to death by a dog. The only difference is that I didn't have my daughter clinging to my back all those years ago.

"Come on, Daddy! Move!" I hear the panicked voice in my ear. I shake my head and see how close we are. I jump two more tables, then to the ground and run like hell.

We make it to the gift shop.

My emotions are getting away from me. On the one hand, Fi and I made it to the gift shop, and we are that much closer to getting the hell out of this zoo. But looking around, it doesn't feel like we are any safer than when we were in the woods.

The doors are unlocked. We quickly ran into the building and slammed the doors behind us. Fi is smiling and I force myself to smile back at her. Our goal was to reach the gift shop and we did it. She feels as though we made it to safety, and I'm not about to tell her that we were still far from safe. If those animals wanted in, they were coming in.

I don't even bother to look for weapons. We're in the fucking gift shop of a zoo, and just what the hell am I going to find? I take a bench and some chairs inside the shop and prop them against the door. The animals are out there just watching us. A wolf and a house cat have replaced the deer and pig and are tearing apart and eating Julie. My eyes well up.

"What happened to Julie?" Fi asks.

She hadn't seen it happen. Fi doesn't know that I accidentally stabbed and killed Julie. Tears run down my cheeks.

"She fell off the table, sweetie. She… just fell," I say, trying not to cry.

Fi is staring out among the animals. "I'm gonna miss her, Daddy. She was nice."

"Me too, sweetie. I'm gonna miss her too." I watch Fi looking out the door at the animals. In the course of one day, she has become desensitized to violence. My little girl was forced to grow up very quickly.

I go over to the cooler and get us a couple of waters. We drink them in silence, Fi still looking out the door, and me getting lost in my head.

I have a million questions, but the one nagging me the most is, why the animals didn't attack us. They could have taken us down any time they wanted. We were running on top of picnic tables, and it wasn't as if we were thirty feet above them. I just can't put these questions to rest. I feel sick to my stomach thinking about Julie, but I am trying to remain strong for Fi.

Then it hit me. "Julie... sick..." My mind is racing as I try to figure out what the hell is going on. My eyes grow wide. "That can't be it," I say. Fi is staring at me.

"What, Daddy?" she asks, confused.

There is no point in trying to hide what I am thinking. With everything Fi has seen and been through today, she deserves to get an explanation. It might help her process everything.

"Well, sweetie, I can't help but keep wondering why those animals didn't get us as we were running to the gift shop."

"Is it because you're really fast, Daddy?"

I smile. I really love this kid. "No, sweetie. The animals got Brice and Jason almost as soon as we started heading for the doors here." The pieces are coming together. "They didn't go after Julie until I..." I stop myself before I say "stabbed her." Fi is looking at me, but that's it. They didn't attack Julie until after she was injured.

The animals were thinning out our ranks by eliminating the injured. Brice had possibly broken ribs, Jason's collarbone was shattered, and Julie... Julie was injured. Fi and I only have a couple of scratches on us. Nothing more. We are healthy and uninjured.

Instead of these thoughts making me feel better, they are starting to make me feel more uneasy.

Why the fuck aren't they attacking the healthy? Do they have other plans for us? I think.

Then another thought slams into my mind. We never found the bodies of the kids taken from us back in the woods. Where are they?

5

Sils Research Lab

Butsko is going over the history of Jim, "patient zero." Since Wilder and his men brought him to the facility, he's been placed in complete isolation and sedated, although it hasn't seemed as though he's needed the drugs.

As doctors and lab technicians are doing their hourly checks, one seems to notice activity from the subject. "Sir," the lab tech says to Butsko. "Could you come over here?" Everyone in the room walked over to see what the tech was looking at.

Jim is just lying there.

"Sir," one of the doctors says. "It looks as if he's dreaming." The man is looking at the read out from the electroencephalograph (EEG), which is, of course, not registering anything. For all accounts and purposes, Jim is dead.

"I agree, Sir," another doctor says excitedly. "We have rapid eye movement. I think the subject is dreaming."

Butsko frowns. "Dreaming," he whispers. Then he says, "What the hell... no, scratch that." Butsko tries to organize his thoughts. "How the hell can a dead man dream, and what could he possibly be dreaming about?" No one has any answers.

"It's not so much what he's dreaming about, Sir," the first doctor replies. "It's more of what the dreaming is doing for him." Everyone stops and looks at the doctor.

"Go on, Williams," Butsko says.

"We still don't know the exact function of REM sleep, but there are a couple of theories. One suggests that certain memories are consolidated during REM sleep, thereby strengthening the relevant or important memories and weeding out less important ones." Williams stops to let that sink in.

"Okay," Butsko says. "That doesn't seem to be relevant here at all."

"I agree," Williams says. "Another theory postulates that REM sleep is required in order for our neurotransmitters to recover and regain full sensitivity. Almost like recharging the batteries in our heads." He pauses long enough to see if there were any readouts coming from the EEG. There aren't. He continues, "The theory I'm partial to, called the Ontogenetic Hypothesis, says REM sleep is so important because it helps develop the brain through neural stimulation. We know that REM sleep in newborns helps them develop their nervous system by forging more mature neural connections."

Butsko looks at Williams. "In English please."

"Okay," Williams replies. "Think of it like this: every night you shut down your computer into hibernation mode. Now, instead of all functions ceasing, say another program kicks in that might clean up the hard drive and reorganize all the information to make it more efficient and, in a sense, 'smarter.'"

All eyes are still on him. Finally, another doctor, Levine, interrupts, "If I may," he says. "So even though your computer seems to be doing nothing after you shut it down, it's still performing various functions in order to make sense out of all the information it received during the day."

"So the brain, while in REM sleep, is making itself better and rejuvenating itself?" Butsko asks.

"Essentially, yes," Levine responds.

"Which brings us back to my original question about our subject over here," Butsko says, nodding toward Jim, still laying on the table. "What could a dead man's brain possibly be trying to process and reorganize?"

Before anyone can answer, the lab tech closest to Jim yells, "Holy shit!" Everyone runs over to the containment chamber that Jim is in. "His... his eyes, Sir," the tech says. "He opened his eyes."

***

Jim can feel himself swimming in darkness: a warm, embracing darkness. He isn't scared to be out here all alone. He knows something special is happening inside him. He can feel a new purpose emerging.

Right now, all he has is a hunger.

The drugs being pumped into his system in steady intervals are helping to keep the hunger at bay for now. He can feel it just under the surface, always present.

He hears all the doctors and experts theorizing about what is going on. He is interested because he wants to know what is happening to him. He is curious, but not scared. The hunger lets him know that he is still alive and has some bigger purpose to fulfill. He is aware of what is going on.

On various occasions, he hears different doctors saying he is dead. He hears them say he has no pulse and that he isn't breathing.

If I'm dead, he thinks, *then how can I even ask this question? I'm not dead. I'm something else.*

The sedatives have stopped having an effect on his system long ago. He knows this and feels (no, *knows*) he can get up anytime he wants to.

Now is one of those times.

He opens and closes his eyes quickly to see who is around him. Immediately, he hears a racket as doctors and tech gather around him.

The hunger that seems to be a dull pang in his system is slowly spreading through his entire body. He can't control that hunger any longer. He is beginning to realize what his bigger purpose is.

He is about to fulfill it.

***

"What do you mean he opened his eyes?" Butsko yells at the tech. "He's still out cold."

"Sir," Williams says in a calm voice, "you need to stop thinking about this man as alive or in some kind of coma."

Butsko stares at him.

Wilder decides it was time to get in on this. "Look, guys, I'm not anything remotely close to a doctor, but I've seen and been around more dead people than all of you combined." He lets that point sink in. "This man is dead." Before anyone can say anything, he continues, "Yet, he seems to still retain certain functions, certain living functions like REM sleep. I just said I wasn't a doctor, so tell me: what the fuck is going on here? Is this man dead?"

"Yes," Williams answers, "but not in a traditional sense." Wilder rolls his eyes.

"You're forgetting that he was bitten by an animal that was undergoing experimental trials," Levine reminds everyone.

"Okay," Wilder says, perking up. "That's good. All we need to know is exactly what those experiments were."

"That's the million dollar question," Butsko hisses.

Just at that moment, Butsko's walkie-talkie buzzes. "Butsko," he answers.

"Sir, sir," says a voice excitedly over the phone. "This is Monroe down in the computer lab. We recovered and deciphered the damaged hard drive from the Hudson lab."

Finally, Butsko thinks. *We can finally get some more pieces to the puzzle.* "Go on, Monroe. What the hell are we dealing with here? What kind of virus is coursing through the subject?"

"It's not a virus, Sir," Monroe says, correcting the General. "I wish it were. There's a virus component to these experiments, but the virus is only acting as the host and as an activating mechanism to the main player."

"Stop beating around the bush, Monroe. Get to the point. What the hell are we dealing with here?"

"Think smaller," Monroe says, "way smaller than a virus."

"Are you talking about ..." Williams starts to say, but he is interrupted by Jim leaping off the bed and slamming himself against the solid reinforced cage.

All of them jump back except Wilder, who immediately unholsters his Glock. He has a bead on the subject.

"Stand down, Wilder," Butsko calmly says, placing his hand on the man's shoulder. "That's reinforced polymer, and your bullets are useless against it. There's no way he's gonna get out of there."

The subject suddenly drops to the floor, as if he's just realized he is dead. They stand there looking at Jim's lifeless body.

"Okay," Wilder says, turning to face everyone. "Someone needs to tell me why this dead man keeps waking up and then apparently dying over and over again." He looks everyone in the eyes. No one responds--not because of some bullshit clearance level, but because no one in that room appears to have any answers.

After a few minutes passed, Butsko orders a few men to get into their hazmat suits and put the subject back on the bed. "This time, put the restraints on," Butsko says as the two men walk into the containment room.

Before either man has a chance to shut and seal the door behind them, Jim jumps up and immediately attacks the man closest to him. He is like an animal as he lands on the first guy's back. With no hesitation, he tears off the helmet of the hazmat suit and bites off the soldier's cheek. Blood shoots all over Jim's face and chest as he chews and then spits the piece of cheek onto the floor.

The soldiers are unarmed. Wilder immediately runs to the thick door and is about to go inside.

"Stop!" Butsko yells, but it is too late. Wilder runs into the cage knowing Laning and Reynolds would be right behind him for backup.

Jim throws the cheek-less soldier head first into the wall of the cage, immediately knocking him out. He then turns to the other soldier, and with the speed and strength of an attacking tiger, rips through the back of his hazmat suit and bites into the base of the soldier's neck, severing his spine. They both drop to the floor as blood shoots everywhere. Jim continues to tear into the man's neck as he chews on the exposed spinal cord.

Wilder aims and fires two rounds in quick succession. He hits the subject once in the back and the other in his shoulder.

Jim jumps off the bloodied soldier and looks Wilder right in the eyes. Wilder immediately shoots off another three rounds, hitting him dead center in his chest. Jim goes down.

"Sir, sir," comes a panicked voice through the intercom system on the wall. "Sir, are you there?" the voice is pleading.

"Yes, I'm here!" Butsko shouts into the intercom. "We have a situation we're dealing with right now." Jim is laying still on the ground. For now.

They all hear screams over the intercom. "What the hell is going on over there?" Butsko shouts.

"The animals, Sir." The voice on the intercom is breaking up, almost as if the man talking can't keep his finger on the 'talk' button.

Butsko's eyes go wide. "Take a deep breath, soldier, and tell me what the hell is going on over there." Wilder nods to Laning and Reynolds and the two of them run toward the lab that houses all the animals.

"Mitchell and Torrence are dead, Sir," the soldier reports. "The animals just started going crazy. The monkey attacked Mitchell and then opened the cages to the other animals. Oh my God!" he shouts. "Riley is bleeding real bad, Sir. They're killing them! Those fucking animals are killing them!"

"I need you to calm down," Butsko says. "What is your position?"

"I... I'm in the office in the animal lab. I'm under the desk now. Wait. I think I hear something... aaaahhhhhhh!" The line goes dead. The last thing they hear over the intercom is something that sounds like a dog growling.

Butsko is pale white. "What the fuck are we dealing with here?" he asks no one in particular.

"Behind you!" shouts one of the lab techs. Wilder spins around to see Jim has gotten back up and is running straight toward him. Wilder reacted with three burst shots. He shoots a round into Jeff's chest, quickly followed by a round to his head. He does this three times in a row. There is no way he is getting back up.

Three soldiers run into the lab and Butsko tells them to lock it down. Then he and Wilder run to the animal lab. As they get closer, they hear gunfire and screams as animals continue to tear through soldiers and lab techs alike. The animals are beginning to spill out into the main corridor.

"Lock that room down!" Butsko shouts to no one in particular. "Nothing gets out of that lab!" He doesn't even know if anyone inside the lab was still alive.

***

Laning and Reynolds reach the lab and can hear the screams even before they open the thick door. Laning runs into the room first, his Glock raised before him, firing and hitting anything on four feet. Reynolds has his back, making sure nothing is behind them. Lanning feels overwhelmed. The animals are all throughout the lab. Some are crawling on the walls, some on the ceiling, and most of them are running wild on the ground.

Laning looks around as he fires his pistol, trying to see if he can locate any techs or other soldiers who might still be alive. He sees four bodies on the floor. None of them are moving. He turns to say something to Reynolds when he sees a house cat sailing through the air, seconds away from landing on Reynolds' shoulder. He raises his gun, but the shot isn't there.

"Reynolds!" Laning yells over to him. "Get down." On instinct, Reynolds immediately hits the ground. When you've been in and survived as many battles as Reynolds has, they know that when someone yells 'duck,' you duck.

Reynolds rolls to the left as he hits the ground. Laning fires and hit the cat in the chest, propelling it across the room and slamming it into the wall. When he looks down at Reynolds, he knows they are far from safe.

A large dog has spotted Reynolds on the floor and is creeping closer to him. Laning has run over to the closest body to check for any signs of life. There is none. The lab tech's throat has been torn out and one of his eyes is dangling on his cheek, hanging by the optical nerve.

When he turns to check on Reynolds, he stops dead in his tracks. The dog has already advanced on Reynolds and has him pinned to the ground. Laning sees Reynolds trying to raise his gun up enough to fire off a round, but the weight of the dog keeps him down. The dog opens its slobbering mouth and lowers its huge head. In one snapping bite, the dog rips off Reynolds' lower jaw, exposing jagged bone and his tongue. As his exposed tongue wags back and forth, a raccoon pounces on his chest and tore out his tongue.

Laning empties his gun into the dog that butchered Reynolds. As he reloads, he can hear Wilder and Butsko shouting in the hallway. He knows the animals are getting out, but there is nothing he can do. He is out-manned, or "animal-ed," as the case might be. He is in survival mode. The mission is lost and now he just needs to survive to fight another day.

Just as he sees Wilder walking into the lab, something catches his eye to his right. He turns with his gun raised and manages to get off two rounds before his arm a tiger removes his arm with one swipe of its claws. Laning screams as he sees the tiger getting ready to come in for the kill.

The last thing he ever sees is the unnatural gaping jaws of the beast coming down on him.

6

The gift shop looks untouched. Everything is where it always is. After Fi and I drink some water, we have some snacks. I feel a little more energized and am ready to get us the fuck out of there.

I keep Fi close to me at all times. I haven't fooled myself for one second into thinking that we are safe behind these glass doors. I look out the front window that overlooks the parking lot. I guess my car is about fifty feet away. It may as well have been two-thousand feet away.

We are out of options. There is only one thing to do: make a run for the car and hope the animals will leave us alone like they did when we ran to the gift shop. I can't help that negative voice deep inside my head from asking, *How much longer do you think your luck is gonna hold out?*

Behind the register is a small office that has a desk, a chair, a coat rack, and not much else. Unless I can MacGyver an adding machine into a shotgun, there is nothing in the office of use. I notice a closet door behind the coat rack. "What the hell?" I say. "Let's see what's in the closet."

"Be careful, Daddy," Fi says as she reaches out and prevents my hand from opening the closet door.

I look down at her, wink, and nod. I turned the door handle slowly and crack the door open.

Nothing jumps out.

I open it wider and immediately jump on top of Fi as something comes into view. One thought goes through my mind, *This is how it ends: looking in a closet.*

"What are you doing, Daddy?" Fi says underneath me.

I look up slowly and notice the "creature" isn't moving. "Sorry, sweetie," I say as I stand, helping Fi to her feet. "I saw the…" I let my thought trail off as I stab a finger toward the thing in the closet.

I take a closer look and realize the creature is actually a thick foam body suit, like the kind used to train attack dogs. This is a good find. A plan is coming together. I grab the suit and look it over, making sure there are no holes and that it isn't falling apart. I ignore the most obvious question: Why the hell does the zoo have a foam protective suit? My guess is that, since they're an animal rescue preserve, they have to go out and get a wild animal every once in a while.

I try the suit on to see if it is bulky enough to fit the two of us. I should have known that would have been way too easy. I remove the suit and tell Fi she is going to wear it and that we were are to make a run for the car. I put her into the suit and she completely disappears into it.

Fuck, I think. If I attempt to cut the suit down for Fi, it would probably fall apart and become useless. Nothing is easy today.

"Okay, Fi," I say changing the plan, "I want you to get into the suit, keeping your hands, head, and feet tucked into it."

"Like a turtle, right, Daddy?"

"That's right, just like a turtle. I'm gonna carry you and run to the car." I don't like this plan at all, but we are running out of time and options. These fuckers could attack at any moment.

As she gets into the suit, I run back into the office and grab the coat rack. It is six feet tall and made of oak, a nice hardwood. I break off the little knobs used to hang the coats, leaving sharpened spikes on all of them. I then pick it up and smash the base on the floor until it breaks off. I now have a makeshift spear. It's not much, but it's more protection than I had forty-five seconds ago.

I pick Fi up in the suit and am surprised at how light it is. The weight isn't a problem, but it is very bulky.

"No matter what happens, Fi," I say as I walk to the front door, "don't get out of the suit. Stay inside."

"Okay, Daddy," the muffled voice says. Then she adds, "I'm scared."

"Me too, sweetie, but we're almost out of here. They haven't attacked us yet, so maybe they won't again this time." I really want to believe that.

"Maybe they don't want us to leave," Fi says softly.

I stop for a second to think about that. All day these animals have been demonstrating extreme aggression and elevated intelligence. Could they possibly be that smart? Do they actually have a plan? Is that why they took the children? Because they had plans for them? They did seem to be targeting the injured, but earlier in the day, they seemed to be attacking and killing anyone, healthy or not. Nothing is making sense.

I finally answer, "They may not want us to leave, sweetie, but we have to try." Her silence speaks volumes.

I carry Fi to the front door and look out. Some of the animals are beginning to gather in the front. I can't tell if they are trying to block our path to the car or if they are just curious to see how stupid we are. It's probably both.

I open the front door and forget about the little bell hooked up to it. I can't help but think the tiny 'dinging' sounds like a dinner bell for these animals. I shake the thought from my head.

I can't get through the door carrying Fi in that suit and my spear. I walk through the door first, holding up the spear, and then guide Fi out. As soon as she clears the door, I swoop her up. More animals are gathering around.

To the right of us stand three deer, a llama, and a cow. They watch us as I slowly walk down the handicapped ramp. Behind them, four lemurs and two ostriches join the group. None of the animals seem to notice each other, as they were all focused on us.

I then feel something brush by my legs. I freeze as I feel the fur of some animal glide past me. I realize I am holding my breath. I slowly exhale. It is a wolf, another goddamn wolf. It came through the back door, the one that opens up into the zoo. This is too much. Why are these fucking animals toying with us? The wolf walks five feet past me and then stops to face me. There is something in its mouth. I squint to try to make it out and realize it is the big floppy hat that Julie wore earlier today. It drops the hat on the ground and I notice dried blood all around the wolf's mouth.

This wolf is fucking taunting me.

Anger wells inside of me. I want to run over and kick that son of a bitch wolf so hard that its ribs shatter. I want to see it die slowly, and then I feel the weight of the coat rack in my right hand. I set Fi down and, without hesitating or giving that fucking wolf any idea of what I am about to do, run forward and impale it onto the jagged tip of the spear. It lets out a tiny whimper as I force it to the ground. I twist the spear harder into the wolf's body. I can't see clear enough to know exactly where I've hit the wolf, but I know I've impaled it.

I pulled the spear out of the wolf completely, and without hesitating, rammed it toward its head as hard as I can. I feel the hard wood connect as its skull shatters from the force.

The wolf is dead. I stand there, staring at it, feeling a small victory and a little justice for Julie. Deep down, I know I will never get over what I did to Julie, no matter how many animals I kill.

More and more animals are gathering and I am preparing for an attack. I look over my shoulder and see that some of the animals have filled the gift shop. I don't get the feeling we are about to be overrun by these beasts. In fact, I don't think they care one bit that I just killed one of their own right in front of them.

"They're blocking the way behind us," I say. "They are making sure we don't try to go back into the gift shop and back into the zoo."

"What, Daddy?" Fi screams in a muffled shout.

"Nothing, sweetie" I say, gathering her into my arms. "Just talking to myself." I have no intention of going back into the zoo, because forward is our only way out.

Kicking the dead wolf aside, I notice four donkeys, two African lions, six goats, and three pot-bellied pigs gathered to our left. In another five minutes, we're going to have every fucking animal from the zoo here.

I continue to walk slowly in the direction of the car. The animals are just sitting there, watching as I carry Fi inside the bulky foam suit in one arm and the coat rack-spear in my other. I think about the ending to Alfred Hitchcock's *The Birds*. All those birds, thousands and thousands, just sitting around, watching Rod Taylor walking to his car. After a night of brutal attacks, they'd all just decided to let him go. The parallel here is uncanny.

Except this isn't a movie. There is no director sitting off to the side ready to yell "Cut!" when I get to the car.

We are thirty feet away from my vehicle. The animals are moving with us, but never get closer than ten feet. A horrible thought runs through my head.

Did I have my car keys?

Between jumping off the train, running away, and fighting these animals, I have no idea if I still have my keys on me. There is no way to check unless I either put down my only weapon or my only daughter.

I lower myself onto one knee and place the rack-spear on the ground. As I stand, one the African tigers begins circling us.

I reach into my pocket for my keys. Relief washes over me as I felt the cool metal.

I lowered myself back down and reach for the spear.

Nothing.

I search frantically with my free hand, never taking my eyes off the animals or the tiger. It's gone. I look down quickly. I may not be able to see details anymore, but I sure as hell could still see the outline of a six-foot bloody spear.

It isn't there.

"The lion," I hiss through clenched teeth. Scanning around, looking for the lion, I see it sitting ten feet away. It is staring at me and has its front paw resting on the spear.

We're twenty-five feet from the car and without a weapon, but I have the car keys. I'll take that as a small victory. I turn away from the lion and move closer to the car, taking bigger steps. I'm getting fed up playing this game. *If you want us, come and get us, but I'm done pussy-footing around.*

As we get within ten feet of the car, I put Fi down next to me. I pull out my keys and pushed the button to unlock the doors. The "beep beep" noise slices through the eerie silence and all the animals jump to their feet all at once.

My heart is racing the closer we get. As Fi lumbers towards the car, I realized I would have to take her out of the suit in order to get her into the back seat. That is going to take time, too much time. My K-bar combat knife is still stuck in Julie's chest underneath a picnic table, but I remember that I left another knife in the trunk, my eight-inch Gerber Mark II. I'm not crazy enough to try and fight off any of the animals, but the knife is sharp enough to slice right down the back of the foam suit.

I feel hope as I put the plan together in my head. I want to avoid any confrontation. They aren't attacking us, even though I've killed the wolf. I plan on just getting the knife, cutting Fi out of the foam suit, throwing her in the back seat, and getting the hell out. Simple plan, right?

With the press of a button, I place Fi against the front passenger door and tell her to keep all her extremities inside the protective suit. I'm scared to leave her alone while I get the Gerber knife out of the trunk, but I have no other choice. By using both hands, I could get into the trunk, find the knife, and get to Fi faster than with one hand.

Attacks were happening all over the zoo at this point. The monkeys and lemurs were out of their cages jumping on anyone close by. They were ripping flesh from bone like they were peeling a grape. The zoo was a chorus of screams and cries.

The bears had gotten out of their display cage. One disappeared into the woods while the other remained at the zoo and looked to be relaxing after having mauled a family of five. The parents were dead and the three young children all had broken bones to prevent them from running off. The youngest, a five-year-old boy, was slowing sinking into shock; his fibula, the bone right underneath the kneecap, had shredded his flesh and the jagged edges were exposed.

By far, the worst attacks had come from the larger cats. African lions, Bengal tigers, cougars, bobcats, leopards, and jaguars, had all become killing machines, wandering around killing anyone, regardless of age.

The entire attack had taken less than an hour. From the time Madison was bitten by the goat, until the moment the iguanas slipped away into the woods, a total of fifty-four minutes had passed. In fifty-four minutes, the zoo had become a slaughtering ground and not one human being remained breathing.

In about eight hours' time, those bodies, at least the ones that weren't completely devoured or torn apart, would again begin to breathe. They would breathe with a new kind of life inside them, a life full of hunger that yearned and ached to propagate itself.

I make my way to the trunk, keeping what is left of my eyesight on Fi. I slide my hand into my front pocket to get my car keys. The animals seem to be interested in Fi, but keep their distance. An ostrich appears to be the most interested in Fi and her protective cocoon.

I pull out my keychain, being careful not to hit the "open doors" or "panic" buttons, but just as they clear my pocket, the keys jingle together. A dog in the front immediately stands and cocks its head as the keys dance together. My effort to silence them was useless. The damage is done. All the animals around us seem even more interested in what we are doing.

My heart starts to race. I can almost feel a beam of hope shining on Fi and me. When the chips are this stacked up against you, any small victory becomes something you cling to with everything you got.

I find the knife quickly. It is right where I stashed it under my dirty work coats. Considering the higher level of intelligence these animals have been displaying, I tuck the knife into my waistband and hide it under my shirt. When I turn, I could feel hundreds of beady eyes boring into me. One of the lemurs slowly approaches me. It looks like a harmless little runt, but I've seen what these animals, big and small alike, are capable of. Ten feet to my left, I can vaguely make out the tiger standing there. I look at the cat as I kick the lemur away.

The tiger doesn't move. I can't see its eyes, but I am sure it is staring right at me.

I shut the trunk, trying not to make too much noise. I know by now that I couldn't spook these animals. They weren't normal anymore. Their intelligence, strength, aggression, and motor skills have been elevated. They are in complete control of their behaviors and actions. What scares me is that their plan could change at any moment.

The trunk closes with a dull "thud." The animals appear to be getting closer to us. Fi has hardly moved an inch.

"Are you okay, sweetie?" I whisper loudly to her.

"Yes, Daddy, but this suit is getting really hot."

"Well, we're gonna get you out of it now. I need you to stand perfectly still. I'm going to cut you out."

"Daddy..." she starts to protest.

"It's okay, sweetie," I say, trying to calm her down. "I'll have you out of the suit in no time." I take the knife out and drop the sheath to the ground. The eight animals closest to us creep a little closer to see what I am doing.

I slip the knife into the suit right around Fi's lower back. It is like putting a hot knife into butter. I pull the foam away the knife effortlessly glides through it. In six seconds, I have made a slit from her lower back up to the base of her neck.

The animals are all coming in for a closer look. A horrible thought raced through my mind. What if they are all just waiting for me to get her out of the protective suit? What if they attack her as soon as she is free from the foam? What if they want to eat the coconut meat, but don't want to crack the hard shell themselves? It is too late to second-guess my plan. We are out of time, and trying to figure out what these animals are planning is completely counter-productive.

I slip my hands into the seam I've just made with the knife and spread open the foam suit. I can feel Fi's body heat escape through the opening I have just made. Poor girl is burning up in there. I fold the suit over and expose her to the outside air. She takes a big gulp of fresh air and coughs a little bit, but then smiles when she sees me standing next to her.

"Okay, sweetie," I say quietly as I open the rear passenger door. "As soon as I open the door, I want you to jump in. We need to get the hell out of here fast." She is looking behind me at the animals.

"Daddy," she says. "The animals ..."

She doesn't finish her thought. I can hear the fear in her voice and imagine that the animals are getting closer. The closer we are to getting away from them, the closer they get to us.

"It's gonna be okay, sweetie. Just get ready to jump into the back seat." I can see the animals on the other side of the car closing in on us. Our time is up. We have to make our move right now or end up like the others in the retention pond.

I open both the front and rear passenger doors at the same time. I grab Fi around her waist with the intention of pulling her out of the lower part of the foam suit. My plan doesn't work. Instead, her feet get caught, and as I put her into the back seat, I realize her lower half was still snared.

The animals are starting to make their move. The monkeys and lemurs are coming first. My adrenaline starts to pump. We are so close to getting out of here.

"Fuck!" I scream as I start kicking the monkeys as they rush us. They don't seem be in kill mode. God knows if they were, we'd be dead by now. It feels as though they are just trying to slow us down.

"Get in, sweetie!" I yell as I push her into the back seat. I push hard to try and get the lower part of the suit into the back as well. It isn't budging. "Pull up your feet, Fi." I'm trying not to panic. I can see the faint outline of something running right toward me. As it gets closer, I can make out that it is a lemur. I lift my foot and stomp on its head. I feel the skull cave in under my shoe. Brain and gore stick to the underside of my shoe.

"Pull your knees up so they clear the door." I am pushing her legs hard so I won't slam the car door on her.

"I'm trying, Daddy!" she yells in a panic. "I think I'm stuck!"

I push harder but realize it is in vain. We are out of time. I can feel fur brushing against my legs. The animals are going to attack soon. I back away from the car and grab the door. I throw the door shut as hard as I can, hoping the sheer force will make the latch catch through the thick foam.

The car door pops open.

I muster all my strength and try again. I hear a weak thud and it seems as though the car door has caught. The thick foam is sticking out, but it appears to be staying shut. I turn to get into the passenger door.

I am met by at least thirty different animals. They are all two to three feet away and I can see the blood lust in their eyes. I bend down and quickly pick up the Gerber knife. As I stand, a deer jumps off the roof of the car. I barely see it in time through the corner of my eye. I hold the knife up and it impales itself on the eight-inch blade. The weight of the deer as it falls to the ground makes me lose my grip on the knife. Without hesitating, I turn to jump into the open passenger door. The whole time I am kicking and trying to stomp on any animal that comes close to me. I still can't help but think that they aren't really attacking us.

I grab the doorframe and am about to jump in when I come eye to eye with one of the wolf hybrids. We are so close that I can see every detail on its face. Its eyes make me shiver in fear. They have the icy stare of a killer, but there is something more. I don't feel a life force behind its eyes. All this time I've thought these animals have had some kind of higher plan and purpose, but now, as I look into this beast's eyes, all I see is murder and survival. It wants to survive, and I feel its survival depends on me.

"Daddy, hurry!" Fi screams from the back seat. She hasn't seen the wolf yet. Without thinking, I reach out to grab the beast. It doesn't flinch as my hands dart for its head. In fact, it seems to move closer, allowing me to get a better grip on it. I wrap my right arm around its neck and pull it towards me. As I do, Fi finally sees the wolf and screams. When I instinctively turn to look at my screaming daughter, the wolf lowers its head and slips free of my strangle hold around its neck. Then, in one fluid motion, it lunges and sinks its teeth into me. I scream as its teeth rips through my shoulder.

Instead of thrashing its head around and tearing my shoulder apart, the wolf opens its mouth and releases me from its jaws. I immediately shuffle back towards the car door, open it, and kick the wolf in the face. My blood is still dripping out of its mouth as it just looks at me, not even fazed by my kick.

It stands there, staring me down. Fi is still screaming in the back seat. Just when I think the wolf is going to finish me off, it hops over me and jumps over the car. I sit there for a few seconds, stunned that I am still breathing. The pain rips through my shoulder and Fi's screams bring me back. I dart into the passenger seat so I can close the door. Just as I am about to secure it, an ostrich sneaks its head in. I pull hard and decapitate it.

I fucking hate ostriches.

I get behind the wheel and start the car. "It's okay, Fi!" I shout, trying to talk over her screams. "We're gonna be okay. We're getting out of here."

I start backing up the car, hoping to run over ten to fifteen of those fucking animals. I look out the rearview mirror and notice the animals are moving away from the car--not scattering like they were scared of the car, but moving back to allow us room to get out. The parking lot is just dirt ground and sand, and dust is everywhere as I gun the engine for the exit.

My eyes are really bad by this point, and under normal circumstances, I would never have gotten behind the wheel of a car. But nothing about today was normal.

I floor it and hit a pothole in the lot. The vibrations shake the car violently and the back door next to Fi pops open.

"Daddy!" Fi screamed.

I'm afraid to stop. We are still in the parking lot, and even through the dust in the air I can see the outlines of a lot of animals still watching us.

"Hold on, sweetie!" I yell into the back seat. "Let me get some distance from the animals and then I'll close the door."

Too late.

I hear Fi scream louder than ever before. I look back and see a small marmoset jumping into the backseat with Fi.

Fi put her hands up as the marmoset lunges toward her. By luck, it jumps right into her open hands. She holds it at arm's length and I quickly jam on the brakes. I reach around, put my hands on top of Fi's, and begin to squeeze with all my force.

"Squeeze, honey!" I yell. I can feel her hands tightening as we both close our fists around the marmoset's body. I feel bones snap and organs squish. It lets out a little yelp as its eyes explode from their sockets. Then it is dead.

We both sit there for a second, staring at the pile of gore in our hands.

"Open your hands, sweetie," I say. She stares at the blood and gore dripping through her fingers and out of her palms.

"Sweetie," I say a little louder. "It's okay. You can open your hands." I throw the crushed animal out the open door. Fi is able to free her feet from the foam suit and kicks the remnants of it out the door. She reaches over and pulls her door shut. We look at each other and hug.

She then sits down in the back and puts on the seat belt.

I drive away fast.

I don't look in the rearview mirror.

Why bother? I know what I would find.

As we drive away from the zoo down Rawhide Trail, my mind races a mile a minute. I am trying to make sense of what has happened. Why did the animals attack us? Why did they let us go? A pain shoots through my shoulder and I know I have to go to the hospital. How the hell am I going to explain that a wolf bit me?

Regardless, I know that everything is going to be all right. I may have gotten bitten, but Fi is okay. I protected my little girl against all odds. I can't help but smile, even though it is a sour.

"I'm sorry, Julie," I whisper as tears fill my eyes. "I'm so sorry."

"What, Daddy?" says the tired voice from the back seat.

"Nothing, sweetie," I say as I try to choke back the tears.

My little girl is going to be okay. That's what matters. This whole time I've wondered if I'd be able to step up in the face of danger. All this time I've thought that, if I just had the opportunity, I'd prove to everyone that I was brave. Maybe that would even alleviate the guilt of doing nothing as I watched Dave being torn apart all those years ago.

None of that matters, as redemption is nothing but a Hollywood plot device. The world isn't so black and white. Well, maybe it is. I protected my little girl, and that's the only thing that matters.

I reach for my cell phone so I can call my wife and tell her to meet us at the hospital. As I begin to dial, I hear the faint sounds of helicopters in the distance.

"Hi, honey," I start to say as my wife answers the phone, but I don't get any more words out. I break into tears.

I turned onto Circle Drive and see that Fi has fallen asleep. When I am able to talk again, I tell my wife about what has happened at the zoo. She is silent as she lets me tell the story at my own pace.

Fi sleeps in the back seat, no doubt dreaming about monsters.

As I turn onto Highway 290, I hear the helicopters getting louder.

AFTERWARDS

Two days after the incident at the Austin Zoo
Avery Ranch Development, Austin, TX

Kim and Bryan are walking home from school. They live in a
neighborhood where the school is just minutes from their house.
Their parents love the fact that they don't have to take the school
bus. Maybe they can postpone their kids' exposure to bad words
another couple of years.

Kim is nine going on thirty-eight, and Bryan is six years old.
They always wait for each other after the final school bell rings.
Their parents know they have a couple of great kids. They always
look after each other and rarely ever fight.

They walk along Staked Plains Loop to get to their house on
Hattery Lane. Both their parents work, but one always tries to
make it home in time to meet the kids after school. Today, their
mother, Janice, gets stuck in a meeting. She sends Kim a text
telling them she will be a little late, but to go straight home and she
will meet them there. Kim likes it when her parents are late. She
feels like the adult in the house. Plus, she likes taking care of
Bryan.

"Come on, Kim," Bryan says as he starts running toward the
park. "Let's play before we go home." Bryan is a little short for
his age, but makes up for it by being fearless. He isn't afraid of
the bigger kids in the school and loves to climb tall trees. The
trees in the park are his favorite. The trees around his house, like

most in the new development, are still way too small to climb, but here in the park they are huge. Perfect for climbing.

"No, Bryan!" Kim calls back to him. "Mom told us to go straight home." Bryan is already to the park. Kim rolls her eyes. "Children," she says out loud as she runs to catch up with her brother. Truth is, she loves to play at the park, but she also wants to show her mom how grown up she is and that she can follow instructions.

"Okay, Bryan," Kim says as she finally catches up to Bryan next to the slide. "We can play for ten minutes and that's it."

Bryan knows when his older sister is in no mood for negotiations and agrees. He immediately runs over to his favorite oak tree and begins to climb.

Kim looks around the park. There are two metal benches at each end of the park under the shady trees. There are definitely bigger parks around their house, but this one is the most convenient on their way home from school. It has two slides, a small rock-climbing wall, and a large playhouse structure complete with monkey bars.

Kim is climbing up the ladder to go down the slide when she notices a small dog lying under a tree. She isn't sure what kind it was, but it reminds her of the dog from the *Benji* movies. She descends the ladder and approaches the animal slowly, saying stuff like, "Hi there, cutie. My name's Kim. What are you doing out here all alone?" The dog pricks up its ears, but doesn't react like some of the dogs her friends have. It raises its head, but doesn't seem too energetic.

When Kim is about ten feet away from the dog, she gets down on one knee and holds out her hand, making clicking sounds with her tongue. The dog just looks at her.

"Hey! What are you doing?" Bryan yells as he runs over. "Don't get too close to that dog."

"I'm not, doofus," she says, smiling. "I'm just trying to see if it has a collar and if it's lost."

"I don't see one," Bryan says.

"Well, it must be someone's dog," Kim reasons. "There's a lot of houses around here. It must have gotten out of the backyard."

"Well, what should we do?" Bryan asks. "He looks hungry."

"We could take him home and give him a little food," Kim suggests. "Then we could take a picture of him and put 'Lost Dog' signs up all over the neighborhood."

"What about Booger?" Bryan asks, thinking about the five-year-old tabby cat at home. "Booger's not real good with other pets."

"We'll keep the dog out in the garage," Kim says. The dog bolts to a standing position, almost as if it understands what Kim is saying. It's ready to follow its new friends to their house.

"There's no way we're keeping that dog," Kim and Bryan's dad, Bob, says. "Besides, you both know better than to approach and bring home a stray." It isn't that Bob dislikes dogs. He just knows his kids are too young to be able to handle the responsibility. There is no way in hell he is going to wake up at six in the morning to take it out for a walk.

They are standing in the garage, watching the dog eat out of the bowl. They had to resort to giving it some cat food, but it doesn't seem to mind.

"I think your original idea is a very smart one," Bob continues, trying to be positive. "We'll take some pictures with the digital camera and make up some posters to put up around the neighborhood. We're not gonna kick the little fella out on the streets. We'll just find his home." The kids smile and hug their dad.

They set up a little bed for the dog in the garage with some old towels for the night. They will take some pictures in the morning.

At midnight, the dog's eyes shoot open. It is tired and just wants to sleep, but there is something urging it to wake up. It is hungry again. It was used to being hungry before, but this hunger makes it ache. It couldn't ignore the hunger. It doesn't realize it, but whatever is inside it needs to eat and feed in order to accomplish its goals.

The dog stands and scratches the garage door that leads into the house. Its claws seem longer, stronger than a few weeks ago. Eventually, Bob comes downstairs to see what all the noise is.

"This is exactly why I don't want a dog," he says. "Everyone's asleep and good old dad is down here taking care of this dog."

He walks over to the door leading into the garage and bangs on it a little. "Quiet in there, poochie. Go back into your bed." The dog replies with some whimpers and pathetic noises.

"For fuck's sake," Bob says as he begins to open the door. "What's wro…"

As soon as the door is wide enough to fit through, the dog jumps and sinks its teeth into Bob's throat. He makes a wet, gurgling noise as he falls to his knees. His eyes are wide with fear as he realizes what is happening.

To his left, their cat Booger hisses. Bob is starting to lose consciousness as the blood sprays from his carotid. No one can lose that much blood in that little time and stay conscious. He grabs at his throat only to find that the dog has taken a chunk of it out. Even if he could stand up long enough to get a dishtowel, he would never be able to stop the bleeding.

He falls face-first to the kitchen floor. He feels a coldness he's never experienced as the blood continues to drain. He hears a violent hiss and can see the dog has forgotten him and has moved on to Booger. Booger's eyes are wide with panic as that dog pins him to the floor and tears into his belly. Booger dies instantly as the shock of being eviscerated hits his system.

Bob's last thoughts are of his family as he sees the dog heading toward the stairs.

The dog is fast and quiet--too quiet, in fact, for a dog. It seems as though some primal instinct, some latent predatory memory, has been unlocked from some dormant gene. It silently walks upstairs and first goes into the mother's room. It is over quickly as the dog bites her on the hand. She makes it easy enough, as one hand hangs off the side of the bed. It knows it only needed to give her a little nip, but that primal lust takes it over. It bites down with such ferocity that it removes two of her fingers before she even wakes up.

Her screams wake the rest of the house. The kids run into the room to find the dog standing next to the bed and their mom screaming while holding a bloody hand with missing fingers.

Bryan breaks their silence first. "Mommy, what's going on?" The dog stands there, looking at him and Kim, almost as if deciding who to attack first.

Its primal instinct tell it to go after the boy. Like a shot out of a gun, the dog launches at Bryan, its claws tearing through his Lightening McQueen pajamas and deep into his thigh. He screams in pain as he drops to the floor.

Kim is in shock, but realizes that if she doesn't move quickly, she'll be next. She sees one of her father's work boots on the ground. He is in construction and she knows there is something called a "steel toe" in it. She isn't sure exactly that meant, but she knows it is hard.

The dog lunges and she raises the boot. The dog slams into the sole and falls to the ground. Without hesitating, she starts beating the dog, making sure she uses the toe part to smash into the dog.

The dog lays there, not making a sound. It put its head on the floor. When Kim is satisfied that no living thing could withstand such a beating, she drops the boot. She tries to console her brother, but sees that her mom is losing a lot of blood. She hands her mom a t-shirt lying on the floor and her mom wraps it around her hand. She starts looking around in a panic.

"Where's your dad, kids?" she asks, trying to calm down.

Kim suddenly realized that her dad is nowhere to be found. "I don't know, Mom. I don't see him anywhere."

The mother reaches over to the phone and starts dialing the number for the ambulance. "Sweetie," she says in a calm voice to Kim. "Can you go downstairs and get me a bowl of ice?"

Kim looks at her, confused.

"I need to put my fingers on ice so the doctors can put them back on at the hospital," she explains calmly. Then she looks down at Bryan and says, "Come up here, sweetie. Come up onto the bed with Mommy." Bryan jumps onto the bed and starts crying.

"Why did that dog do this, Mommy?" Bryan says between tears.

"I don't know, sweetie," his mom answers, but is interrupted by a voice on the other end of the phone. "Hi... yes. I need an ambulance immediately. My family was attacked by a dog. Yes, a dog," Kim starts to walk out of the room as she hears her mom tell the emergency operator their house address. As she walks past the dog, she stops for a second and stares at it. So many questions races through her mind. When she turns to leave the bedroom, the dog extends its paw and scratches Kim on the heel of her left foot. She lets out a little gasp, but thinks she will look stupid if she cries out and runs to her mother. Her mother's lost two fingers and Bryan has deep gashes in his thigh. She rubs the spot where the claws got her and walks downstairs to get the ice for her mom, calling for her dad. It doesn't make sense for him to be gone. Maybe he is in the downstairs bathroom. He often goes there if he can't sleep. He would sit there and read so as not to wake up the rest of the family.

She walks through the living room and sees the kitchen light on. "Daddy, are you in the kitchen?"

Upstairs, Bryan and his mom sit on the bed. She is able to slow the bleeding with some clothes on the floor and Bryan is beginning to calm down. She hasn't yet heard the icemaker and is wondering what is taking Kim so long. The thought of more animals in the house cross her mind, but she knows it is just paranoid thinking.

"Kim!" she yells. "Kim! Are you all right?"

She can faintly hear the ambulance sirens.

As they grow louder, a blood-curdling scream tears through the house.

Kim has found her daddy.

Barton Creek Community, Austin TX.   2:00pm

Daniel pulls onto Wimberly Lane off of Barton Creek Boulevard. He got a call from dispatch twenty minutes ago that there was a wild animal, possibly feral, in the Barton Creek area-- an upscale community with a private golf club. He figures some rich douche bag had a deer or two eating his manicured lawn and called it in as a wild animal.

Daniel is thirty-nine-years-old and never thought he'd end up in the animal control business. In his younger years, he was actively involved in Greenpeace and PETA. In 1985, he ran away from home at age fifteen in order to "fight the good fight," as he'd called it. He'd been on the Greenpeace ship *Rainbow Warrior* when it was bombed and sunk by the French government. His wife keeps telling him he should write a book about those days, but now he drives around capturing wild animals, mostly stray dogs and cats and the occasional aggressive raccoon. It's not like the he'd done at Greenpeace, but, as he tells himself, when you have a family, you need to "get real." He'd do anything for his wife and four kids, even if it meant compromising some of his principles. At least by being in animal control he is still able to help some animals.

He pulls onto Wimberly Cove and drives slowly as he looks between the houses and in the woods surrounding the area. Being a cove, it dead-ends into the woods, and he figures it is a pretty good area for any animal, wild or not, to hide. As he passes the last house and approaches the dead end, he sees the tops of three trees shaking.

"If this is another goddamn call about a turkey vulture, I'm gonna be pissed," he says. He can understand why people would get freaked out. The birds are huge and can have a wingspan of seventy-two inches. Plus, they aren't very afraid of humans. They can stare a person down and make them run in the opposite direction. If it happened to be a turkey vulture, there isn't much he can do about it.

He parks his van about fifty feet from the end of the cove and gets some of his equipment. He puts on some thick foam hand, arm and leg protectors. You can never be too safe. He walks to the edge of the woods, whistles, and then waits. He doesn't see or hear any movement. As he lowers his hand to get his walkie-talkie to call dispatch, something buzzes by him to the right, going very fast. He shoots his head up, but whatever it was is long gone. He even starts to doubt that he actually saw anything. He laughs at himself and turns to go back to the van.

This time, something *does* move, and this time he sees it. He hears weird noises, almost like heavy breathing, and something that sounds like claws scurrying up a tree.

"Hello!" he yells. "Who's out there?"

He is answered by the fading sound of the trees rustling to his left. He takes a step deeper into the woods, leaving the paved surface of the cove behind him. He hears more of that weird heavy breathing sound, but can't tell which direction it is coming from.

He shoots his head to the left and catches a glimpse of what looks to be a skunk. He shakes his head as he mumbles, "Daniel, you are losing your mind. Skunks do not climb trees."

He pauses, then blurts out, "A tail... it has a black and white bushy tail." He scans the trees, trying to get a look at whatever it was. He guesses the tail was a good two feet long and figures whatever animal is attached to it has to be around five feet tall.

"What the hell could that be?" he says. He knows whatever it was isn't found naturally in these woods. He walks back to his van and looks in a few books to figure out what it could be. When he finds nothing even remotely fitting the description of a 'five foot skunk-like animal with a long tail,' he turns to his iPhone and Googles it. As he waits for a result, he walks back to the woods and continues looking for the creature.

"Finally," he says, looking at his iPhone. "What the fuck?"

The only animal that vague fits his description is a Colobus monkey, and they sure as hell aren't found in Austin, Texas, or even America for that matter.

He grabs his walkie-talkie without taking his eyes off the trees. As he presses the button to call dispatch, the large, skunk-like looking Colobus monkey comes hurdling from the trees above him, its claws extended and teeth bared. The last thought he has before the monkey slammed into him is, *Monkeys don't make that kind of noise.*

Daniel wakes up in the grass. It is dark, he is dazed, and has no idea where he is. His body is full of aches. His head is pounding, his muscles are sore. Even his teeth are hurting, but the worst pain comes from his right shoulder. He reaches over and feels the dried blood on his jacket.

He jumps to his feet as he remembers being attacked by something. He looks around to make sure he is alone and that the creature isn't still here. *Colobus monkey*, he remembers. The thing that attacked him sure as hell looked like the picture on his phone.

He suddenly realizes that he is standing in total darkness. He looks around and sees where his van is parked near some of the houses down at the other end of the cove.

He looks at his watch. 11:47 P.M..

"What the fuck?" he says. "I've been out cold for over nine hours."

He slides his shirt off his right shoulder to take a look at the wound. Judging by the puncture marks, it must have bitten him deep. He touches the bite and expects pain, but only feels a dull throb.

Great, he thinks. *It's infected and going numb on me already.*

He could understand passing out from the shock of being attacked by some large monkey, but for over nine hours? He feels a warmth throughout his body, kind of like drinking hot coffee after being outside on a really cold day.

As he stands there, the warmth inside of him turns into a faint hunger. *I'm starving,* he thinks as he realizes he hasn't eaten anything since noon. As he walks back to the van, he hears the walkie-talkie on the ground over by where he passed out. The dispatcher asks where the hell he is and if he is all right.

"I'm alright," he says, staring at the walkie-talkie, "I'm just really hungry."

That faint hunger he had a moment ago begins to grow. It isn't just a hunger that emanates from his stomach. His whole body feels hungry as he climbs into the van. He seems to have a clear focus on things now, and needs to eat and satisfy his hunger. Deep in his mind, he knows something bad will happen to him if he doesn't eat something. He pulls out his phone to call his wife.

"Hi," he says in a deadpan voice.

"Jesus Christ, Daniel!" comes the frantic voice on the other end of the line. "Where the hell have you been? Are you okay? Work has been looking for you."

"I'm fine," he says. "I'm on my way home now."

"On your way home?" she repeats. "Do you have any idea how late it is?"

"I had a little nap is all," he says as he stares out the windshield. "I'm coming home and I'm really hungry." He looks at his eyes in the rearview mirror and is shocked to see his blue eyes have turned grey.

He smiles.

"I'm fine, honey," he continues, "I'm just really hungry."

"Are you sure you're okay?" his wife asks. "You don't sound like yourself."

"I promise I'm great," he says as he continues to stare into his own lifeless eyes. "I'll be home in about fifteen minutes." Before she can say anything, he adds, "I'm just hungry honey. Really hungry."

Sils Research Facility, Outside Killeen, Texas

The room is still. Nothing is moving any longer. Animals and humans alike are still on the ground. Most of the animals are dead from the Rangers' attack, and those not dead have entered a state of stasis as their bodies try to repair the damage caused by the Rangers' bullets.

The humans littering the floor are worse off. Reynolds is missing his lower jaw and has lost a lot of blood, but the change occurring in his body will eventually repair those injuries. He won't grow another jaw, but he will wake up. Eventually. Laning had already entered a deep REM stage. His "sleep" won't take as long as Reynolds' will.

Butsko and Wilder are trying to figure out what has happened, and how those animals escaped and attacked. As they'd run to try and help, Jim had escaped and managed to chew his way through six lab techs before Wilder was able to bring him down.

Everything appears calm as soldiers, lab techs and men in hazmat gear run around, trying to clean up and contain the aftermath.

Reynolds and Laning are placed inside hazmat containment bags as they are prepared for transport. Reynolds is still a long way off from waking with the hunger, but as the men lift Laning onto the gurney, his eyes shoot open.

He looks around as he feels the hunger growing inside him.

It won't be long now. It won't be long at all.

Arboretum Area, Austin, TX

I wake in a cold sweat. This seems to be the norm now. I've woken up this way the last couple nights. It's only been two days since the events at the zoo. "Events." That's a nice way of describing what happened. A lot of people lost their lives that day. The thing that really scares me is that I've never heard anything about it on the news. My wife, Sarah, had met Fi and I at the emergency room around four o'clock that day. By the time we got there, the pain in my shoulder had already started to fade away-- which was strange, because I hadn't taken so much as a Tylenol after being bitten.

It took about an hour to see a doctor. A nurse had looked at my shoulder and said that it didn't look bad, that the wound appeared to be closing already. I'd gone into one of the bathrooms to see for myself. The nurse had been right. It looked as though it was almost completely healed. I'd stayed anyway to get a shot of antibiotic, just to be safe. When I finally got to see the doctor, he'd asked where I got my wound. Something inside me prevented me from telling him it was an animal bite. I didn't think he'd believe me and by this time, it looked like a bruise.

I told him I'd tripped and slammed my shoulder against a concrete wall. I didn't even ask for an antibiotic shot like initially planned because that would have raised too many questions. He'd sent me away with a topical cream. I've never filled the prescription.

When we finally got home, Fi and I told Sarah all about what had happened at the zoo. She'd sat in silence, stunned at what we were telling her. I've always been honest and open with Sarah, but I just couldn't get myself to tell her about what I'd done to Julie. I told her how much she'd helped me protect Fi, but not that she was the only person who hadn't died from an animal attack. That's a memory I will suffer alone.

In the middle of telling our story, she'd gone over to the TV and put it on the local news. There had been nothing about the massacre at the zoo.

As we'd tried to relate our entire tale, Fi had sat on my lap on the couch. She wouldn't leave my side. Her head rested against my chest, and after relating a particularly violent part of our experience, I would playfully throw her down on the couch and hold her arms, tickling and buzzing her stomach with my mouth. Fi always loved it when I did that. I'd started to get the feeling that Sarah hadn't completely believed us, but I couldn't blame her. Even I had trouble believing it. I'd finally taken Fi to bed and read her some stories. I knew she was exhausted, but also knew that she had some horrible images just waiting to greet her as soon as she closed her eyes. I figured she'd be crawling into our bed later that night and most likely for several weeks.

As I left her room that night, she'd said something to me that I will never forget.

"Daddy," she'd said while trying to fight off sleep. "You're my hero."

"What you're telling me is really out there, John," my wife had said as I'd rejoined her on the couch. "Way out there, even for you."

"Do you think I made all this shit up and convinced Fi to play along?" I'd asked, getting angry.

"Of course not, sweetie. I just find it hard to believe there was a massacre at the zoo, and there is absolutely no mention of it on the news."

That had bothered me as well. I'd told her about Brice and Jason and the connection with Sean.

"Maybe you should have told that doctor about the wolf biting you," Sarah had said, concerned.

I'd taken off my shirt to show her my 'injured' shoulder. There had barely been a scratch on it. "He would have thought I was crazy if I told him that, only hours before, a wolf bit me. I'm starting to doubt that a fucking wolf bit me."

"What if those animals were carrying some kind of virus?" she'd asked.

I couldn't think of anything to say to make her feel better. "Look, I'm really tired and my eye still hurts. I'm gonna call it a night."

I'd taken about three drops of Azopt to try to get my eye straight. It'd cleared up slowly and I knew that sleep would be the best thing for both my eye and my body.

That night, I think I went from being awake to falling into a very deep sleep in seconds. I don't remember having any dreams that night. I was grateful for that. I was afraid I would see the surprised look on Julie's face as the knife sank into her belly when I closed my eyes. I wouldn't be able to handle that. Mercifully, I was so exhausted that I fell straight into a deep REM sleep. This would also be the last night I would sleep through the entire night without waking up in a cold sweat.

It was also the last night where I would wake up without a voracious hunger.

I slept thirteen hours last night. Sarah had said she'd been worried a few times and had tried to wake me up. She'd pushed me and yelled my name, but said I'd slept through every attempt to wake me up. At one point, she'd taken my pulse and had been about to call an ambulance.

Sarah said I'd looked dead, and any doctor would have agreed with her.

As she was calling the ambulance, my leg had twitched and I'd begun breathing again. After that, she'd let me sleep, checking in on me every half hour.

I still can't recall anything particular about that night of deep sleep. I don't remember having any dreams, but I have vague recollections of feelings. I can remember feeling a warmth throughout my entire body and the feeling that everything was going to be different when I woke up.

After my thirteen-hour slumber, I wake feeling better than I ever had. Usually on rare days when I get more than seven hours of sleep, I wake feeling more tired than when I went to bed. Not this time. This time I wake feeling that warmth inside me, but there is something else. Something like...

...a hunger.

Not the usual 'I-just-slept-thirteen-hours-and-need-a-hearty-breakfast' hunger. This hunger is hiding behind that warmth and keeps intensifying the longer I don't eat. This hunger spreads throughout my body and goes far beyond the pit of my stomach. Every inch of my body is experiencing this hunger, and every part of me wants to consume and eat.

The hunger is also become something other than about food.

It's turning into a craving, but I still can't figure out what it is. It goes beyond simply satisfying my hunger. It is an urge, a desire to fulfill some sort of purpose. I need to figure out what that purpose is, and the hunger is consuming me to the point where I can't think about anything else.

Pulling my shirt over my head, the hunger in me is stronger than it ever has been. The warmth is becoming a furnace. My skin is hot to the touch. Walking down the stairs to the kitchen, I know what it is the hunger wants from me. It is so clear and obvious that I feel stupid for not recognizing it before.

Sarah is in the kitchen, making breakfast.

"Good morning sleepy head," Sarah says. "You had me scared to death a few times last night."

I walk past the kitchen ignoring Sarah's greeting. Fi is sitting on the couch watching her favorite television show, *Charlie and Lola.* Fi barely notices me as I slowly walk toward her.

Sitting down next to her. The burning inside me grows hotter.

"Morning, Daddy," she says cheerily.

I stared at Fi, as I finally start to understood what my hunger wants from me.

"Morning, sweetie," I say, watching her show. "I think someone is about to get a visit from the tickle monster," I finally say, turning to her. She giggles as she pulls a couch pillow closer to her body.

I extend my arms, wiggle my fingers as I slowly lean over her …

…my hunger is so clear now. I feel stupid for not recognizing it before …

I take the pillow away from her body as I grab her arms, just like I've done a thousand times before. She is playfully screaming as we fall onto the couch.

… the hunger inside me has finally revealed its purpose …

I start tickling her tummy with my mouth, making a "buzzing" noise. Fi always laughs so hard when I do that.

… everything around me dissolves as my purpose become clear …

Fi hasn't noticed that I've pulled her t-shirt up a little bit, exposing her tummy. The skin is soft and I can still smell the soap on her from her bath last night.

… my world goes black as I move in to fulfill my new purpose …

My "buzzing" stops as I run my teeth down her ribs. She is still laughing and I can hear her trying to catch her breath. I let her inhale …

… there is nothing left inside of me except my purpose. I am finally going to satisfy that burning hunger …

As Fi inhales, I sink my teeth into her soft flesh. Her screams of laughter quickly become screams of pain and horror. The man she called her hero just days ago is tearing into her flesh. Her blood fills my mouth as her mother comes running into the room.

Sarah freezes at the sight before her.

I have already opened up my little girl's stomach, and her intestines start unspooling off the couch and onto the ground. Fi's screaming becomes less intense with each breath. Her life is draining from her, yet I know I am also passing something on to her.

… I finally feel satisfied. My hunger is subsiding, for now. I finally understand my hunger, my desire. I am fulfilling my new purpose. I am passing along what is inside me …

It wants to live on, and I will do anything to fulfill its desires.

And I do.

Scott Shoyer has had a love affair with the horror genre since seeing The Last House on the Left (1972) and Cannibal Ferox at the tender age of nine. In college, Scott studied philosophy and after earning his Ph.D. in 19th Century German Political Philosophy, moved to Austin, TX to be with his girlfriend. They married in 2003 and have 2 children, Braeden (10) and Fia (7). Scott went back into the "family business" and became an Executive Chef, running some of the busiest kitchens in Austin.

Scott also runs the popular and successful website http://www.anythinghorror.com where he writes about the various facets of the world of horror. He spends many late nights dividing his time between writing for his website and writing horror novels, novellas, and short stories.

Scott is writing the sequel to Outbreak: The Hunger and plans to further explore the zombie world he created in a series of novellas. He is also busy outlining several other new horror projects.

CHECK OUT OTHER GREAT ZOMBIE NOVELS

Z BURBIA
by Jake Bible

Whispering Pines is a classic, quiet, private American subdivision on the edge of Asheville, NC, set in the pristine Blue Ridge Mountains. Which is good since the zombie apocalypse has come to Western North Carolina and really put suburban living to the test!

Surrounded by a sea of the undead, the residents of Whispering Pines have adapted their bucolic life of block parties to scavenging parties, common area groundskeeping to immediate area warfare, neighborhood beautification to neighborhood fortification.

But, even in the best of times, suburban living has its ups and downs what with nosy neighbors, a strict Home Owners' Association, and a property management company that believes the words "strict interpretation" are holy words when applied to the HOA covenants. Now with the zombie apocalypse upon them even those innocuous, daily irritations quickly become dramatic struggles for personal identity, family security, and straight up survival.

ZOMBIE RULES
by David Achord

Zach Gunderson's life sucked and then the zombie apocalypse began.

Rick, an aging Vietnam veteran, alcoholic, and prepper, convinces Zach that the apocalypse is on the horizon. The two of them take refuge at a remote farm. As the zombie plague rages, they face a terrifying fight for survival.

They soon learn however that the walking dead are not the only monsters.

 SEVERED**PRESS**

⑤ facebook.com/severedpress
◎ twitter.com/severedpress

CHECK OUT OTHER GREAT ZOMBIE NOVELS

900 MILES
by S. Johnathan Davis

John is a killer, but that wasn't his day job before the Apocalypse.

In a harrowing 900 mile race against time to get to his wife just as the dead begin to rise, John, a business man trapped in New York, soon learns that the zombies are the least of his worries, as he sees first-hand the horror of what man is capable of with no rules, no consequences and death at every turn.

Teaming up with an ex-army pilot named Kyle, they escape New York only to stumble across a man who says that he has the key to a rumored underground stronghold called Avalon..... Will they find safety? Will they make it to Johns wife before it's too late?

Get ready to follow John and Kyle in this fast paced thriller that mixes zombie horror with gladiator style arena action!

WHITE FLAG OF THE DEAD
by Joseph Talluto

Millions died when the Enillo Virus swept the earth. Millions more were lost when the victims of the plague refused to stay dead, instead rising to slaughter and feed on those left alive. For survivors like John Talon and his son Jake, they are faced with a choice: Do they submit to the dead, raising the white flag of surrender? Or do they find the will to fight, to try and hang on to the last shreds or humanity?

SEVEREDPRESS

CHECK OUT OTHER GREAT ZOMBIE NOVELS

VACCINATION
by Phillip Tomasso

What if the H7N9 vaccination wasn't just a preventative measure against swine flu?

It seemed like the flu came out of nowhere and yet, in no time at all the government manufactured a vaccination. Were lab workers diligent, or could the virus itself have been man-made? Chase McKinney works as a dispatcher at 9-1-1. Taking emergency calls, it becomes immediately obvious that the entire city is infected with the walking dead. His first goal is to reach and save his two children.

Could the walls built by the U.S.A. to keep out illegal aliens, and the fact the Mexican government could not afford to vaccinate their citizens against the flu, make the southern border the only plausible destination for safety?

ZOMBIE, INC
by Chris Dougherty

"WELCOME! To Zombie, Inc. The United Five State Republic's leading manufacturer of zombie defense systems! In business since 2027, Zombie, Inc. puts YOU first. YOUR safety is our MAIN GOAL! Our many home defense options - from Ze Fence® to Ze Popper® to Ze Shed® - fit every need and every budget. Use Scan Code "TELL ME MORE!" for your FREE, in-home*, no obligation consultation! *Schedule your appointment with the confidence that you will NEVER HAVE TO LEAVE YOUR HOME! It isn't safe out there and we know it better than most! Our sales staff is FULLY TRAINED to handle any and all adversarial encounters with the living and the undead". Twenty-five years after the deadly plague, the United Five State Republic's most successful company, Zombie, Inc., is in trouble. Will a simple case of dwindling supply and lessening demand be the end of them or will Zombie, Inc. find a way, however unpalatable, to survive?

Made in the USA
Lexington, KY
08 March 2019